All
Night
with a
Rogue

All Night

with a

Rogue

Alexandra Hawkins

St. Martin's Paperbacks

This is a work of fiction. All of the characters, organizations, and events portrayed in this novel are either products of the author's imagination or are used fictitiously.

ALL NIGHT WITH A ROGUE

Copyright © 2010 by Alexandra Hawkins.
Excerpt from *Till Dawn with the Devil* copyright © 2010 by Alexandra Hawkins.

All rights reserved.

For information address St. Martin's Press, 175 Fifth Avenue, New York, NY 10010.

ISBN: 978-0-312-58019-3

Printed in the United States of America

St. Martin's Paperbacks edition / February 2010

St. Martin's Paperbacks are published by St. Martin's Press, 175 Fifth Avenue, New York, NY 10010.

10 9 8 7 6 5 4 3 2 1

This book is dedicated to my amazing editor,
Monique Patterson—and our mutual appreciation
for unrepentant bad boys.

Acknowledgments

With appreciation, I would like to thank Liam Shannon for lending his expertise and assisting me with the Latin phrases in this book.

Virtue has a veil, vice a mask.

—VICTOR HUGO (1802–1885)

Chapter One

London, May 27, 1820

SEDUCTION WAS NOT foremost in Lady Juliana Ivers's thoughts. However, the same could not have been said for her escort, Mr. Engelheart. The moment she had agreed to step out onto the upper garden terrace with him, her amiable supper companion at Lord and Lady Lettlecott's prestigious ball had turned into a lecherous, brutish knave.

So naturally Juliana ended up in the Lettlecotts' hazel tree.

Juliana pressed her lips against the comforting trunk and uttered a brief prayer of appreciation for the beautiful old tree that had been coppiced in its youth, four distinct trunks radiated out from the ground at thirty, fifty, and seventy-degree angles. In spite of the hindrance of her evening dress, she had managed to use one of the opposing low-lying trunks as a step as she carefully inched her way high enough for the foliage to conceal her.

Her beautiful dress was ruined.

The stylish frock of white satin with pearl and jet beads dangling from the short sleeves was now etched with smudges of dirt and lichen from the trunk of the tree. The higher confusion of corkscrew branches and spiky serrated leaves caught at the jet beads and flounces adorning the bottom of her skirt and her upswept hair. Even her sandal slippers and white kid gloves had not been spared the abuse.

Maman would likely despair over the loss. The tumultuous five years following her husband's unexpected death had cast their family on the precipice of financial ruin. Maman had done her best to provide for their basic needs and the considerable investment needed to launch Juliana and her two older sisters, Cordelia and Lucilla, into polite society. When Maman had summoned a modiste from London to their rather unassuming house in Norfolk, the widowed Marchioness of Duncombe had vowed to see each of her daughters married and their future secured.

She would undoubtedly be shocked to see Juliana perched in a tree as she tried to escape the potential suitor.

"Lady Juliana!"

She froze at the sound of Mr. Engelheart's voice. In the distance, Juliana could hear the merry tempo of string instruments and a tambourine as the musicians in the ballroom played the old ballad "Blow the Candle Out." It was a cautionary tale of a young lady and her apprentice lover. Without a doubt, the song added a certain irony to Juliana's predicament. One that would be likely lost on her lovelorn supper companion.

Juliana had hoped Mr. Engelheart would have given up by now. After she had broken free from his unwanted embrace, she had spun around and escaped down the polished stone steps that led into the Lettlecotts' expansive back gardens. The moonlight and flickering lanterns that lit up the meandering paths had bolstered her nerve. She had assumed that the gentleman would have surrendered with dignity.

Sadly, the man's head was as thick as his hands were clumsy.

Her illuminated path to freedom also fired Mr. Engelheart's passion to catch his slippery quarry. She veered off the gravel paths into a small thicket. The time had come for drastic measures.

Hence the hazel tree.

"Lady Juliana?" Mr. Engelheart was close enough that she heard the fine tremor in his inflection. "You have nothing to fear from me. I just want to escort you safely into the ballroom."

He paused and listened to the night sounds for some clue to her whereabouts.

Juliana's lips thinned as she wondered how long would she have to remain in the tree? Minutes? An hour? The rest of the evening?

Juliana shifted her body in an attempt to scoot down from her perch. A faint hiss escaped Juliana's lips as the sharp point of a broken branch punctured her stocking and scratched her left calf. Leaves rustled a warning as she struggled to free herself. Her struggles only made matters worse. Portions of her skirt were snagged, and the more she moved, the higher the hem crept up her legs. She was soundly caught by this wretched tree!

Then soft feminine laughter floated like pollen on a spring breeze, and Juliana came to a halt at the throaty sound.

"Catch me if you dare," the unidentified woman called out to someone, probably her lover, as she unknowingly raced toward the tree Juliana was starting to view as her own.

There was the sound of multiple footfalls on the gravel path and a brief tussle. It was followed by a high-pitched burst of laughter. Clearly the lady had been caught by her male companion.

However, sheer panic set in when a dark-haired woman adorned in a black bombazine dress carelessly brushed against the nearby shrubbery and staggered toward the bench next to the hazel tree. She slipped onto the bench and extended her outstretched gloved hand to the man casually strolling into Juliana's line of vision and for some reason her heart immediately began to pound.

This gentleman was no Mr. Engelheart. He moved stealthily, like a well-fed predator in his prime. His dark hair was long and straight. Most of the length was tied in a queue at the back of his nape. However, some of the dark, glossy ends had escaped during his playful romp with his lover and the ends curled slightly at his jawbone. Juliana could only see intriguing glimpses of his face. Her elevated position and the shadowy thicket deprived her of details, but Juliana sensed his gaze was fixed on the lady beckoning him to join her on the bench.

"I have been waiting all evening for this," the woman purred.

Juliana's forehead furrowed in puzzlement. The woman's voice sounded dreadfully familiar.

"Half the fun is the chase," the man said, his low, smooth tones trailing down Juliana's spine like phantom fingers. He clasped his companion's wrist, drawing her up so that her breasts were flush against his chest. "Besides, I doubt you want an audience when we fuck."

Juliana's breath caught and she found her eyes locked on this depraved gentleman in fascination.

He lowered his head and claimed the woman's lips. For a few minutes, the only sounds were breathy gasps and moist sucking sounds of fervent kissing.

"Or maybe you do," the man chuckled with something akin to admiration in his silky, rich tone. He tugged on her full sleeve and bared her left shoulder. The woman clutched him tightly and moaned when he put his mouth on the exposed flesh.

Juliana peeked down as the woman uttered a wordless sound of need. She slipped her hands into the man's coat, her fingers splayed over his inner waistcoat. From her perch, Juliana recognized the bird egg–sized diamond pinned to the front of the woman's gown. Juliana's lip curled into a sneer. She had been wrong about the color of the dress. It was a dark blue rather than black. The gaudy diamond winked at her. The amorous lady below was her hostess, Lady Lettlecott. The same odious woman who had cheerfully paired Juliana earlier with the lecherous Mr. Engelheart. She did not recognize the lady's companion, but he was *not* Lord Lettlecott.

"Sin, it has been too long since our last meeting," the countess said breathlessly, losing her concentration when he cupped the swell of her right breast and worshiped the flesh with his mouth. "I—I was beginning to feel . . ."—she sucked in her breath—"undesired."

Sin paused in his sensual ministrations and touched Lady Lettlecott's cheek with undisguised affection. "If you move your hand lower, you can feel my desire, Abby. All the same, let's not complicate our friendship with messy sentiment that neither one of us wants. Our needs are pathetically basic. Fortunately for you, I'm in the mood to accommodate you."

Juliana blinked at the man's detached bluntness. She hugged the tree trunk, watching Lady Lettlecott struggle about in Sin's embrace as if she was trying to raise her hand to slap him. The man seized the lady's wrists with one hand as he delivered a firm swat to her backside.

"Behave!" he growled.

Juliana grinned at the countess's well-deserved comeuppance. This was more entertaining than any drama Juliana had ever witnessed in a ballroom, and the *ton* was notorious for public spectacles.

"Do you really want to fight me, Abby?" Sin separated the countess's hands and nipped one of her palms with his teeth. For chastisement, it was mild and oddly sensual. Juliana's stomach fluttered in response.

Lady Lettlecott evidently agreed with Juliana's private assessment. The lady ceased her futile struggles and leaned heavily against him. She moaned, signaling her surrender to his overwhelming dominance.

"You are so wicked, Sin. If I had any sense, I should

leave that preening cock you are so proud of stiff and aching."

Sin released her wrists and stepped back. "Then leave," he replied, sounding almost bored by her threat. He sat down on the bench, resting his left arm casually on the back of the bench. "This quiet spot and my hand are more than enough for the delicate chore, my dear."

Juliana's eyes widened in shock and she craned her neck to glimpse even more of the gentleman who Lady Lettlecott thought was worth the risk of inciting her husband's wrath. She could not see Sin's face at all from this angle, though she deduced from his confidence and movements that he was undoubtedly handsome. She had met the Earl of Lettlecott on her arrival. He possessed an admirable face, and Juliana doubted his wife would settle for an inferior specimen of manhood.

"There was a time when you claimed that you liked it best when *I* used my hands on your flesh," the countess said, edging close enough so that her skirts brushed his knee.

"Did I?" he said; his soft, patronizing tone was enough to make Juliana grit her teeth.

Sin had slumped down into an informal sprawl on the bench, his long legs spread out in front of him. Lady Lettlecott seemed to be staring between his legs intensely. Juliana conceded that she was curious, too, about this so-called magnificent testament of maleness concealed within his trousers. As she had lived a sheltered life, her knowledge of the male body was woefully incomplete. What was it about Sin that warranted such rapt attention from Lady Lettlecott?

To Juliana's surprise, Sin did not seem troubled by

the countess's frank perusal. In fact, Juliana sensed that he was enjoying his companion's brazen actions. Without making a sound, Juliana lifted her upper torso slightly to the left of the sturdy branch. She ignored the burning sensation in her eyes as she strained to see beyond the enigmatic shadows just above the man's muscular thighs.

Lady Lettlecott slowly moved into the V created from Sin's outstretched legs. Wordlessly she knelt down between his legs so her upturned face was inches from the buttons adorning the front of his trousers. "Perhaps a demonstration is in order, my lord." Her hands lovingly stroked the intimate contours on display.

Here? No! She would not dare! . . . Would she?

Not trusting herself, Juliana clamped her hand over her mouth. Egad, this was not happening! The faint sounds of fabric sliding over fabric and the countess's sigh of appreciation at what she had uncovered confirmed that Juliana was about to become the unwilling spectator of a lovers' tryst. It took an immeasurable amount of inner fortitude to quell her mounting panic.

"Oh, Sin, my love, I will perish if you deny me a taste!"

Juliana cringed, unwilling to dwell on what portion of Sin the countess wanted to taste. Juliana had never kissed a man, let alone examined his—what had the countess called it?—his preening cock? Lady Lettlecott, conversely, seemed to have an unnatural obsession and familiarity with it.

If she and Sin discovered Juliana, what would they do to her? Offer payment for her silence? Threats? Violence? She felt her throat constrict as half a dozen choices flashed through her mind like repeating lightning strikes on her skull.

A murmur of encouragement rumbled deep from Sin's throat. Juliana shivered at the wild masculine sound of abandonment. She rubbed the sudden ache in her breasts. The poor constricted flesh was mashed by her corset and the unyielding hardness of the trunk. She yearned for the moment when her maid would free her from her clothing to ease the tightness that she felt all the way down to her stomach. Below, Sin widened his stance, giving the kneeling woman better access to his defining attributes.

Juliana bit her lips to suppress her soft groan. Her legs instinctively tightened around the trunk of the hazel tree, pressing the hard roughened surface against her feminine core. In spite of the coolness of the evening, she felt hot and light-headed. If she did not calm her rattled nerves, she was going to do something to give herself away like fainting and falling out of the cursed tree!

In an agitated gesture, she dragged her hand from her hair, causing the unexpected to happen. One of the tiny white plumes tucked into her upswept tresses slipped free. Without thinking, Juliana reached out to grasp the errant two-inch curl of fluff that was destined to be her downfall. The lissome plume evaded her fingers, dancing on the breeze created by her frantic motion. It silently drifted down to the couple.

Juliana brought her fist to her mouth and silently prayed. Both Lady Lettlecott and Sin were distracted for the moment. Perhaps the tiny feather would remain unnoticed. The husky moans and disconcertingly wet smacking noises coming from below heartened Juliana.

Until the fragile white plume landed on the top of the countess's dark tresses. Even in the moonlight, it was a stark beacon. Juliana held her breath. She mentally willed the plume to catch another breeze and disappear into the inky blackness of the ground.

Fly!

Any hope she harbored was dashed when Sin's fingers moved from his lover's shoulder to the lady's hair. To the traitorous plume. His shoulders stiffened as he held up the feather, rubbing the light down between his fingers as he wordlessly contemplated its origins. Then without warning, Sin tipped his head back and stared directly into Juliana's troubled gaze.

Alexius Lothar Braverton, Marquess of Sinclair, or simply Sin to his friends, had made the most of his five and twenty years. His privileged existence was filled with excessive indulgences, the forbidden, and oftentimes the perilous. Very few things in life surprised him. That was, until he looked up into the branches of the hazel tree and saw the pale, frightened face of a young woman.

The air in his lungs burst from his lips.

Abby, naturally, thought her skillful tongue and the measure of his cock were the reasons for his lapse of control. Alexius was content to let her believe he was enthralled. The countess's soft tongue curling and lapping the full length of him was pleasurable, even if his interest had drifted decidedly upward. Besides, if he exposed the little interloper, he would never learn why she was watching them from the tree.

And, yes, he was . . . intrigued.

From his vantage point, her appealing looks caught his jaded eye. Long blond corkscrew curls were draped chaotically around her oval face, hanging like the golden catkins of the hazel tree. A pair of languid almond-shaped eyes balanced the delicate slope of her nose, and the rounded curve of her chin made his fingers itch to inspect each line. Her skin was pale, luminous, like the moon overhead. Whether it was natural or from fear he could only guess. Her full lips parted, as if she struggled to draw air into her chest.

Who the devil was she?

Was she spying for Lettlecott? Alexius immediately discarded the idea. Boredom rather than desire had driven him into Abby's clinging arms this evening. He could have taken the lusty countess anywhere. Their decision to use the back gardens had been merely a whim. No one, not even a suspicious husband, would have thought to plant spies in the trees.

And a pretty one, as well.

The sharp press of Abby's nails against Sin's sensitive baubles caused him to return to more important matters. If left to her own devices, the lady would score a man's tender flesh with her teeth and nails.

"Here now, my dear, as pleasurable as that is," he said, pulling her up with one hand, "we'll give my tickle tail a chance to recover." Ignoring her wordless protest, he tucked his turgid cock back into his trousers and fastened the two buttons above his right hipbone. Modesty was not his primary motivation. Alexius doubted the pretty wench in the tree could see much in the gloom. He just wanted to get through the evening without crescent-shaped welts on his bloody tackle.

Alexius teased the nipple peeking from the edge of the countess's bodice with his finger. "It seems impolite to keep you on your knees."

Abby flowed like warm wine onto his lap. "I seem to recall that you prefer your women on their knees and their mouths filled to cease their useless prattle."

The corner of his mouth lifted into a genuine smirk. The comment certainly sounded like something he might have spouted in the past. "Perhaps I have changed."

Abby laughed at the absurdity of the notion. "Oh, Sin, you are many things. Reckless . . . calculating." Abby pushed his hair away from his face, pressing tiny kisses down the line of his jaw as she tried to sum up his nature. "Inventive, passionate, crude . . . sometimes cruel. You are a self-seeking scoundrel. A breaker of hearts. And a jaded bastard. Nevertheless, at this moment, you are mine!" Her hands slid around his neck, slipping beneath the secured wrappings of his cravat. He felt the sting of her nails cut into his skin, drawing blood.

So Abby had marked him, after all.

Alexius did not bother to contest her opinion of his character. His friends would heartily agree. He had been all of those things at one time or another. A lady would be foolish to trust him with her heart or her body. That was one of the reasons why a woman like Abby appealed to him.

When he took a lover, he learned her body so he knew it as well as his own. He knew exactly how much pressure to apply to make a woman quiver in his arms. What pace to set with his agile fingers to make her sigh and cry out his name. Alexius was just one of countless lovers Abby had taken since she had given Lettlecott his heir. In truth, Alexius was not even her favorite.

A second pregnancy and the birth of another son had kept Alexius out of her greedy hands for more than eighteen months. However, Abby had recently weaned her infant son, and she had expressed a desire to renew her and Alexius's acquaintance. He had been mildly interested. Earlier this evening, he had faced the choice of spending the evening fondling sweet Abby's breasts or playing cards with his friends and Lettlecott's cronies.

He should have stayed in the card room.

Fortunately, his mercurial nature sensed a new game was afoot, and he openly embraced it.

Alexius looked up and wide, solemn eyes met his stare. He grinned up at her, calculating the possibilities of his good fortune.

Alexius helped Abby to her feet. Abby looked startled. "What is this? You have not—we have not—"

"Alas, there is no time."

With his hand firmly on her elbow, he led her away from the tree. "We have tarried too long. I thought I heard someone call your name from the upper terrace."

The first hint of fear flashed in Abby's eyes. "Why did you not speak of this sooner?"

His smile was unapologetic. "I was distracted."

The countess muttered an unladylike curse as she reassured herself that her dress and hair were in place. "Remain here. It would be unseemly if we both appeared to be taking air in the gardens."

Abby kissed him quickly on the lips. "I look forward to our next meeting." She let her fingers linger on his cheek for a few seconds before she dashed back toward the house.

Abby viewed him as a secret lover to be used and discarded at whim. Alexius had allowed the countess to cling to her illusion because it suited him. What the countess failed to understand was that he had taken and pleasured her at *his* whim. Like all the women who came before her, Abby belonged to him until he tired of the game.

With anticipation vibrating through his aroused body, Alexius turned and headed back for the hazel tree.

God's hooks, Sin was walking toward her!

The man was aptly named. With him on his feet and striding toward the tree with a lazy grace, Juliana understood why Lady Lettlecott risked a beating or worse for this man. Sin was the most beautiful man Juliana had ever encountered. Granted, she and her sisters had lived rather sequestered lives since their father had died and a distant cousin had claimed the Duncombe title along with their beloved home. Even so, Juliana's natural instincts hummed with a secret pleasure that muted her earlier fear.

He was older, mayhap twenty-five or twenty-six. His face was riveting, all slashing angles across his cheeks, nose, and jawbone. Hatless, the tousled black hair that had escaped his queue softened those uncompromising planes. Juliana was certain his eyes, too, enhanced his masculine beauty, but he would need to get closer for her to inspect them. She noticed as he approached that there was a slight plumpness to his lower lip and a hint of self-mockery that twisted his mouth. It might beckon an unwary lady—not her, of course—to risk her virtue by begging for a kiss. Oh, good grief, he was tall. Lean corded muscle and sinew moved seductively under his expensively tailored coat and tan-colored trousers that indicated that he was a gentleman.

Now that he was almost upon her, Juliana could not stop blushing. She kept thinking about the intimate way he had touched Lady Lettlecott. The countess had mewed and rolled her feverish body against him, and Sin *knew* Juliana was watching!

Even in the varying levels of shadows, the gleam in his eyes seemed like an unspoken challenge. No longer concerned about the noise she might make, Juliana tried to scoot down the tree trunk before he reached her, only to remember that her skirts were caught on the shoots and branches.

"Well, well, it isn't every day that I encounter a tree sprite," Sin drawled, bracing a palm against the slanted trunk that held her prisoner. His amusement was palpable.

And annoying.

Juliana impatiently blew the strand of hair obscuring her vision. "You know very well that I am not a tree sprite."

"Or mayhap you are a *lybbestre*. Tell me, my lady: is it true that moonlight is the source of your power and beauty?" Oh, the scoundrel, as Lady Lettlecott named him, was thoroughly enjoying himself on Juliana's behalf.

"I am not a sorceress," she said through clenched teeth. Her fear had gradually waned when it was plain

that Sin had no intention of alerting the countess to
Juliana's presence. While she was forced to watch the
wicked rake dally with his married mistress, the night
air had chilled Juliana. She was tired and her arms
ached from the strength she had exerted to avoid discovery. In her frame of mind, mocking her predicament
was a dangerous sport.

She glared down at him. "Go away."

Sin gave her a measured stare, before his gaze traveled down the length of her body to her exposed legs.
Her stockings and garters were visible to his perusal,
and she cringed at the several inches of bare skin he
could see above her garter on her left thigh. Even her
mother had not viewed Juliana's body so intimately
since she was a small child.

The man sensed her growing agitation and sighed.
"Very well. I shall leave you to your magic and moonlight—" He stepped away from the tree. His shoulders
bowed as he stoically accepted her rejection.

"Pray, my lord, hold!" Juliana blurted out before she
thought better of asking the devil to help her. "I need
your assistance. I am soundly caught." She kicked her
legs to demonstrate her dire predicament.

The swift grin he flashed at her revealed that she
had neatly ensnared herself in the subtle trap he had
set. "Indeed, you are, my lady."

He had thought her merely appealing? The blond *lybbestre* was spectacular! All of the physical attributes
Sin had admired from afar had only improved with
proximity. He seized the heavy bench at the base of the

tree and dragged it closer to her side. Climbing up, he used one of the other low-angled trunks to balance his stance. If she had not seemed so vexed with him and her predicament, he might have touched her cheek to test its petal-soft smoothness for himself.

Instead, he concentrated on her legs. By god, it was no hardship on his eyes. The poor lady had managed to tangle her skirt and petticoat in the branches. The gentle curves of her calves and a tantalizing hint of thigh were exposed for his hungry gaze. He patted one of the hazel tree's trunks, paying silent tribute to it for the lovely prize it had caught for him. If he had known what awaited him, he would have shoved Abby off his lap and sent her back to the house sooner for a chance to dally with this delightful wench.

Unable to resist, he stroked one of her legs with his palm. The blonde shrieked as if he had hurt her. The panicked reaction doused his enthusiasm a little. Whoever she was, she was unused to a man's hands on her body. Or she belonged to another man. Sin scowled, immediately disliking the notion. In the past, he had been able to work around such a hindrance when it suited him.

Like now.

"Steady, my dear lady. You'll bring others to your side, and I highly doubt either one of us wants the attention." Sin paused and waited for her consent.

She gave him a shaky nod.

"Good girl," he said approvingly like he was speaking to a fractious mare. Sin leaned in and peered at her legs. He heard her soft gasp. He uttered a low curse, noting her torn stockings and the spots of blood that had soaked through. "Christ, what a mess you've made," he muttered, sure her leg was stinging as much as the back of his neck. "You've bloodied your leg with your night mischief!"

"Night mischief?"

Sin turned his face away so she could not see his grin. Her outrage had fired her blood, and it was heating parts of him as well. He was certain the little tree witch was livid that he dared to scold her when she had caught him dallying with someone else's wife. What would she do, he mused, if he told her that he had changed his mind about Abby the second he had seen her peering down from the tree's foliage? His hand was unsteady when he placed it on her leg. What would she do if he bent his head down and tasted the hollow at the back of her knee with his tongue?

Alexius snorted.

She would probably try to plant her dainty foot in his arrogant mug.

What a sad, sorry state he was in. Lust had a way of stewing a man's wits, so much so that it twisted a man's cravings for a lady in a manner that even the thought of her committing violence against him made his cock twitch.

Painfully aroused, Alexius was sorely tempted to show the little innocent how rapidly temper could change into blind passion. The bruises and scratches would be worth it.

"I had a very good reason for climbing this tree, Mr. Sin," she said, oblivious to the battle he was waging within himself. "You might find this difficult to believe, but none of my reasons had anything to do with *you* or Lady Lettlecott!"

His lips twitched as if he was fighting not to laugh at her petulant tone. "So now I can add spying and eavesdropping to your growing list of misdeeds."

Sin patted her calf in sympathy, and to his delight, she growled at him. Her response provoked a throaty chuckle. "There, there, I was merely teasing. And it's simply 'Sin.' After all we have shared I think it is only fair that we are on informal terms. And you are?"

She ignored the question. Sin would have been disappointed if she had made it too easy for him. Sulky, the blonde closed her eyes, blocking out the knowledge that he was touching her. He kept the pressure of his fingers light and impersonal. A whiff of a light feminine scent teased his nose as he worked. She smelled of crushed hazel leaves, wood, and violets. All he wanted to do was bury his face between her legs and discover all of her unique scents.

Her body trembled under his gentle ministrations.

"Are you cold?" he inquired politely. "My coat would help warm you."

She opened her eyes and angled her neck so she could watch him unthread the fabric of her dress from the branches. "You are kind to offer, but I will be warm again when I return to the house."

"So you are one of Lettlecott's guests."

Her brows rose in mild curiosity. "Did you think I was a servant?"

Sin shook his head, his gaze directed on his task. "No. Your dress and speech are too refined." He did not mention that Abby was a trifle vain. She would have sacked any maid who outshone her own beauty. "I did, however, suspect that you might try to lie."

"Why would I lie?"

Aware of every move that she made, from the corner of his eye Sin watched as she kneaded a cramped muscle in her neck. She rested her cheek on her arm to relieve the discomfort.

"I have no intention of telling you anything about myself."

Juliana stopped breathing when Sin stroked her garter with the pad of his thumb. "You are not as forgettable as you might think, my mysterious *lybbestre*. You have skin that glows in the moonlight. Gold spun silk for hair, and lips that remind of ripe wood strawberries. Your eyes—," he began, but she cut him off.

"Pray, not another word." She leaned on her elbow to brace herself into more of a sitting position. "You cannot see the color of my eyes, you dolt!" she said, ruthlessly cutting off his praise. The fluttering in her heart had more to do with annoyance, she tried to tell herself, rather than pleasure at his practiced flattery. The man probably paid every woman he encountered the same compliments. "Even I cannot see the color of your eyes!"

The abrupt tension in his body unsettled her. Maybe she had gone too far? Finally, he said, "Then you will have to take a risk and move closer." The edge in his tone made her want to apologize. Before she could, he added, "You are free."

Without asking her permission, Sin plucked her from her perch and cradled her in his arms with an ease that astounded her. He was so warm Juliana wanted to instinctively burrow against him, soaking his heat into her bones. As her unguarded yearning registered, she stiffened in his embrace.

Juliana whispered against his coat, "You are holding me too tightly."

On a muffled oath, Sin jumped down from the bench, causing their bodies to bump against each other. The impact was strong enough to rattle her teeth.

Juliana had closed her eyes and now refused to open them. "You can put me down."

"What color are my eyes?"

Her eyes fluttered open at the unexpected question and she looked up and directly into his. Juliana only had the filtered moonlight and Lettlecott's distant lanterns to assist her, but her vision had acclimated to her dark surroundings. She saw Sin quite clearly. Framed with dark long eyelashes she saw intelligence, humor, and an emotional intensity she did not quite understand just beneath the gleaming surface of those expressive orbs. Sin had also proved he was capable of kindness. He had not delivered her to Lady Lettlecott when he had his chance. Nor had he abandoned Juliana, when her shame over her awkward predicament had caused her to be rude to him. The countess had said that Sin was capable of cruelty, and there was no reason to doubt the woman. She knew the man far more intimately than Juliana ever would dare.

However, that was not what he had asked her.

"Brown," she said, squinting as she drew closer. "No, wait. A hint of dark green and mayhap some gold. Hazel, I believe."

Hazel.

Just like the tree.

Was her fate to be ensnared by Sin as thoroughly?

The triumphant smile faded from her lips. It was then that she realized Sin's mouth was a hair's breadth away from hers. A sudden strong wind could have satisfied her curiosity and ended her just-realized torment.

No, this was wrong. *He* was all wrong for her. He could be married, a rake, or a fortune hunter. Her mother had plans for Juliana and her sisters. Whoever Sin was, she was certain that he did not fit in Maman's grand schemes. Juliana cleared her throat, breaking the spell of enchantment. Blinking rapidly, she turned her face away and cast her eyes downward to the ground.

"I need to return to the house, my lord," she said, hating the rawness in her voice. "My family. They will be concerned by my absence."

His slow reaction hinted at his reluctance to release her. Her legs wobbled as her satin slippers touched the soft ground covering.

"Green."

She started at his abrupt tone. "I beg your pardon?"

"Your eyes. The hue is reminiscent of the dark leaves of the Dog Rose in August."

He released his firm grip on her arms, and the night air washed away the warmth she had stolen from his embrace. She crossed her arms over her breasts. "I should go."

Sin took a step forward. Arms spread, he gestured at the wooden bench. "Or you could tarry and tell me why you were hiding in Lettlecott's hazel tree."

Juliana smiled sheepishly at his outrageous offer. Their unusual meeting should not have invited shared confidences. So why was she tempted to remain? She wrinkled her nose and shook her head. "I have family awaiting me indoors. Besides, your countess might return."

Juliana backed away from him, letting the shadows swallow her.

"Abby belongs to Lettlecott," Sin said quietly. "Not I."

"You might want to remind her of that fact, the next time she unbuttons your trousers," Juliana snapped back, and then winced. She would have happily cut out her tongue if she could have taken back her sharp words.

Sin's low, hearty laughter enveloped her. It slipped beneath her skin even as Juliana quickened her pace to put as much distance between them as possible.

Alexius listened to the woman's footfalls and shook his head in disbelief at her foolishness. She was likely to break an ankle fleeing from him at such a reckless pace. He could have assured her that he had no intention of pursuing her. There was a chance that she might have believed him.

Of course, it would have been a lie.

Walking back to the bench, he crouched down and scanned the ground. Where was it? There. Alexius plucked up the forgotten white plume and held it up for inspection.

There was nothing extraordinary about the tiny piece of fluff. Nothing. Still, it did not stop him from tucking the feather into the tiny pocket of his waistcoat.

It was then that Alexius recalled that his sulky *lybbestre* had not told him her name.

No matter.

The mystery of her identity was part of the sensual game they would play together. No woman had ever been able to resist Sin for long.

Chapter Two

ALEXIUS NODDED TO the two burly guards as they opened the double doors to Nox, one of the more notorious clubs in London. Situated at 44 King Street between Covent Garden and the private clubs of St. James, Nox was an exclusive den of corruption whose members provided titillating gossip for the *ton* each spring.

As one of the founding members, Alexius was often the focus of innuendo and full-blown scandals; however, such notoriety was common for the men bearing the Sinclair title.

"Good evening, Lord Sinclair." Berus, the steward of Nox, inclined his head respectfully. He removed the heavy black cloak from Alexius's shoulders and passed the outer garment to a waiting footman. "We were not expecting you this evening."

Alexius handed the servant his silk top hat. "My plans for the evening have taken an unexpected turn,

Berus." Energetic music and the shouts from enthusiastic gamblers beckoned behind closed doors. "It sounds like we have a full house."

The eighty-five-year-old house once belonged to the current Duke of Huntsley's grandmother. When she had died, she had specified in her will that the house and all its contents would pass to her beloved grandson. Six years earlier, the duke, or Hunter as he was called by his friends, had generously offered to donate the house for their little club. In a joint financial endeavor, Sin and his friends had renovated the old King Street house into an elegant, if not disreputable, meeting place. It had been Frost, the not-always-so-sensible Earl of Chillingsworth, who had suggested that they open the first floor of their club to guests and potential club candidates. All seven founding members had concurred. Over the years, the drinking and gambling had provided substantial revenue for the treasury that covered the servants' wages and the club's upkeep.

"Busier than usual for a Saturday evening, but nothing me and the staff can't handle, my lord," Berus said, removing a key from his waistcoat. He inserted the shank into the keyhole and gave the ornate bow an efficient twist. "You will find that you are not the only member whose plans took an unexpected turn this evening."

The steward opened the door. Overhead, painted on a rectangular stained-glass panel was the Latin phrase "*Virtus Deseritur,*" which translated into "virtue is forsaken." The panel had been a generous gift from someone's former mistress, though the astute widow's name had been long forgotten. Over time, the phrase became an apt motto for their little club.

Upstairs was the private sanctuary of the Lords of Vice. The appellation had been bestowed upon the seven of them years earlier after a prank had gone horribly awry. Afterward, several angry members of the *ton* had christened them with the nefarious title and Alexius and his friends were perverse enough to embrace it.

Access to the upper floors was restricted. Berus and his men were paid handsomely to ensure the uninvited were kept out. "Do you require anything else before I return to my duties, Lord Sinclair?"

"No, that will be all."

Alexius heard the heavy oak door close and the metal locking mechanism slide into place as he climbed the stairs. Ahead he could hear the familiar crack as one ivory ball collided with another. Masculine and feminine laughter greeted him when he entered the room.

Only four of the seven founding members of their club were present this evening. Reign, who seemed determined to ignore the stifling duties as Earl of Rainecourt, was stretched out on the sofa with a female companion tucked under each arm. Vane, the Earl of Vanewright, was across the room on another sofa cuddling a very affectionate wench on his lap while Saint, the Marquess of Sainthill, and Frost, the Earl of Chillingsworth, strategically circled the twelve-feet by six-feet billiard table positioned in the middle of the room.

Reign ground his dark head of hair into the back of the sofa as he twisted his face in the general direction of the doorway. His expression flashed from surprise to genuine pleasure. "Sin! Egad, you've made a short evening of it. You have my sympathies."

"Good evening, gents . . . ladies," Alexius said, settling into the chair to his left. "Berus says we have a full house this evening."

"Apparently so," Saint said, his keen gaze focused on the billiard table. His tone implied that the activity below meant little to him.

Reign murmured something in the blonde's ear, causing her to giggle. Sensing Alexius's casual regard, the earl's dark blue gaze shifted to him. "What happened to the Lettlecotts?"

Alexius pressed the back of his hand to his mouth to stifle a yawn. "Nothing. They seemed hearty and hale when I took my leave."

Vane gave the woman sitting on his lap a playful shove. "Mary, my flirtatious minx, be a dear and pour Sin some brandy. It should dull the edge of his sarcastic tongue and spare us a bloodletting."

The two white ivory balls collided, the hollow sound morbidly reminding him of skulls clacking together. Frost grunted in satisfaction as Saint's ivory ball disappeared into a corner pocket.

"Do you wish to concede this game, Saint, or shall I humiliate you further?"

The Marquess of Sainthill pointed his cue at his opponent. Contrary to what his nickname implied, Saint could be quite devilish when provoked. Alexius shifted in his chair, his muscles tensing at the subtle threat of violence emanating from the players. This would not be the first time that he and the others had separated Saint and Frost.

Saint sneered. "Just play, you cocky arse. Either

way, at the end of the night, my blunt still ends up in your bloody purse."

" 'Ere you go, milord," Vane's brown-haired minx said, dangling the glass of brandy in front of his face. When Alexius accepted the offered glass, the lady interpreted his actions as an invitation and slid gracefully onto his lap.

"I do not believe we have been properly introduced, my dear," he said dryly as the generous chit worked her clever little tongue into his ear. "What is your name?"

Everyone laughed, which had been his intention. The enthusiastic flirt on his lap had bathed herself in a heavy floral scent that offended his nose, but she had a sweet face, clean hair, and wore a dress that displayed her enticing wares as effectively as a shopkeeper's front window display.

"I'm Mary, my lord," she said, glancing back at Vane for his support.

"Or you may pick another name if you fancy something exotic," Vane added cheerfully, unperturbed that his lady for the night was fondling one of his best friends. "Is that not so, love?"

"Indeed, it is." She leaned closer and whispered into Alexius's ear, "I can be anyone you desire."

Her offer summoned the unbidden visage of the mysterious lady he had encountered in the Lettlecotts' gardens. Those expressive green eyes, so wary and yet curious, had made an impression on him. He looked forward to the hour when he would encounter the lady again. For now, he banished the intriguing *lybbestre* from his thoughts and concentrated on the female on his lap.

"You're one of Madam V's girls, are you not?" Alexius inquired, lazily wondering if the lady was also a pickpocket. Her hand had delved beneath his coat and he could feel her unfastening the buttons of his waistcoat.

"Aye, that's right," Mary said, her brown eyes warming with pride. "The madam sent us to you fine gents with her compliments."

Madam Venna was the proprietress of the Golden Pearl, a brothel that provided a rather extraordinary creative selection of carnal indulgences for its discerning patrons. Alexius suspected it was Madam V's royal admirers who allowed her to run her establishment unmolested by the local constables.

"Your mistress is generous," Reign said, nibbling on the brunette's lips as he fondled the blonde leaning against his right side. The man was thoroughly enjoying the lion's share of the madam's gift, and if Alexius knew his friend, neither lady would be neglected.

The brunette clinging to Reign added, "Madam Venna appreciates the business our visits to Nox bring about." She gave Saint a sly glance. "Lord Sainthill, the madam wanted me to convey her personal condolences on the departure of your latest mistress. If you require anything, the madam has offered to see to your, uh, demands personally."

Saint slammed his cue down on the billiards table with enough force to silence the room. He took a threatening step toward the brunette but seemed to collect himself as she cringed against Reign. "Tell Madam Venna," he said, snatching up his cue. "Tell her . . . Her pity is unnecessary and her offer bores me."

That was Saint for you. He could be polite while telling a lady to go to hell. Alexius could only speculate on what had transpired between the lovely Madame V and Saint, but it had ended unpleasantly.

Vane cleared his throat. It was a pathetic attempt to change the subject, but even he seemed willing to ignore Saint's unexpected outburst. "Sin, did Berus mention that your sister has sent several messengers to the club this afternoon?"

Damn.

Alexius finished his brandy. "No," he said curtly while Mary, bless her, trotted off without being asked to refill his glass. Why was Belinda searching for him? Already aggravated by whatever crisis his sister was planning to draw him into, Alexius scrubbed his face with his hand. He was tired and hoped within the hour he would be too drunk to tackle Belinda's little problem.

"I will call on her tomorrow."

"There, there, Lord Sinclair," Mary said, placing the glass of brandy into his eager hands. Her tone was soothing and almost motherly, but she ruined the chaste image by plopping down onto his lap. "Family matters. They tend to muddle a man's plans, don't ye think?"

"For a pretty girl, you are awfully insightful." Alexius toasted her clever brain by raising his glass and imbibing. Mary giggled and squirmed closer as if she hoped to share his coat with him.

For a silent invitation, hers was endearingly transparent.

The pretty whore was letting him know in her unsubtle manner that she was his for the evening. All he had to do was accept her generous offer. Alexius measured her narrow waist with his hands. His thoughts once again drifted to the beautiful green-eyed blonde who had not trusted him with her name.

Utterly insulting.

Even though he had spared her from the Countess of Lettlecott's ire, the ungrateful chit had not thought his good deed worthy of a boon. Sighing, he lifted Mary off his lap and steadied her while she found her feet. He patted her affectionately on the rump.

Mary's brow lifted in puzzlement.

Alexius was sympathetic. He was equally bewildered by his decision.

"Off you go," he said, encouraging her toward Vane. "My friend will appreciate you this evening more than I."

Vane gave Alexius a questioning glance when Mary rejoined him on the sofa. Alexius shrugged and sipped his brandy. This was hardly the moment to announce to his drunken companions that a willing whore would not satisfy the lust simmering in his loins when he craved a more elusive challenge.

Frost howled in triumph as he holed the winning ball. His friends cheered, and in spite of Saint's flash of temper, he accepted their ribbing with admirable grace.

"Another game, Saint?" Alexius suggested. "I didn't have the opportunity to wager on Frost this last game."

Saint muttered an obscenity under his breath. With a pointed look at Reign, Saint rolled the cue between his palms. "Any thought on how I might improve my odds?"

Reign's slow smile was truly evil.

"I might, indeed." He spoke quietly to the brunette.

She cast several quick glances at Frost and nodded. "Frost, my friend, what say you if we added a slight challenge to this new game?"

The Earl of Chillingsworth snorted. "If you double the wager."

"Done!" Reign extricated himself from the two beauties and climbed to his feet. "Gentlemen?" he asked, looking at his friends for concurrence.

From Saint's expression Alexius concluded that he and Reign had concocted a plan long before the first game had been played. It was even possible that Saint had deliberately forfeited the earlier game to lure Frost into a false sense of confidence.

Not that Frost needed any encouragement.

The man possessed the arrogance of five men.

Vane shrugged, so Alexius spoke for both of them. "Agreed."

Reign offered his hand to the brunette. She appeared a little skittish, but she tucked her hand into his and allowed him to escort her over to Frost.

"Lord Chillingsworth, your challenge."

The prostitute tolerated Frost's sullen perusal like a professional. Of the three, she likely would not have been the earl's first choice. Alexius, like the rest of the occupants in the room, was privately wondering what Reign had ordered the brunette to do.

The earl's eyes flared with interest when her fingers touched the two vertical buttons near his right hipbone. She unfastened his trousers with a practiced ease, and with her gaze fixed on Frost's she braced her hands on his hips while she slowly lowered herself until she was on her knees.

"If I may?" The brunette purred in approval as she freed Frost from his trousers.

The prostitute's head blocked Alexius's view, but Frost's face told its own story. He was aroused and willing to play billiards by Reign's rules.

Without warning, Frost's blissful expression vanished and his jaw clenched as his competitive spirit resurfaced. Reign had underestimated Frost's desire to win. Nothing could distract him from claiming his victory, not even the tantalizing wench on her knees.

"Do your worst."

Even so, there was no doubt in Alexius's mind that Frost fully intended to bed the brunette who was teasing him to the point of madness with her nimble tongue.

After he trounced Saint in a game of billiards.

With the lip of the glass of brandy touching his lips, Alexius watched both professionals in action. When his eyes were half-closed, it was simple to imagine the blond *lybbestre* at his feet, her green eyes shimmering with desire.

All he had to do was find her again.

Chapter Three

SOFTLY HUMMING A snippet of a melody from the previous evening, Juliana was making her way downstairs to join her mother and sisters in the breakfast room. She was in high spirits this morning, though she loathed dwelling on the reasons. It certainly had nothing to do with the charming rogue she had encountered by chance in the Lettlecotts' gardens. Indeed, the very notion was ridiculous. Their brief exchange could barely be described as a conversation.

No, perhaps the true source of her high spirits was that she had finally reconciled herself to her fate. Since her mother had announced that they would be spending the season in London, Juliana had suffered bouts of unease about the entire affair.

And why should she not?

Her family's position in polite society had plummeted considerably since her father's demise five years earlier from a sudden weakness in his heart. Sadly, the kind, genial Marquess of Duncombe had died an impoverished man. As he had lacked the business sense of his predecessors, what money the marquess had inherited swiftly evaporated as his family increased. What had spared them the fate of debtor's prison was his skill at the gaming tables. Up to the day he died, her father had maintained a delicate balance of credit and winnings.

No one, not even her mother, had been aware how precarious their financial circumstances had become, that was, until a distant cousin had arrived at Ivers Hall to claim the Duncombe title.

Oliver Bristow, the new Lord Duncombe, was everything his predecessor had not been when it came to business. Bristow's investments had paid off handsomely, and for a brief time her mother had believed their cousin would save the Ivers family.

That was not the case.

The then-twenty-five-year-old Lord Duncombe might have been adequate in looks and brought wealth to the title again; however, he did not possess an ounce of compassion for the widowed marchioness and her three daughters.

Instead of paying off Juliana's father's creditors, the new Lord Duncombe gave the family lectures. For hours and hours, the dreadful man pontificated on his predecessor's weakness, recklessness, and the burden her father had settled on his family. She had watched her mother's slender shoulders bow with each condemnation, and what hope Juliana might have felt upon meeting the young lord had winked out of existence.

Satisfied that the widow understood her new position in the family, Lord Duncombe offered to increase her annuity on one condition. The widow and her daughters had to vacate Ivers Hall at once. Literally overnight, the servants had packed the family's personal belongings and they were taken to a small cottage Lord Duncombe had rented on their behalf.

The marquess had thought he had rid himself of his impoverished relatives. Arrogant, rigid, and judgmental, he had assumed the widow would accept his charity for her daughters' sake and shut herself away from the *ton*.

The gentleman, however, had sorely misjudged Lady Duncombe's character.

An unintelligible cry of exasperation resounded from the study of their rented town house, shaking Juliana from her musings. She swiftly altered her course from the breakfast room to the small study. Something had upset her mother. She rarely made use of the study at such an early hour.

As Juliana peered within, she discovered her mother seated at the oversized mahogany desk. There were several sheets of paper scattered on the desk; however, it was the one in her hand that was the source of the lady's outrage.

Juliana suddenly lost all desire for breakfast.

The scowl on her mother's face warned that new trials were brewing for their little family. And nothing had been simple for them since Juliana's father's death.

"Trouble, Maman?" Juliana politely inquired, trying to keep her growing anxiety hidden.

The Marchioness of Duncombe started at her youngest daughter's voice. She slapped her hand over her heart. "Juliana, you gave me a tremendous fright! What are you doing here? Have you eaten breakfast, my dear child?" She set aside the paper she had been reading, and with deliberate care she removed her spectacles.

Maman's warm, blue eyes sharpened on her youngest daughter. With her forty-sixth birthday approaching, Hester Ivers, Lady Duncombe did not look like a woman who had three daughters ready for the marriage market. Her blond hair, a lovely mix of brown and gold, was tucked into a matronly lace cap. She wore a blue-gray morning dress that seemed to hang from her frame, a sign that she had lost more weight. Panic fluttered in Juliana's empty stomach at the thought that she and her sisters might lose their mother as well.

Juliana swallowed the lump of misery thickening in her throat. "No. I was just coming down the stairs when I heard you cry out." Juliana approached the desk and glanced down at the paper. It was not a bill from a creditor, as she had feared, but rather some personal correspondence. "Are you unwell? Has something happened?"

Her mother laid her palm on the letter before Juliana could pick it up. "It is nothing," Lady Duncombe said dismissively, crushing the letter to prove her point.

Pursing her lips as she stared down at the crumpled ball of paper in her mother's clenched fist, Juliana could think of several relatives and well-meaning friends who could provoke such a response from the marchioness. As Juliana debated about making a childish grab for the letter, her face must have revealed her intentions.

With a dramatic sigh of surrender, her mother said, "Did I ever tell you and your sisters that single-mindedness can be deemed unappealing to a potential husband, unless the intent is obedience?"

Lady Duncombe touched two fingers to her own forehead. "It also gives you the most unattractive lines—"

Before Juliana could stop herself, she covered the offending lines with her hand. Disgusted that she had fallen for the distracting ruse, her hand came down in a slashing gesture. "Oh, for goodness' sake, Maman! Tell me the truth. Who sent the letter?"

Her mother's shoulders sagged. "He knows."

Juliana resisted the urge to stomp her foot down in frustration. "It is early, Maman. Could you be less evasive?"

"Oliver knows we are currently residing in London." She opened her hand, glowering at the ruined paper that represented the figurehead of their family. "And he doesn't approve."

Although she was the youngest, Juliana understood her mother better than her elder sisters, Cordelia and Lucilla. Juliana had learned to pay attention to the marchioness's clever omissions.

"Oh, Maman." Juliana joined her mother on the other side of the desk and knelt in front of her. "Look me in the eye, and swear that you did not write Lord Duncombe."

"There have been expenses that I had not anticipated."

Juliana groaned and pressed her knuckles into her lips. For five years, they had been at the mercy of their cousin's whims. Like her husband before her, Lady

Duncombe had sought her fortune at the card tables. Once a casual player in the elegant card rooms around London, she believed that her skills were akin to her husband's. While her successes had bought the women certain freedoms, her occasional losses kept them indebted to Lord Duncombe.

"What was I to do? The bill for the mantua maker alone exceeded my calculations." Lady Duncombe clasped both of Juliana's hands and settled them on her lap. "And lately, there have been several evenings when the cards have not favored me. I only asked Oliver for a small loan."

Juliana conjured the marquess's stern visage, his thin lips pressed together in disapproval. She shuddered, banishing his face from her mind. From the moment he had inherited the Duncombe title, the marquess had displayed nothing but contempt for his predecessor's widow and her daughters.

"Maman, Lord Duncombe has made it clear on numerous occasions that he considers this branch of the family a nuisance and an inconvenient drain of his time and resources."

"Not all, my love. I recall a summer when he was rather taken with you. In fact . . ." She trailed off, then seemed to collect herself and focus on the subject at hand. "Of course, he will do his duty!"

Juliana closed her eyes, striving for patience. With a shake of her head, she kissed her mother's hands. "And *you* promised that we would remain in the country, the last time you asked him to cover your losses."

Lady Duncombe smiled, recalling the encounter. "Oliver was rather vexed at me, was he not?"

Lord Duncombe was a judgmental, sanctimonious prig. "Our impoverished circumstances shame our cousin, Maman. He will view our stay in London as a blatant act of defiance."

"I will admit that I do not understand the gentleman. He is nothing like your father," Lady Duncombe said crossly. "London is where you girls need to be this season. If one or all of you make solid matches in town, then our unfortunate circumstances will come to an end. We will no longer have to appeal to his generous nature."

Generous nature, my foot!

Lord Duncombe took perverse pleasure in placing his polished boot on Lady Duncombe's throat and watching her squirm. Juliana despised the odious man for his callous disposition. Nor did she like the hard, calculating look in his eyes when his gaze happened to settle on her.

"I assume Lord Duncombe rejected your appeal for a temporary loan." Juliana slowly straightened, allowing the blood to ease back into her cramped legs. She braced herself against the edge of the desk.

Her mother blinked at her. "What?" She dismissed Juliana's assumption with a wave of her hand. "Of course. He made his disappointment quite clear in his letter."

Indeed. Lord Duncombe was always precise and articulate when expressing his disappointments in the Ivers family.

"He has ordered us to return to the country," Juliana's mother said offhandedly. She did not seem upset by the command.

"Should I order the servants to start packing?" Juliana asked, masking the relief she felt that for once her mother's plans for her daughters had been hindered before they could come to fruition.

Although Juliana loathed confessing the words aloud, she privately feared Lord Duncombe. He would not forgive her mother's defiance, and the unknown consequences were likely to affect them all.

"Why? My plans for you girls are coming along nicely. Cordelia and Lucilla already have gentlemen leaving their cards." Lady Duncombe's eyes narrowed on Juliana as if she were a puzzle her mother had yet to solve. "Perhaps we should lower the bodice of all your dresses?"

Not without a fight.

"Maman, my dresses are fine," Juliana said, crossing her arms. "What about Lord Duncombe?"

Her mother shrugged her shoulders daintily. "We will address the matter when he joins us in London."

Chapter Four

"YOUR NOTE SPOKE of a favor."

"Ah, Alexius, you try my patience," Belinda Snow, Countess of Gredell, said crisply, her light brown eyes flashing in vexation. "Six hours have elapsed since the messenger delivered my note to your residence."

Alexius dutifully brushed his lips against his older sister's subtly rouged cheek. "I was not at home when your imperial summons arrived, Belle. I came as soon as I was aware that you required my services."

Adorned in a claret and ivory evening dress, his sister reclined against the chaise longue as if she were a queen. With her long black hair swept high and bound with slender serpentine ropes of gold chain and pearls, Belinda definitely had the airs of one.

She tilted her chin just high enough to look down her nose at him. It was quite a feat, since he was standing over her. "Where were you?"

Alexius stiffened at her accusatory tone. He was not accustomed to explaining himself to anyone. If she had been his mistress, rather than his older sister, he would have walked out the door and out of her life. With a careless grace, he removed his frock coat.

"Many years have passed since I was accountable to you, little mother," he said lightly; the hint of affection in his inflection took the sting out of his words. Alexius draped the coat over the nearest chair. His relationship with his half sister was complicated, one he never discussed with others, including his closest friends. However, he understood where his loyalties lay.

As a peace offering, he picked up the silver bowl containing a lopsided pyramid of plump sugared grapes from the table and extended the bowl to her. "May I offer you something to chew on besides my tough hide, love?"

Belinda plucked a grape from the bowl. Her light brown eyes narrowed, conveying her disappointment. "You were fondling with one of your whores, I wager."

Alexius grinned at her outrageous remark. He leaned forward and returned the silver bowl to the table. Belinda sounded jealous. However, her possessiveness was not of a carnal nature. His sister simply disliked him putting his needs above hers.

"Just *one*?" he teased, sliding down to the floor until his back reclined against the cushion of the chaise longue. "Belle, truly, you cut me to the quick."

"Fine. Mock my words, my pain," Belinda said heatedly as she sat up, burying the right side of his body with a prodigious amount of silk and petticoat. "In many ways, you remind me of our father."

For spiteful remarks, this one hit the target.

Shoving her skirts aside, Alexius grabbed his sister by the wrist. "That was beneath you." His grip became punishing when she attempted to pull away. "Especially since you desire a favor from me."

Belinda's expression became instantly contrite. "Forgive me."

On a muttered oath, Alexius released her. He climbed onto his feet and crossed the room to the narrow cart that displayed several wines and his favorite brandy. "This favor. What do you require from me?" He sent her a sharp glance while he poured brandy into a glass.

Fumbling for a handkerchief, Belinda sniffed delicately and blotted the tender flesh beneath her eyes. With a quiet sincerity, Belinda said, "I want you to seduce Lady Juliana Ivers."

Alexius tried not to choke on the mouthful of brandy he had just swallowed. He gritted his teeth as the liquor burned a path down to his gut. "Christ! You little hypocrite. Just moments earlier, you were chastising me for dallying with my whores. Now you are ordering me into a lady's bed?"

"This is entirely different," Belinda countered defensively.

Unconvinced, he cocked his left brow. "Indeed? How so?"

She gave him an exasperated look. "You bed any pretty wench who catches your eye. Why on earth are you balking about a silly virgin?"

Alexius took a healthy swallow of his brandy and shut his eyes so he did not have to see the silent plea in

Belinda's gaze. "Lady Juliana is a virgin," he said, not trusting his hearing. What his sister desired brought him uncomfortably close to the past.

Some of his distaste must have been evident on his face. Or maybe Belinda understood him better than anyone else in the world. She rose up from the chaise longue and tentatively approached him. "Do not give me a look, Alexius. Considering the lady's daring with certain gentlemen of the *ton*, Lady Juliana's innocence is debatable, if nonexistent. Trust me; this horrible creature is nothing like your dearly departed mother. I was wrong before when I said that you reminded me of our father. You are nothing like him," she said fiercely, cupping the underside of his jaw.

It was a lie, but Alexius understood why his sister preferred to shy away from the truth. In many ways, he was his father's son, and there was little about his sire that was commendable, except for the fact that the elder Sinclair was dead.

Alexius leaned against her palm, noting the apology in her liquid brown eyes before he pulled away. He also saw her determination. A sense of foreboding washed over him. A determined Belle was a dangerous Belle. He was not blind to his sister's faults. If he refused to help her, his sister would find another gentleman to assist her. There was no telling what price another man might demand of Belinda, or how far she was willing to go to exact her revenge for a real or imaginary slight.

Alexius clasped her shoulders and stared intently into her eyes. "I am unfamiliar with Lady Juliana. Who is she? What has she done?"

Belinda's mouth moved wordlessly before she hoarsely uttered, "She stole from me the affections of the man I hope to marry!"

As if the confession sapped the last of her strength, his sister collapsed against him in a noisy fit of hysteria.

Although Alexius had thought himself rather jaded to a lady's tears, he was not unmoved by his sister's misery. He dipped low and picked her up into his arms. With her trembling form pressed tightly to his chest, he returned to the chaise longue and lowered them both onto the soft cushions.

"Tell me about Lady Juliana," he murmured softly against Belinda's ear.

At first, Belinda made little sense to him. She cried and spoke in disjointed sentences, punctuating her words by pounding her fist against his chest. From her tearful explanation, Alexius pieced together the cunning and spiteful nature of Lady Juliana Ivers.

The vain chit viewed herself as Belinda's equal in beauty and position in the *ton*. His sister explained that she had initially tried to guide the young lady, but jealousy and resentment had soured their budding friendship. According to his sister, Lady Juliana had already turned this season into an unpleasant and ruthless competition. Any gentleman who displayed the slightest interest in Alexius's sister was lured away by the blond siren's machinations.

Alexius and his friends had played similar mischievous games with the ladies of the *ton*. So had his sister. Though in her current mood, she was likely to deny it. He did not begrudge Lady Juliana her games. Nevertheless, the lady had gravely miscalculated her influence within the *ton* when she had selected Belinda as her rival. The unknown chit had earned his ire for hurting his sister, and there were few who would openly court his wrath.

"The others . . . Oh, I cared little for their departure," Belinda said, pausing to indelicately blow her nose. She waved the handkerchief dismissively. "But Lord Kyd! He has been a devoted and ardent companion for three seasons. I have sensed for some time that he has been working up the courage to offer for my hand—"

Belinda pressed the sodden handkerchief to her mouth and hiccupped. "Yesterday, he had sent a note with his regrets that he would not be able to join me in my theater box that evening. I had decided to attend the theater without him." She shivered as the horror of the evening assailed her. "Who did I espy in Lady Juliana's rented box but my beloved Lord Kyd!"

"Kyd is an arse."

Alexius had been unaware that his sister had been contemplating marriage again. That bounder of a husband, Gredell, had been moldering in his grave for five years. Belinda had seemed content with her lord's absence as long as she had access to his purse.

"You leave Lord Kyd alone! He's my beloved arse, and I will not surrender him to the wiles of Lady Juliana," Belinda said, her bout of melancholy waning with the rise of her anger.

Alexius rubbed his sister's back as he mentally pondered his choices. "I could approach Lady Juliana. A simple warning might suffice."

Belinda dismissed the suggestion with a vigorous shake of her head. "I, however, will not be satisfied with a simple warning, Alexius. Lady Juliana Ivers has mocked and humiliated me in front of the *ton*. I want—" She suddenly went silent.

"What do you want, Belle?" he coaxed, already knowing her reply.

"I want to teach the arrogant chit a lesson." His sister stared lovingly at him while her hand tenderly cupped his cheek. "You are so beautiful, Alexius. I want Lady Juliana to be seduced and cast aside by the one man I know she cannot have."

A slight dimple formed in his right cheek as Alexius grinned at his sister. "Such faith, Belle. What makes you think I will be impervious to Lady Juliana's infamous charms?"

Belinda leaned closer, kissing him lightly on the lips. "Because you, my handsome brother," she said, her brown eyes shimmering with confidence, "belong wholly to *me*."

Chapter Five

"I FEEL RIDICULOUS."

Cordelia's nose crinkled charmingly as she gave Juliana's bonnet and dress a critical glance. At the age of four and twenty, Cordelia had had the pleasure of the social whirl of a season in London six years earlier, before their father's death had forced the family to remain in the country. Although the season had not ended with a marriage offer, Juliana and Lucilla viewed their elder sister as an expert in matters of etiquette and fashion.

"Is it the bonnet? I will admit the brim on the bonnet is larger than our older ones."

Lucilla touched the wide brim of her own leghorn bonnet. "I rather like it," she said, fondling the tangled cascade of yellow and green ribbons pinned to the crown. Their new bonnets and dresses with matching parasols all seemed like an adventure to her.

Juliana fingered the fanciful mix of greenery, flowers, and fat bows adorning her crown and brim in stoic silence. She had already complained to her mother that the fresh flowers were likely to attract bees, but she had merely brushed aside her daughter's complaints.

"The bonnet is not as annoying as this carriage ride through the park," Juliana grumbled. "I would have preferred walking with Maman and Mrs. Maddock."

Unless Juliana turned her head, the oversized brim limited her view so that she could only view the carriages that passed them from the opposite direction. The scrutiny from the gentlemen and ladies was unsettling, as if she and her sisters were something to analyze, ridicule, and dismiss.

Lucilla smiled coyly at two gentlemen on horseback who tipped their hats at the trio as they rode past the women. She might have thought twice about the flirtation if she had put on her spectacles.

"Well, I think all of this is rather grand!"

"You think everything is grand," Juliana shot back. "You certainly have been annoyingly cheerful ever since you learned that Mr. Stepkins had followed you to London like a heartsick puppy."

"Mr. Stepkins has nothing to do with my high spirits," Lucilla said with a haughty toss of her chin. "I cannot help if the gentleman favors my company above all others."

Juliana yawned. She had grown weary of discussing her sister's suitor months ago. "Mayhap he favors how free you are with your kisses."

"Apologize immediately!" Lucilla squealed with outrage.

"Ladies," Cordelia said quietly.

Two ladies in the passing carriage peered at them with undisguised interest.

Lucilla curled her upper lip. Her pale green eyes reminded Juliana of cool, impenetrable marble. "You are just envious that I have garnered such devotion and friendship that Mr. Stepkins could not bear to be separated from me while all you have for company is an old pianoforte in the stuffy drawing room."

It was mean-spirited of her to attack the one activity that truly gave Juliana pleasure. Music had eased her grief when the family had to carry on without their father, and gave her companionship when she was lonely.

She was not jealous of her sister.

Still, Juliana could not resist retaliating in kind. "The pianoforte is more entertaining than listening to Mr. Stepkins drone on about the new horse he purchased or the latest gossip he overheard. I daresay, he likely followed you to town because you are the only lady in England who does not fall asleep when he opens his mouth."

"Ooph!"

Lucilla kicked Juliana sharply in the ankle.

"The word is 'oaf,' and it aptly describes your hamfisted suitor." Juliana sent the point of her closed parasol into the top of her sister's leather shoe. "Nearsighted harpy!"

"Juliana! Lucilla!" Cordelia scolded them, though her light blue eyes were twinkling with suppressed humor. "Maman would be horrified if she witnessed this bickering. She wants us to make a good impression, and both of you are behaving like ill-mannered children."

Juliana leaned forward. "Driver, turn about and return us to our mother."

"Aye, miss."

"You have no right to issue orders!" Lucilla said, twisting around to counter her younger sister's command. "You there—"

"Let the order stand, Lucilla," Cordelia advised dryly. "If you and Juliana persist, this shameful display will likely end in fisticuffs."

Juliana giggled at the notion of facing their mother with a blackened eye or bloodied lip. When they were girls, the trio had engaged in some very unladylike behavior. Even though Lucilla was to blame, their mother would not tolerate squabbling and her daughters would all suffer her ire. "We could always open a booth at a fair and sell tickets."

Cordelia smiled. "While that might be an inventive and amusing way to solve our family's financial woes, I doubt Maman would approve."

"When Mr. Stepkins asks Maman for my hand in marriage, I will insist that Maman come live with us," Lucilla announced, a not-so-subtle reminder that she currently was in the best position to help their family.

Juliana shared a commiserating look with Cordelia. Lucilla was simply being Lucilla, but there were times when the rivalry was irksome.

"That is very generous of you, Lucilla," Juliana said to placate her sibling. "However, Maman enjoys her cards too much to ever give them up."

"That means one of us should find a wealthy gentleman," Cordelia added.

Both Cordelia and Lucilla were welcome to hunt for a wealthy gentleman to marry. When pursuing a gentleman, Juliana had higher ambitions than marriage. She had already met one such gentleman. He was well mannered, friendly, and had no interest in courting her. Lord Kyd also shared her appreciation for music and seemed quite amenable to helping her find a publisher for her musical compositions.

His friendship had made her family's stay in London bearable.

"If Maman has her way, she will be matching all three of us with titled gentlemen with hefty purses," Lucilla said, looking pensive. She was probably wondering what she was going to do about her devoted Mr. Stepkins.

Juliana turned her head and stared at their driver's back. The wide brim of her hopeless hat served to shield her from the prying gazes of the *ton*. Absently she waved away a hovering bumblebee as her thoughts drifted to Lord Kyd. She hoped that she would encounter him this evening and that he would save her from her mother's matchmaking.

"Who has caught your eye?"

Alexius's gaze shifted from the ballroom to the gentleman beside him. Fifteen minutes earlier, he had excused himself from the card table, leaving his friends to empty the purses of Lord and Lady Kempe's guests. Alexius was surprised that Hugh Wells Mordare, or Dare as he was commonly called, had followed him, since the man preferred games of chance to the riskier games played by the ladies of the *ton*.

"My sister."

So he was not being exactly truthful. Seconds before Dare had intruded, Alexius had been searching the crowd for the mysterious blonde who had not lingered around for a proper introduction.

"Berus had mentioned that the countess had sent several messengers to Nox," Dare said, his somber blue-gray gaze casually drifting from guest to guest. "What does she want from you?"

Dare was a cynical soul when it came to family and their demands. Years earlier, he had been betrayed by his brother and the woman Dare had loved. The experience had left him embittered and his family divided. It did not take much intuition for Alexius to predict how his friend might react to Belle's small favor.

"Perhaps Belle was simply missing me."

Dare glanced back at Alexius, bemused that his friend would suggestion anything so ridiculously naïve. "No offense, Sin, but most ladies, and your sister, in particular, always have a reason."

It was a shrewd observation that Alexius could not dispute.

"Is there a reason why we have not moved on to another house?" Vane demanded as he strolled up to them. "Hunter fell asleep in the middle of the game; Saint is winning, which is annoying Frost, so he is doing his best to provoke Kempe's heir into a fight."

Christ.

"That will get him and the rest of us tossed out onto our arses," Dare muttered.

Alexius had been mildly surprised that Lord and Lady Kempe had bothered to send the Lords of Vice invitations. Nevertheless, a man's title and wealth went a long way to smoothing his less savory habits. Lady Kempe, undoubtedly, hoped to do some matchmaking.

Alexius said to his friends, "I need a word with my sister, and then we can depart." He pointed at Dare. "Keep Frost from killing Kempe's whelp."

Alexius walked away, intending to circle the perimeter of the ballroom once before he and his friends took their leave. He had lied about his need to see his sister. Belle had not mentioned to him that she would be attending the Kempes' ball. Nor was he interested in seeking out her rival, Lady Juliana Ivers.

The lady he desired was elusive. If he did not find her here, there were other ballrooms, other nights.

As he mulled over whether or not there was time to walk the ballroom again before Frost or the others strained their welcome, Alexius's vision was obscured by gloved fingers.

"Sin," the low feminine voice sighed, as if his name were a benediction. "Oh, you dreadfully wicked man. Where have you been hiding?"

Alexius smiled at the exasperation he sensed in the question. "Nell, my lovely hussy, the real mystery is: why are you here? I thought you were visiting Bath."

The Countess of Lawrie's hands lifted from his eyes so he could turn around and properly greet the lady who occasionally shared his bed when the notion suited them both. Only three inches shorter than him, the twenty-four-year-old dark-haired beauty was staring at him as if she wanted to nibble her way down his body.

Since they were in public, however, he bowed over her hand and she curtsied. There was a twinkle of mischief in her dark blue eyes that always seemed to taunt him into being wicked. He had met her six years ago when she was eighteen and he was nineteen. The elderly husband her greedy father had secured for her had already left her a widow. Fortunately, the earl had also bequeathed a small fortune to his young countess. Free of her tyrannical father and a restrictive enfeebled husband, Lady Lawrie had dedicated herself to spending her dead husband's wealth and enjoying her lovers.

Nell pouted as Alexius straightened. "You were correct. Cadoux was utterly tiresome out of bed. I left him at Royal Crescent, or thereabouts," she said with a dismissive flick of her fingers.

"You are remaining in town for the season?"

"But of course." She surveyed Lord and Lady Kempe's ballroom with a sanguine expression. "With you at my side, we shall keep the gossips and the *ton* amused for weeks."

An energetic, naughty minx, Nell was just the lady to shake the ennui that had been gradually stealing his enthusiasm about remaining in London. As a lover, she had been creative and generous. There had been odd times when Alexius had genuinely missed her as she had moved on to other lovers.

"London would have been boring without you," he said, deciding that talking with the lady next to him would be more entertaining than pursuing his mystery lady or seducing the vain Lady Juliana Ivers. There was comfort in the familiar, which was an indication how far he had fallen into his odd melancholy. "Would you prefer— Oh, Christ."

"What is it?"

There she was. His mysterious *lybbestre*, an inviting vision in violet. Her hand was on the arm of Lord Kyd's as they promenaded back to their positions of their set. If Belle had been present to witness her lover's delight as he grinned boyishly at his dancing partner, she would have happily murdered them both.

As if sensing Alexius's scrutiny, his *lybbestre* glanced at him. He seized Nell's hand and dragged her behind one of the marble colonnades.

"Sin, what on earth—?"

The last thing he wanted was for the lady to see him with Lady Lawrie. He and Nell shared an intimacy that was apparent even to the casual observer, and if the blonde inquired about them there was an endless supply of gossip that could fill her ears about their relationship.

He had to get rid of Nell.

Alexius stared intently at the countess, wondering what to do with her.

As she misunderstood the intensity radiating off him like heat waves, Nell's dark blue eyes softened. "Sin?"

"This ballroom is stuffy. Care to take a walk?" Without giving her a chance to reply, Alexius pushed his companion toward the closest door. Assuming that he was in the mood to play games, Nell was willingly to indulge him.

Chapter Six

"WHAT AN AMAZING coincidence that I encountered you and your family at the park this afternoon," Lord Kyd said, escorting Juliana away from the dancers.

"My mother would describe it as providence," Juliana said wryly. "I must confess that I had been quarreling with Lucilla when we came upon you, Mrs. Maddock, and Maman. Your presence prevented us from continuing our appalling behavior."

"Do you often fight with your sisters?"

"I do not think I should answer such a question, Juliana said teasingly. "After all, if you are going to conduct business on my behalf, I would not want to give you the impression that I am difficult."

"I have a particular fondness for temperamental ladies," he countered, the corner of his mouth curling in an appealing manner. "After reviewing the music compositions that you entrusted to me, I am willing to indulge your artistic disposition."

"Oh, my goodness." Lord Kyd straightened and cocked his head to the side as he recognized someone. She peered in the direction that he was gazing but could not find the cause for the resignation in his tone.

Concern marked her brow as Juliana asked, "Something troubling?"

"No, no," the baron denied briskly. "I had hoped that we might dance again; however, I have other business matters that need my attention. Immediately. Another time, perhaps?"

Lord Kyd clasped her extended hand and bowed.

"Of course."

The indulgent smile on Juliana's face faded as she discreetly observed the baron as he made his way to the other side of the ballroom. Her eyes narrowed. Oh, she had been right about the trouble, she mused, watching him as he paid his respects to the one person determined to ruin her stay in London. Lady Gredell. After a brief greeting, the couple disappeared through the doorway that led to the outer front hall.

Juliana clasped her hands together and released the breath she was holding. The tightness in her chest eased at the couple's departure. Although it was none of her business, she could not fathom why Lord Kyd would consort with such a dreadful woman.

"I have the devil's own luck," a masculine voice drawled, interrupting Juliana's uncharitable thoughts about the disagreeable countess. "For me to find a pretty wallflower just begging to be plucked."

"Vincent Bishop, Earl of Chillingsworth," the handsome stranger said, his hand scrolling with a mid-air flourish as he bowed. "My friends call me Frost. And your name, my lovely?"

"Lady Juliana Ivers," she replied unthinkingly, the manners her mother had drilled into her coming to the forefront. She curtsied as she discreetly searched for her mother and sisters.

Juliana did not understand her rising need to flee from this gentleman. While Lord Kyd had shyly gazed at her with a combination of quiet awe and respect, Lord Chillingsworth's gaze was unswerving and intimate.

In spite of his boldness, the earl appeared to be exactly what her mother was seeking for her daughters. He was titled, and the refined quality of his coat, the heavy gold seal ring on his right hand, and the silver buckles on his polished shoes indicated wealth. Oh, and his face. If fallen angels walked the earth, this gentleman could have been mistaken for one. A strong narrowed jaw, piercing turquoise eyes, and black hair that fell in artful disarray, the ends brushing his cravat. The fact that he was astonishingly handsome, too, would have only encouraged Juliana's mother to secure him for one of her daughters.

If Lady Duncombe saw them together, it would be disastrous.

"Forgive me, my lord; my mother and sisters are waiting for me," Juliana said, edging away from the earl. She did not want to be rude, but she sensed any subtlety would be lost on this gentleman.

Lord Chillingsworth stepped in front of her. "Dance with me."

"I really must return to my family."

"You did not seem to mind tarrying with Lord Kyd," he said, backing her up against one of the colonnades.

"Lord Kyd is a friend of the family," she brazenly lied. With her back against the marble, Juliana inched her way around until she could walk to the next column. "We share a mutual appreciation for music."

"I like music," he said, casually pursuing her as she moved from the colonnade to a closed door. "And I like to share."

Juliana's intuition clanged like a bell in her head, warning her that the earl might not be remarking about his love of music. The back of her head connected with the solid oak door.

This was getting a trifle awkward.

"Lord Chillingsworth, please!"

Juliana started when he braced each hand on the wooden frame of the door, effectively cutting off her escape. "You beg so sweetly, Lady Juliana," he said, lowering his head. "How will you taste?"

Her eyes widened as the scoundrel kissed her on the mouth. Or perhaps "plundered" was more apt. There was a muffled squeak of surprise when he grasped her upper arms. Juliana felt the flick of his tongue along the edge of her teeth. Her brief struggle for freedom seemed to inflame his ardor. She reached behind her for the door latch and pushed.

The door swung wide on its well-oiled hinges, and locked together they staggered into the room. They bounced against the door and collided with a high wingback chair. Juliana thought her back would snap in half from the weight of the earl on top of her.

The brute had the audacity to laugh.

It was too much for a sheltered lady.

"Get off of me!" she said, her voice laced with maidenly outrage.

"Frost?"

Both Juliana and Lord Chillingsworth stiffened upon hearing his nickname. Although she could not place it, the masculine voice seemed vaguely familiar. She twisted her neck in an attempt to identify the gentleman who had witnessed their humiliating entrance.

Good grief, it was *him*!

She shoved frantically at the earl's chest.

Across the room, there stood the gentleman who had been trysting with Lady Lettlecott in her gardens. The man who seemed to be the living and breathing essence of all things wicked and forbidden.

Sin.

And the gentleman was not alone. With his back partially facing them, his large muscular frame was shielding a dark-haired lady who was prudently adjusting her bodice.

Exactly how many mistresses did Sin have in town?

Juliana tore her gaze away from the couple and glared at her captor. This awkward predicament was plainly his fault!

Lord Chillingsworth, the unrepentant fool, did not seem uncomfortable that he had been caught groping her. He straightened and pulled Juliana against him, his hand resting possessively on her left hip. "Sin, what are you—?" He broke off and grinned. "Nell! This is indeed a pleasant surprise. I thought you were in Bath with some French bas—?"

The earl bit his tongue, suddenly recalling the lady at his side.

"It appears that I prefer the English ones to French," the lady saucily drawled, slipping her arm around Sin's waist.

"The trouble is, you keep choosing the wrong gent," the earl teased; his ease with the unknown lady revealed that the trio had been friends for some time. "And Sin is the worst."

"I fear some habits are too troublesome to break."

Lord Chillingsworth and Sin's companion laughed.

For some reason, the woman shifted her shrewd attention to Juliana. "Do you not agree, my dear?"

Juliana preferred being ignored by the trio.

Sin was staring at her. She could feel the weight of it as her eyelids lowered; her gloved fingers were digging into the back of the dark green wingback chair. She shifted her stance, shrugging off the earl's hand on her hip.

He let his arm drop to his side, but he remained too close for Juliana's comfort.

"Frost, you have been remiss in introducing us to your lovely companion," Sin murmured, ignoring the banter of his friends.

"Not remiss, my friend, just possessive since I found her first," the earl said, bringing one of her hands to his mouth and kissing her knuckles. "Nevertheless, it eases my mind knowing that Nell will keep you well occupied."

Juliana saw no purpose in pointing out to Lord

Chillingsworth that she had encountered Sin at the Lettlecotts'.

"My lady, may I present Alexius Braverton, Marquess of Sinclair, and his dear friend the Countess of Lawrie." He broadly gestured at her as if she were some sort of prize. "My friends, this is Lady Juliana Ivers."

Lord Sinclair flinched as if he recognized her name. "Lady Juliana Ivers," he said evenly.

He did not seem pleased by the revelation.

Juliana hastily curtsied. "A pleasure, Lady Lawrie . . . Lord Sinclair." She sidestepped Lord Chillingsworth's hand and backed away toward the doorway. "I have to—forgive me—my mother and sisters await my return."

Without giving anyone a chance to stop her, she bolted from the small parlor.

"What an odd, nervous mouse," remarked Nell.

Alexius walked to the doorway and searched the passageway. Not surprisingly, it was empty. The lady had vanished. He wondered if she had been telling them the truth about seeking out her mother and sisters or if it had been a ruse to escape what had turned into an awkward encounter.

Christ, what a surprise.

His mysterious blond *lybbestre* was Lady Juliana Ivers.

One had to appreciate the irony.

"You ruined everything," Frost said, his voice rich with disgust.

Nell crossed over to the sofa and sat down. "Us?" She glared at Alexius. "I told you to lock the door."

"There seemed to be little point," Alexius countered.

"We both saw the error of our ways before any damage had been done."

The countess tipped her chin upward and purred, "Oh, I might have left a scratch or two."

Tangling with Nell again had been a very bad idea.

Lust had never been the problem between them. They had both enjoyed the carnal side of their relationship. Regrettably, it was Nell's emotional needs Alexius could never quite satisfy, and he gradually became distant with her increasing demands. This led them both eventually to find solace in the arms of other lovers; however, he and Nell always seemed to circle back to each other at odd times.

This time, he was to blame, Alexius silently mused. He should not have allowed Nell to kiss him.

She had viewed his lack of resistance as a sign that he had wanted to resume their relationship. As it was, the eager lady had managed to partially tug one of her breasts free from her bodice when Frost and Lady Juliana had stumbled into the room.

"Odd," Alexius said to Nell. "I felt nothing."

Frost was too frustrated with his own disappointment to notice the couple's exchange. "I will admit the lady was skittish, but she was beginning to thaw. I might have coaxed the lady to indulge in a little mischief if the parlor had been empty."

Alexius's face snapped in Frost's direction. Unadulterated rage washed over him at the thought of his friend touching Lady Juliana. He had seen her first.

Frost smirked at his friend. "What is wrong with you? Were you hoping that I would share?"

A small mound of violet satin spared Alexius from responding to his friend's taunt. He strode over to the chair and snatched up the fabric. It was Lady Juliana's reticule. It was small and delicate like its owner.

"She must have dropped it when she was fighting you off."

"I resent that remark," Frost said with mock outrage. "The lady was most definitely warming to my touch."

Alexius silently disagreed. According to his sister, Lady Juliana was chasing after the well-mannered Lord Kyd. Frost's aggressiveness probably terrified her.

And Alexius was about to test her reaction to him.

His grip tightened on the reticule. "I will return the reticule to her."

Frost's blue eyes narrowed in suspicion. "Why you?" he demanded.

Nell stirred, also unhappy with Alexius's announcement. "Frost wants the little mouse. Let him return it."

"Be reasonable. Lady Juliana will be with her mother and sisters," Alexius reminded them. "Mothers tend to hide their daughters when Frost shows any interest."

"He speaks the truth. It is a curse." Frost dropped down beside Nell and leaned his head against her shoulder as if seeking comfort.

The countess sighed, laying her cheek against the top of the earl's head. "Poor Frost. What shall we do with you?"

Frost used his finger to trace the outline of her bodice. "If I may be bold, I have a few humble suggestions."

Alexius left the parlor with Nell's high-pitched

laughter ringing in his ears. Though Frost had not been the countess's first choice, she would take him into her bed, letting him soothe away the hurt Alexius's rejection had caused.

Alexius had other quarry: the lady in the violet dress.

Chapter Seven

"WHERE DID YOU go? Maman said that you were dancing with Lord Kyd, and then you vanished." Lucilla beckoned Juliana closer. At their mother's insistence, her sister was also attired in violet. There were subtle differences, since Juliana's dress was edged with different trim that had been dyed a darker hue. Cordelia wore yet another style.

"Did you go out into the gardens with him?"

Juliana was scandalized by the suggestion. "What an outlandish thing to say! Lord Kyd is a gentleman, and nothing more than a friend. I—" She abruptly shut her mouth.

The only thing worse than slipping out into the dark gardens with a gentleman she barely knew was letting Lord Chillingsworth kiss her in the Kempes' small parlor. Lord Sinclair and Lady Lawrie were unlikely chaperones. Juliana suspected that she and the earl had interrupted something intimate between the pair. Thankfully, she had been spared the details.

Lord Sinclair seemed to have ladies tossing themselves at his feet wherever he went. Thank goodness she was immune to the madness!

"What?"

Juliana gave her sister an impatient glance. "I retired to one of the small parlors to recover from dancing."

Lucilla nodded, accepting her explanation. "Well, Maman was looking for you. She wanted to be the first to share the good news."

"What good news?"

"Cordelia has a new suitor," Lucilla said, clearly thrilled that she was in the position to share the news with Juliana before anyone else. "Look over there. They are sitting on one of the benches near the open doors."

For once, Lucilla was not exaggerating. Across the ballroom, their elder sister was chatting enthusiastically with a rather handsome gentleman. "Who is he?"

"Lord Fisken," Lucilla confided. "Maman has learned that he is thirty years old, has never been married, no mistresses or scandals lingering in his past, and is heir to an earldom."

Juliana blinked at the wealth of information her mother was able to gather in such a short period of time. "He sounds like the perfect gentleman for our Cordelia."

"I heartily agree," the marchioness said, walking up to her daughters. She had chosen a plum-colored dress to complement her daughters' dresses. "Mrs. Maddock told me that the earl is currently worth five thousand annually."

Lucilla's eyes widened at the amount. "Indeed."

Poor Lucilla had nothing else to say on the matter. She suspected that Lucilla's suitor, Mr. Stepkins, brought in a fraction of that annual amount. The two elder sisters were highly competitive. The fact that Cordelia had caught the eye of a wealthy nobleman was bound to be a source of friction between the two sisters.

"Rumor has it that Fisken has a keen eye for quality horseflesh," a masculine voice interjected. "His stables in the country are the stuff of legend."

Juliana gasped and whirled about to confront him. *Sin.*

"*You*," she said, wanting to cringe at the inanity of her response to him.

He inclined his head. "Forgive me for eavesdropping. I have always wondered what ladies discuss when gentlemen are out of earshot."

Juliana slowly dipped low into an elegant curtsy. "I pray you are well-mannered enough to allow us to keep our secrets."

She was very aware that her mother and Lucilla were awaiting an explanation as to how she had come to know the handsome, flirtatious gentleman.

Lord Sinclair quirked a brow upward at her breathless reply. "I believe this is yours."

Her reticule looked so small in his large gloved hands.

"T-thank you, my lord." She took the cloth bag from him and sent a helpless look to her mother. "Maman, may I present to you the Marquess of Sinclair."

Her gaze shifted back to the man the *ton* called Sin.

"My lord, this is my mother, the Marchioness of Dun-combe, and my sister, Lady Lucilla Ivers."

"Lady Duncombe . . . Lady Lucilla," he murmured, politely taking their extended hands in turn and bow-ing. "What providence that your daughter forgot her reticule. Her carelessness gave me the opportunity to introduce myself to the prettiest ladies at the ball."

Lucilla tittered at Sin's flattery. Juliana gave her an in-credulous look. How easily Mr. Stepkins was forgotten.

Her mother's smile was reserved as she studied the nobleman. "You are generous with your compliments, Lord Sinclair. How is it that you know my Juliana?"

That was indeed an excellent question!

Juliana was curious about the marquess's reply. The two occasions she had encountered the man, he'd had a different lady in his arms. Maman was hoping to find a husband for Juliana and her sisters. Lord Sinclair would never do.

"Your daughter did not tell you?" Sin appeared dis-appointed that Juliana had not gossiped about him. "Lady Lettlecott introduced us."

Juliana almost sputtered at his audacity. However, to correct Sin would only lead to questions that she pre-ferred not to address.

"Really?" Her mother gave her youngest daughter a hard stare. "What a shame that we departed from the Lettlecotts' early. Otherwise, we might have been prop-erly introduced."

The marquess acknowledged the slight rebuke with a gracious nod.

"Regrettably that evening I was pressed into another commitment, and my conversation with Lady Juliana came to an end too quickly." When his gaze switched to hers, Juliana felt her heartbeat quicken. "With your permission, of course, I would like to continue our discussion about—"

"Music," Juliana hastily supplied. It was the one subject she could pontificate about for hours, and one guaranteed to discourage her mother and sister from joining.

"Is this what you were discussing in the Kempes' small parlor?" Lucilla asked slyly.

Juliana's cheeks flushed with color as she contemplated how she would quietly murder her sibling when they were alone.

"Alas, I did not come across Lady Juliana until she was leaving the room." His roguish eyes shimmering with mischief, he asked, "By the bye, who was the enviable gentleman that caused you to forget your reticule?"

Lady Duncombe's eyebrows disappeared into her turban. The gentleman was deliberately tormenting Juliana. Sin's not-so-innocent question had shifted her mother's shrewd regard and placed it squarely on her.

"There were several people in the parlor, Lord Sinclair," she said, recalling the rising panic she had experienced as Lord Chillingsworth had thoroughly kissed her. "This is rather shameful to admit, but I was rather bored by the conversation and did not pay attention to the round of introductions made."

"Juliana!"

She could not decide what appalled her mother more, her daughter's inattention or the fact that Juliana had not tactfully lied about it. The marquess was clearly enjoying the mischief that he had stirred between mother and daughter.

"Walk with me, Lady Juliana," Sin entreated, offering the crook of his arm. "Later, when I escort you back to your family, I am confident that you will not forget my name."

"You lied to my mother."

"So did you."

He seemed privately pleased that she had done so. Perhaps Sin thought she was trying to protect him. It was an erroneous assumption. Truthfully, Juliana did not understand why she had not revealed the marquess's wicked behavior with Lady Lettlecott or even Lady Lawrie to her mother and sister. The revelation would have simplified Juliana's life. She had glimpsed her mother's hopeful expression as she strolled away with Lord Sinclair. Her mother considered the gentleman a potential suitor for her stubborn youngest daughter.

"Where are we going?"

With his hand splayed lightly on her back, he gently urged her to keep ascending the staircase.

"I think this conversation warrants a little privacy, do you not agree?" He led her down a long, narrow hall that the Kempes used as a gallery. Three ladies and their male escort were admiring the art collection, while another couple seemed engrossed in their private discussion.

Sin tried the first door. "It has been a few years since

I have wandered this house—" He peeked inside. "Yes, this room will suffice."

He opened the door and waited for her to enter.

"Lord Kempe is an avid collector of mineral specimens," the marquess said, which explained why every bookcase, table, and shelf was filled with rock specimens both large and small, delicately beautiful and oversized chunks of uninspiring stone.

Juliana picked up a pretty green stone that she could not identify. "Are you a collector, too?"

"Christ, no!"

Perhaps Lord Sinclair was not a collector of stones, but a lady's heart was what he coveted, Juliana privately mused. He savored the hunt, took possession, and for a while he admired his prize before he dashed off in pursuit of another.

Juliana could understand the marquess's appeal. There was something thrilling to be standing next to a beast so beautiful and untamed. The trick was to remember that wild things had a nasty habit of biting the unwary. Juliana silently vowed never to forget that Sin was a gentleman who lived up to his name. He was dangerously tempting. Decadent and unrepentant.

Even if she had been interested in acquiring a husband, Lord Sinclair was wholly unsuitable.

She returned the stone to its place on the marble table. "My lord—"

He held up a hand to silence her. "Sin or Sinclair, if you please."

"Sinclair, then," Juliana said, moving closer to the small fireplace, since the marquess had made himself comfortable on the sofa. "I suppose you are wondering if I will keep your secrets."

Her words seem to puzzle him.

"My secrets?" he said cautiously.

Juliana scowled at the burning coals in the hearth. "Lady Lettlecott and Lady Lawrie." She shrugged. "I doubt either lady is aware that you are courting both."

She glanced back at him as comprehension gleamed in his eyes. Sin grinned at her discomfort and lazily stretched his arm across the back of the sofa as he watched her. "Ah, I see. And what is the price for your silence, Lady Juliana?"

"Price?" The manner in which he stared at her was making her fidgety. "There is no price."

"So you have yet to set a price?"

"No!" She crossed her arms and glared at Sin. "Are you always so provoking? I do not want anything from you."

"Are you certain? Come away from the fire, Juliana," Sin tenderly commanded. "You will be far more comfortable on the sofa."

Juliana glanced back at the handsome male with his long legs splayed apart with an informality that she envied. He patted the cushion beside him and waited for her to return to him.

"I prefer to remain close to the fire. There is a chill this evening," she added defensively, whirling about and offering him her back.

Sin was a gentleman who unmistakably possessed strong passions. He was used to ladies who acquiesced to his demands. Her refusal might be viewed as a challenge. That had not been her goal at all. However, Juliana suspected that if she joined him on the sofa, Sin would not be content until he gained her complete surrender.

He chuckled at her stubbornness. "Very well, my lady. You leave me no choice." With a muffled sigh, he rose from the sofa like a magnificent animal and positioned himself so that the warmth of his body covered her backside like a warm blanket.

"N-no choice?" Juliana shivered, swayed slightly into the glorious heat emanating from his body.

What should she do? Scream? Run away? Or stay? She should have never agreed to speak with him in private. She should have remained with her mother and sister.

"You are standing too close," Juliana whispered.

"Am I?" His lips brushed her right ear. "The distance feels nigh perfect to me."

The top of her head tingled from his soft caress. It felt as if tiny fairies were dancing about in merry rings in hopes of making her head spin. "What is the point to this flirtation? If this is to silence me—I told you, I want nothing. I have no interest in gossip or your private business."

"Hush." Sin nipped the pearl dangling from her earlobe. His breath teased her ear as his hands curled around her upper arms. "You are gracious to keep my secrets. Nevertheless, I believe our first meetings have given you a false impression with regard to where my true interests lie."

Juliana's heart stumbled in her chest at the notion

that Sin desired her, even though she believed that he was spinning pretty tales to gain what he wanted. "I have tarried here too long. Maman—"

"Knows you are in capable hands," Sin said, a touch of humor lacing his voice. "I wager that you are no longer cold."

Juliana turned her face to the side, inadvertently giving his lips access to her cheek. "The fire—"

"Will not satisfy you," he said simply, drawing them both down until they were on their knees. He widened his parted thighs so her bottom was snug against the apex of his trousers. "It cannot make you burn from within."

She felt the fullness of him as his hips gently undulated against her bottom. The subtle movement sent an electrical current of anticipation racing up her spine while every nerve in her body responded to his unspoken demand. Juliana closed her eyes against the foreign, overwhelming sensations his proximity was triggering.

"Please. No more," she said, her voice cracking. To her utter shame, she was on the verge of tears. Sin likely spent his evenings in the company of courtesans and mistresses. She was an inexperienced child in comparison. "It was foolish of me to stay. This frightens me. *You* frighten me."

Sin stilled his sensual movements. Although he did not pull away as she had hoped, she sensed that he was attempting to leash the side of him that had frightened her. He inhaled deeply and then guided her until she was sitting on the floor next to him. Sin gave her a measured glance. "Lady Juliana frightened? I do not believe it." With the fleshy pad of his thumb, he gently wiped the tear that had escaped the corner of her right eye. "Besides, I am the one who should be scurrying away in terror."

The statement was so absurd, Juliana temporarily forgot about her own fears. "Surely you jest, my lord."

With candlelight shining in his eyes, his gaze held a calculating intensity that she had never beheld in their previous encounters. "No, I do not believe I am," he said, cupping her face in his hands. "I sensed that you were trouble the moment I opened my eyes and saw you peering down at me from the Lettlecotts' hazel tree."

How was she troublesome? The man pursued women the way a hungry cat chased after a fishmonger's cart.

"Well, I think you are the most aggravating gentleman I have ever encountered."

He kissed her sweetly on the mouth to silence her. "You are not alone in your opinion." Sin gave her arms a playful squeeze. "Here now. Up you go."

Juliana frowned as Sin pulled her onto her feet. His abrupt shift in temperament made her head spin. "What game is this?"

"No games, my lady." To her embarrassment, he smoothed her skirts until the fabric covered her ankles. "You just reminded me of a rule I rarely break."

Sin took her by the arm and literally dragged her to the door. He was behaving as if he could not wait until he rid himself of her.

"What rule?" she asked, feeling insulted.

"I do my best to avoid messy emotional entanglements. And you, Lady Juliana, represent the worst sort."

It had been a test.

That was what he had told himself as he and Lady Juliana left the little anteroom that housed Lord Kempe's mineral specimens and strolled down the gallery.

He had been a gentleman.

Of sorts.

The lady was barely mussed from her encounter. He had barely gotten a taste before he had pulled her to her feet and shaken out her rumpled skirts. If not for the bright rosy flags of color on her cheeks, one might never guess the Lady Juliana had been dallying with a gent.

Alexius was not certain why he had ended his delicately balanced game of cat and mouse with her. His sister had deemed Lady Juliana a heartless jade determined to steal Lord Kyd. Belle was wrong. While there was no doubt that the lady had struck up a friendship with the baron, Lady Juliana was neither heartless nor a jade.

She was an innocent.

It should have made a difference to him.

Perhaps it was the tainted blood of his sire running through his veins and arteries. Christ knew he was his father's son. The elder Sinclair had viewed it as an asset. The two wives he buried might have thought differently.

His first wife, Belinda's mother, had been handpicked by Alexius's grandfather. It had been a loveless affair, rife with violence that occurred in and out of the bedchamber. After their daughter had been born, Alexius's father and his marchioness had lived separate lives. According to Alexius's sister, her mother had been beaten so often that it had been believed that she was unable to give her husband his heir.

When Belle was five years old, her mother died from catarrh of the stomach while her husband was enjoying his latest mistress during a hunting party.

He did not grieve for his wife. With his marchioness barely cold, the elder Sinclair set out for London to resume his life of debauchery. He drank obsessively, was prone to fits of temper, and was scandalously imprudent when it came to young ladies.

Alexius's mother, Lady Susan, happened to be one of the nameless ladies his drunken father had carelessly seduced and discarded. Unfortunately for the elder Sinclair, Alexius's mother was the youngest daughter of the Earl of Talmash. The earl happened to wield a great deal of influence politically and within the *ton*.

Upon hearing of his daughter's delicate condition that many thought was the result of violent rape, Lord Talmash gave the elder Sinclair the choice between death and marriage. He wisely chose to marry Lady Susan. The match was not unpalatable to the elder Sinclair, and seven months later the new marchioness proved her usefulness by delivering the Sinclair heir.

In the elder Sinclair's typical selfish fashion, he celebrated the good news of his son's birth in the bed of his mistress. Lady Susan fell into a melancholy that most people claimed she never recovered from. Several months after Alexius's second birthday, his mother perished in a carriage accident. There were whispers that his father had driven his unhappy marchioness into killing herself. It was entirely possible, Alexius silently mused. Both he and Belle had lived under the oppressive hand of their sire.

The elder Sinclair could not tolerate weakness or compassion, and he had beaten those lessons into his children.

Lady Juliana halted as she and Alexius approached the grand staircase. Although it had not been deliberate, his silence had apparently unnerved her.

She released his arm. "It is best if I continue alone."

Alexius inclined his head. "If that is your wish."

"It is, my lord," Lady Juliana said firmly. "My mother hopes to find solid matches for her daughters this season, and you are—"

"Unsuitable?"

She blushed at his blunt honesty.

He was not insulted by the lady's conclusion. The fact that she was not only beautiful but intelligent as well merely heightened his interest in her.

"Yes. Pray do not be offended."

"Oh, I am not," Alexius assured her. He lightly stroked her chin with the pad of his thumb. "I am entirely unsuitable for you."

Lady Juliana hastily nodded. "Good, then we are in agreement."

"Not quite."

"I beg your pardon?"

"While I am wholly unsuitable for marriage, I have every intention of seeing you again."

"I do not think that is wise."

"Mayhap not. However, I cannot be dissuaded," he

said, pulling her into his arms and causing her to cry out in surprise.

His lips hovered tantalizingly just above hers. She expected him to kiss her. It would have been so simple to close the inch between them and satisfy his hunger for the lady. Instead, he released her.

She staggered back a step and clutched the newel.

It pleased him to see that she was disappointed that he had not kissed her. "I give you a word of warning, Lady Juliana. The next time we are together, I will *not* be a gentleman."

Frost did not step out from the shadows until Sin and Lady Juliana were halfway down the staircase. *Interesting*, he thought. He had abandoned the delightful Lady Lawrie to follow Sin because his reaction to Lady Juliana annoyed Frost. There was something between them, though he could not put his finger on it. Curious, he had trailed after them, watching them as they disappeared into the small anteroom. Twenty minutes later, the pair had reemerged into the gallery. Frost had noted Lady Juliana's flushed features and partially wrinkled skirts and Sin's grim expression.

Whatever had occurred in that room had not sated him.

Although Frost could not fathom the source, a sharp flicker of resentment burned in his chest. He and Sin had shared women in the past. Once Frost had tired of the shy, nervous wallflower, he would have happily handed her over to his friend.

Something was wrong with Sin.

If Lady Juliana had somehow bewitched him, Frost was equally determined to break the spell she had cast.

No woman had ever come between him and Sin. Frost intended to make certain that Lady Juliana was not the first.

Chapter Eight

"DO YOU THINK it might rain?"

Juliana glanced back at Cordelia, who was sitting on a blanket beside their mother with a book on her lap. She peered up at the sky and gave the clouds a critical glance.

"Most likely," she said, tossing bread crumbs to the greedy black-headed and herring gulls that snatched the bread in a delightful mid-air display at the water's edge. "You can smell it in the air."

She held up a large piece of bread and laughed as a rather aggressive gull plucked it from her hand.

"We have hours yet before the rain chases us off," the marchioness said, quashing the unspoken suggestion that they should pack up their belongings and return home.

When Lady Duncombe had announced at breakfast that they would be picnicking along the Thames, Juliana and her sisters had been reluctant. The late nights were wearing to both body and mind, and the three sisters had been content to remain at home. However, the marchioness could not be discouraged from having her adventure. With her friends Mrs. Maddock and Lady Harper in tow, they had found a scenic spot near the Richmond Bridge.

It had been a tranquil afternoon, one that reminded Juliana of idyllic afternoons she had enjoyed in the country.

"Come play with us, Juliana," Lucilla shouted as she chased after a small wicker hoop.

"Yes, do join us," Lady Harper said, panting from her exertions. "Unless you intend to feed the birds our entire repast."

Juliana's sister had enticed the thirty-year-old Lady Harper into an energetic game of Les Graces. Armed with a stick in each hand, each was supposed to fling the seven-inch hoop high into the air so the other could catch it with her sticks. For Lucilla and Lady Harper it seemed like a hopeless and sadly graceless endeavor.

Juliana brushed the crumbs from her fingers. "The last time I played the game with Lucilla, she tried to run me through with one of her sticks."

The admission startled Lady Harper. "Good heavens."

Cordelia brought her book up to cover her mouth as both she and Maman laughed.

Lucilla angrily stabbed one of her sticks in Juliana's direction. "That is a bold-faced lie. I merely grazed you."

Juliana brought her hand to her chest. "You hit me

squarely in the heart, dear sister. I would be cold in my grave if not for my corset."

"That would have been tragic," Lord Sinclair said, casually striding toward them. "Perhaps I should add your impenetrable corset to my prayers each night."

Juliana had managed to avoid this particular gentleman for three whole days. How had he found them? And blast his timing for coming along when she had been discussing her undergarment, too!

She scowled at her mother. "I do not believe in coincidences."

The marchioness would not meet Juliana's eye.

Sin was dressed for riding, though the immaculate condition of his clothes suggested that he had come by coach rather than on horseback. His dark brown coat and shirt were free from debris and his cravat still bore the crisp folds that the man's valet had carefully aligned and pressed with a hot iron. Her gaze drifted southerly to his legs, encased within tight leather breeches and polished black boots. Juliana sensed that she was not the only one admiring Sin's muscular legs.

"Good afternoon, Lady Duncombe," he said, offering his hand to steady the marchioness as she stood up to greet him. "Ladies."

Juliana's forehead connected with the palm of her hand. "Maman, tell me that you invited Lord Sinclair to join us?"

Cordelia stood behind their mother. "If you were planning to invite gentlemen, why did you not send a note to Lord Fisken?"

"And Mr. Stepkins?" Lucilla added.

Sin murmured in the marchioness's ear, "Most ladies

are grateful to have gentleman callers. You have your work cut out for you if you hope to find Lady Juliana a husband this season."

Juliana lifted her head so she could glare at him. "I can hear you."

"Oh, you do not know the half of it, Sinclair," the marchioness lamented. "Spare me from an intelligent miss." She shook her head as if disappointed in her youngest daughter. "Why could you not be more like your sisters?"

Both Cordelia and Lucilla grimaced at their mother's remark. "Maman!" they wailed in unison.

A cool drop of rain struck Juliana's cheek. She raised her gaze heavenward and opened her arms wide as she felt several more raindrops strike her on the hand, right shoulder, and top of her head.

She laughed at the irony.

"It appears Mother Nature has foiled your plans, my lord. Another time, perhaps," Juliana said smugly as she knelt down to gather up the blanket.

The gentle rain suddenly turned into a downpour. Lucilla and Lady Harper squealed. They hastily collected baskets and parasols before running toward the carriage. Cordelia was several yards behind them, holding her book over her head in a futile attempt to save her bonnet.

Sin took the rolled-up blanket from Juliana. "With your permission, Lady Duncombe, I would like to escort your daughter home."

"That will not be necessary—," Juliana began.

Her mother accepted the blanket from the marquess. She pursed her lips in contemplation, weighing the impropriety of the gentleman's request against the opportunity of strengthening his interest in Juliana. If her mother had any concerns, she did not voice them aloud. Perhaps she viewed the possible rewards worth the risk.

"I see no reason to deny your request as long as you do not tarry too long over the task."

She kissed Juliana's cheek and dashed up the grassy incline to join the others.

Hand in hand, Sin led her away from her family toward his conveyance. They were not the only pedestrians running for shelter. A patch of slippery mud caught Juliana unawares as her left foot slipped, knocking her off her stride. Before she could cry out, the marquess had pulled her against him.

"Clumsy minx," he teased as he half-carried her to the waiting coach.

Juliana gasped in feigned outrage. "I will have you know that I am quite graceful under drier conditions."

"Indeed. I look forward to a demonstration." Sin gave her a playful shove into the coach's interior. To the coachman he said, "Tarry awhile."

Heedless of the rain dripping off him, the coachman touched the brim of his hat. "Aye, milord."

The door closed behind Sin as he settled in beside her.

" 'Tarry awhile'?" she echoed, her melodic tone burdened with suspicion. "You assured my mother that you would not."

"Dear lady, I did no such thing. If you recall, your mother ran off before I could offer a reply."

Juliana shoved at his shoulder when the marquess shook the rain from his hair like a dog trotting out from a lake's shallow waters. She laughed at his outrageous manner. He reminded her of a mischievous boy. "Are you mad? We cannot stay here. Think of your poor coachman. He is likely to drown in this storm."

The marquess lifted the opposing bench and retrieved a small blanket. He plucked her reticule from her hands and tossed it on the bench. "The man has an umbrella."

Sin did not seem very concerned about his servant.

"That is hardly the point, my lord."

Sin had peeled off one of her gloves before she realized his intentions. He grabbed her other hand to keep her from slipping it behind her back. "Be sensible, Juliana. Whether we are moving or stationary, my coachman's discomfort remains the same."

The soggy glove was discarded with its mate.

Juliana shivered slightly from a sudden chill. "I suppose so."

The marquess kissed the tip of her nose. "Do not fret, my dear. My servants are well compensated and used to my odd whims." He nodded at her bonnet. "Christ, what a frightful mess. Might as well remove it."

Her fingers found the ribbons under her chin. While she meekly obeyed his request, she watched as he removed his coat and gloves. He used the small blanket to blot the rain from his face and hair.

The rain hammered against the coach's roof, drowning out any noise the horses or the coachman might have made. Within the dry confines of the coach, she and Sin were insulated from the elements and for all practical purposes alone.

Juliana's heart quickened at the thought.

"Here now, let me tend to that," Sin said, removing the ruined bonnet from her limp grasp.

Juliana glanced down and assessed her dress. The hem was muddy and there were wet streaks marring her long skirts; however, the dress was salvageable. She started as Lord Sinclair touched her cheek with the edge of the blanket.

"Rain or tears?"

She smiled at his tender query. "Rain." She turned away and tried to peer through the small window that was covered in beaded raindrops and grime. "Do you hope to outlast the storm?"

"Or something," he muttered under his breath.

Before Juliana could question him on his bewildering comment, Sin used two fingers on her chin to guide her face toward his.

"What are you doing?"

"Why, I am kissing you, Juliana."

Her eyes were opened wide when his mouth settled over hers like a warm blanket, effectively silencing her response.

Or protest.

If Juliana had had the will to make one.

Even though her experience with gentlemen was limited, Juliana instinctively sensed that she was being kissed by an expert. With only his lips the man was warming her from the inside out. His caresses were light, almost undemanding, as if he had all the time in the world to taste her.

"I have missed you," he murmured against her skin. "Did you think of me?"

With both hands encircling his right upper arm,

Juliana let her lashes flutter downward as she leaned against him. What harm was there in enjoying Sin's kiss?

Plenty, she silently argued with herself. The man was a rake and rather unapologetic about it, which explained all the former and current mistresses who seemed to be in his life. A sensible lady would remind him of his manners and demand that he drive her home.

And yet . . .

Juliana could not deny the spark of desire between them. When Sin looked at her, her body tingled and warmed under his unguarded perusal. The night they had been alone in Lord Kempe's mineral specimen room, Sin had vowed to make her burn. Since then, his words and the memory of his unyielding body against hers had haunted her until she ached for his touch. Each night, before she had drifted off to sleep, she had thought about his promise that he would not be a gentleman the next time they met and wondered if she truly wanted him to be.

As if sensing she was on the cusp of surrendering, the marquess growled against her mouth, deepening the kiss. His thumb brushed her lower lip, gently parting her lips. She smiled, feeling his tongue against her teeth. It was such an odd sensation, and wholly unexpected. Sin ruthlessly used her surprise to deepen the intimate caress. His tongue swept past her teeth and teased her tongue. Their tongues tangled and danced. The sensation was delightful.

Juliana mumbled her approval.

Wordlessly the marquess coaxed her into tasting him. She advanced when he retreated. Juliana edged closer. Breathless, Sin pulled away. His lips had reddened from their kiss. His charming grin gave her heart a sharp twist.

"I have something for you."

The delicate curve of her right eyebrow lifted in surprise. "What is it?"

He reached within his damp coat and removed a small leather pouch from an inner pocket. "A small token of friendship." His eyes glinted with a hint of mischief. "And affection."

She brought her hand to her mouth as he retrieved a long string of pearls from the leather pouch. Even in the dim interior, the pearls, larger than spring peas, gleamed like moonlight in his large hands. "What have you done? Oh no, this is entirely inappropriate. And expensive," she fussed, though she was privately thrilled that he had thought her worthy of such a present.

"I cannot accept."

Sin was amused by her feeble admonishment. "A pearl necklace will not send me to debtors' prison, my lady." His gift laced between his fingers, he held up his hand.

Tantalizing her.

"No," she said with a shake of her head.

"Do not be childish, Juliana," Sin scolded, his soft mocking words straightening her spine. "The pearls are simply a gift from one friend to another. You have no reason to fear them."

Blast him, Juliana thought uncharitably. He knew just the right thing to say to nudge her into accepting the pearl necklace.

She glared at him. "I am not afraid of you or your pearls."

Sin grinned at her rebellious tone. "Reach out and take my gift. Then you can show me how grateful you are."

Her mouth quivered at the slight edge to his words. Although he seemed eager for her to accept his gift, she could not shake the feeling that there was some hidden meaning to his invitation.

"So there *is* a price, my lord." She fought to hide her disappointment from him. "What do you require?"

"Such the timid mouse. It does not suit you, *lybbestre*," he chided, and then sighed at her distrust. "A proper kiss will suffice."

A proper kiss.

His request was reasonable.

Juliana closed her eyes.

"Oh, it is not quite so simple." He laughed when her eyes snapped open, her eyes narrowed with suspicion. "You must initiate the kiss. I want to taste your passion again."

The coach shuddered as a gust of wind shook the compartment.

Whether she liked it or not, she was trapped in the coach with Sin.

She was also beginning to believe that the marquess was toying with her. She crossed her arms and gave him a contemplative look. "Perhaps I no longer want the pearls."

His beautiful hazel eyes gleamed with confidence.

"Liar."

Juliana's lips parted in shock. "Of all the rude, arrogant—" She struggled to find the right word to hurl at him. "I am not some greedy miss who will grovel for trinkets—"

"I never said that you were, Juliana," he replied, unperturbed by her flash of temper. The pearls softly clicked together as he admired them. "I merely called you a liar because you will want me to give you these pearls. As a matter of fact, I predict that you will beg me."

"Ridiculous."

There was an unspoken challenge in his eyes when his gaze shifted to her face. "Then kiss me, and prove me wrong."

Although the outing had not gone according to plan, Alexius was willing to indulge his impulsive nature. Nor was he disappointed in the results. The unexpected downpour had driven Lady Juliana into his coach and straight into his arms. It was precisely where he wanted her to be. With the string of pearls clutched in his fist, he wondered how far he could push her and not have her bolt from the dry compartment. It would be tiresome if he had to pursue his lovely quarry down the muddied road.

"What game are you playing at, Sinclair?"

The pearls were indeed a game. One of many he had played with countless women. Unbeknownst to Lady Juliana, his gift of pearls was a source of amusement for certain members of the *ton*. Former lovers flaunted his gifts in front of current lovers, and husbands never revealed the naughty games Sin had played with them.

A game he was determined to play with her.

"Just 'Sin,'" he entreated, faintly smiling at what he viewed as a private joke.

Lady Juliana laughed nervously. She wrinkled her nose in a manner that Alexius found charming. "Oh, I do not think so, my lord."

"And why not?" he countered. "All of my friends call me Sin."

Unconvinced, she nibbled her lower lip. "I prefer 'Sinclair.'"

As a sign of his growing impatience, Alexius passed the string of pearls from one hand to the next. He could hardly explain to the lady he intended to seduce that he had utterly earned the sobriquet in a dastardly fashion. "My father was the Sinclair. The abbreviation of the title suited me."

Lady Juliana's Cupid's bow mouth curved upward as amusement twinkled in her eyes. "Somehow I am not surprised."

Her saucy comment added a rosy pink to her cheeks. Damp from the rain, the lady beside him was a vision of loveliness. Limp curls of gold and brown uncoiled loosely around her face as she stared at him through clear green eyes. Minutes earlier, he had glimpsed desire in her eyes when he had pulled away from their kiss. It was gone now, replaced by feminine wariness. However, Alexius was confident that he could rekindle the unspoken invitation once he put his hands on her again.

"Be bold, Juliana," he dared her, noticing her eyes flared at his informality. He leaned closer, enticing her. "Kiss me."

"Close your eyes."

Alexius promptly lowered his eyelids to prevent Lady Juliana from glimpsing his excitement. The soggy hem of her skirts slapped against the bench as she shifted her body so her knees brushed against his. Her warm breath teased his face. Anticipation thrummed through his body. Lady Juliana erroneously believed that she was in control, and that would be her downfall. Alexius was confident in his skills as a lover. Soon his companion would surrender to his tender ministrations. When he was finished, both of them would be well pleasured.

His sister would also be appeased that her rival for Lord Kyd's affections had been vanquished. If the baron had any pride, he would cease to consort with a lady who thoughtlessly offered her favors to another.

When Lady Juliana's lips tentatively brushed against his, Alexius was no longer thinking of his sister. Juliana's breath caressed his face in soft, rapid puffs that smelled faintly of wild spearmint. Was it nerves or excitement? She pressed a gentle kiss against his lower lip. Lust lanced through his gut as his cock swelled, quickening painfully within his trousers.

Alexius craved more than a chaste kiss from her.

"Again," he whispered against her lips. "Take my tongue into your mouth. Taste me."

He felt her small hand on his sleeve. Her mouth claimed his with a confidence he had expected from her. Lady Juliana's lips moved slowly against his, the action so tantalizingly erotic that his cock pressed upward, straining against the fabric of his trousers, seeking its own release.

Soon, he promised himself, *soon*.

Lady Juliana's grip tightened on his arm as she

deepened the kiss. The tip of her tongue flicked against his lips and teeth. There was little finesse, but Alexius felt the sensation all the way down to his toes. Unable to resist, he opened his eyes. With her eyes closed, Lady Juliana's expression almost looked pained as she concentrated on her task.

Alexius might have chuckled at her adorable countenance if she had not taken advantage of his parted lips by sliding her tongue deeper. He groaned against her mouth. The heady scent of woman and her hesitant caresses would be his undoing. The lady would have him ejaculating in his trousers if he did not take control of their love play.

"It was a kiss worthy of pearls," he murmured between kisses.

Before she could guess his intentions, Alexius tugged Lady Juliana onto his lap, allowing the curve of her bottom to slide down his engorged cock until his legs flanked her. She did not seem to notice his desire for her.

"Whatever are you doing, Sinclair?"

He ignored her outrage. "Just 'Sin.' Allow me to demonstrate," he said, dangling the string of pearls in front of her.

Juliana reached for the pearls, determined to end Lord Sinclair—no—rather Sin's games. Unfortunately, the man had mastered all games of chance and trickery. He slipped his free hand under her arm and squeezed her right breast. She yelped. There was no other word to describe surprise and wordless protest. No man had ever dared to touch her breasts.

"The pearls are not yours until I *give* them to you."

She shivered at his rather odd emphasis on a single word. Juliana suspected that what Sin had in mind had nothing to do with placing the string of pearls around her neck.

Juliana had good reason to worry.

The hand on her breast followed the contour of her waist and brazenly moved down to her hip.

"There . . . there," he said, his voice low and soothing when she tried to scramble away from his touch. He held her in place. "This will not hurt."

Every inch of him seemed to be made of bone and thick muscle. Even with yards of skirts and petticoats as a barrier between them, she could feel the heat radiating from his body.

"W-what are you doing?" she shrieked when his questing hand seized a fistful of fabric and began inching a portion of her skirts higher. Juliana turned her face into the side of his neck. "This is highly improper."

His throaty chuckle tickled the tip of her nose. "Yes. Nevertheless, you will like it."

Dear heavens! He had plowed a narrow channel up the center of her skirts so that his fingers brushed her inner thigh. Her stomach tightened in response. Juliana dug her fingernails into his arm to halt his efforts.

"Sinclair . . . Sin, please," she said helplessly, torn between fear and pleasure. He had not lied. He was not hurting her. However, the sensations his bold touch was creating were unfamiliar, overruling her curiosity. "Tell the coachman to take me home."

Sin lightly bit down on her earlobe. "You are overwrought. That will not do."

Sin expertly shifted her so her back sagged against his torso. "Now place your right foot on the opposite bench for support," he coaxed, manipulating her limb as if it were his own.

Even though Sin could not see from his position the length of leg he had exposed by lifting her skirts, Juliana still felt vulnerable. "I have my grandmother's pearls," she blurted out. "I do not need yours."

With practiced finesse, he twirled the string of pearls in his hand, wrapping the length around his first two fingers. "Truly? Then you must be the only female in England who does not crave a pretty trinket for her treasure box."

Any protest was silenced when he caressed her cheek with his pearl-covered fingers and kissed her. Lost in the moment, Juliana forgot about her compromising position. Sin's mouth was a sweet balm to her nerves. She shakily exhaled against his lips.

His hazel eyes beamed with approval. "Much better. Close your eyes and hold on to the feeling."

Juliana hesitated. She did not bother hiding her doubt.

"All friendships begin with a gesture of trust." He kissed her left eyelid and then her right, casually maneuvering her to comply with his request.

She wiggled her shoulders, settling against him with her eyes tightly shut. "Most would warn that rakes and rogues are by their very nature untrustworthy fellows."

Sin's chest shook with a soundless chuckle. "Life would be very dull without risk. Or rakes and rogues." He nuzzled her ear and whispered, "Think of the joy and rewards you would miss out on."

Juliana loathed admitting that the marquess was

correct. Weeks earlier, had she not argued with her mother over the decision to travel to London? Her gambling and defying their cousin's orders to remain in the country had certainly been rife with risk, as was Juliana's private decision to solicit a patron for her musical compositions.

Both her mother and father reveled in taking risks. Why would Juliana and her sisters be any different?

Sin rubbed his chin against her temple. The slight abrasive quality to his chin made Juliana smile. She liked the feeling. His scent was nice, too. A mix of rain, starch, and man. As she cuddled against him, she realized that she liked Alexius Braverton, Marquess of Sinclair, more than was wise for a lady in her current predicament.

Juliana opened her eyelids and tried to straighten at the cool, smooth caress of pearls against her nether folds. She could do little more than lift her head from his shoulder. Sin surrounded her. With his one hand on her right thigh, keeping her skirts split like drapery, and the other touching her intimately between her legs, all she could do was take measured breaths to keep from fainting.

"That's my courageous *lybbestre*," he praised, his voice unsteady as he stroked the pearls he had coiled around his two fingers down her cleft. "No, close your eyes. Just enjoy the feel of the pearls and my fingers."

His unhurried movements contrasted with the pounding tempo of the rainstorm. Juliana reclined the back of her head against the cradle of his shoulder and closed her eyes.

Her lower back arched in unspoken need as Sin teased the soft nubbin of flesh within the folds.

Sin set his teeth lightly into her neck. "Even now, your body prepares itself for me. There is nothing more beautiful than a woman's arousal. The slick wetness coats the pearls and my fingers. The musk of your quim is a heady aphrodisiac, Juliana. My heart races as blood fills my cock to the point of bursting—"

Juliana stirred in his carnal embrace, realizing that she could feel his rigid rod pressing into her backside. Fear fluttered like a butterfly caught in her throat. Sin was a man of strong appetites. No doubt, he expected to ease his cravings with her body.

"Desires can be reined, Juliana," he said, reading the sudden tension in her spine correctly. "Channeled. When I ultimately fill you, there will be a soft mattress cushioning your back so I can devote hours to the pleasurable task."

"Hours?" she croaked out. Juliana shook her head in denial. "Sin, I never . . . we will never . . . it is impossible."

His arms tightened possessively around her. "I will have you, my lady. Eventually. This afternoon is just a taste of what we can share together."

The pearls and his intimate strokes seemed to encourage the wetness between her legs. Cleverly Sin used her body's response to deepen his strokes. His fingers circled her womanly core. Juliana moaned. The tension that had straightened her spine had settled in her lower abdomen.

"No!"

She started as Sin plunged his pearl-wrapped fingers into her core.

"Yes," he hissed in her ear. Faint tremors shook his

body while he slowly, albeit determinedly, pressed deeper. "Christ, you are so tight, so sweet."

Her right foot pushed against the opposite bench as she leaned into Sin. Restlessly her hands moved up and down his arms. His fingers stretched her womanly core with each plunge and retreat. The sensation of being filled was overwhelming, but it was not painful. Her body seemed to welcome Sin, coating and drenching his fingers so he could touch the very heart of her.

"I might die from this."

Laughter burst from her lips at his dramatic statement. Sin was worried about dying? The man was torturing her. With his thick fingers he pushed and prodded until the string of pearls was wholly into her aching core. She wiggled her hips against his arousal and was grimly satisfied at his groan.

"Sin. The pearls—," she began.

"Clench your stomach muscles," he said tersely. "Do you like how the pearls shift and rub within you?"

"Yes!"

Sin was not finished. He gave her core a final thrust and then trailed his fingers up her cleft. As his fingertips found the nubbin of flesh, he circled and teased. "Think about the pearls inside of you. Someday soon, my cock will replace those pearls. Those sweet inner muscles clutching those smooth pearls will be milking my shaft, just begging for me—"

Juliana cried out as the first ripple of pleasure radiated from her core outward. Sin's unseen fingers worked feverishly between her legs, increasing the impact of each wave. Her stomach muscles contracted and her nipples tightened painfully. The undulating waves washed over her and pulled her under.

For one frantic second, she wondered if she could die from the violent bliss Sin had wrung out of her body.

Just when Juliana thought she could not bear it, Sin plunged his fingers into her core. She pressed her face into the crook of his neck. His fingers wiggled inside her, setting off another chain reaction of pleasing ripples. He slowly pulled the dampened string of pearls from her core, which only seemed to prolong the sensation.

As the last lingering ripple faded, Juliana curled herself into Sin's chest. Those wicked pearls of his were coiled into his fist, and her skirts had fallen back into place. It was almost as if nothing had happened.

Her womanly core contracted, aching for his touch.

Sin kissed her forehead. "The pearls suit you. I hope you will wear them for me often."

Juliana trembled. Whether she liked it or not, things had changed between her and Sin. Neither of them would be satisfied until Sin claimed her as he had boasted he would.

She did not know if she had the strength or the desire to resist.

Chapter Nine

"OF COURSE, YOU will wear Lord Sinclair's pearls," Cordelia said as she finished styling Juliana's hair.

Juliana had been staring at the reflection of her bare neck, contemplating whether she should wear Sin's gift. It was a daring statement. If the marquess saw the pearls around Juliana's neck, his arrogance would know no boundaries.

She grimaced while Cordelia tugged a section of hair that she was braiding.

"I do not want to appear ungrateful," Juliana mused aloud. "Still, to wear Sinclair's gift suggests an intimate claim. Oh, my life would be simpler if Maman had let me return the necklace."

"It was a very generous gift," her sister countered. "It is apparent to everyone that Lord Sinclair is quite smitten with you."

"Smitten" was not the word she would have chosen

to describe Sin's interest. It seemed too insipid for the passionate gentleman.

After what had transpired within Sin's coach, Juliana had begged the marquess to keep his gift. She had tried to explain to him that the pearl necklace felt like compensation for allowing him to touch her instead of a gift.

To her relief, Sin had not argued when she had pressed the pearls into his hands and told him that she could not accept such an expensive gift because of the questions it would raise within her own family. His mood had shifted to one of contemplation on the ride back to the town house. He had been courteous when he had walked her to the front door. Nor had he tried to kiss her as she had expected.

And then a small box was delivered to the town house. In spite of her wishes, the mischievous gentleman had given her the string of pearls in a more respectable manner.

Needless to say, her mother was elated when she saw the marquess's gift.

Juliana knew she had been cleverly outmaneuvered. How could she tell her mother that every time she glanced at the string of pearls she thought of Sin's boldness and intimate caresses, which had been the rogue's intention all along?

"Do not fall in love with him, Juliana!" she muttered to her reflection in the mirror. "Men such as Sin have little use for a lady's heart."

Her sister tugged on a length of Juliana's hair. "What are you mumbling about? Such impatience! Give me a minute more and I will be ready for the hairpins," Cordelia said, bringing Juliana back to the present.

With their limited resources, the marchioness had only been able to afford one personal maid. The servant certainly earned her keep by assisting all four ladies in the household. However, on evenings such as this one the maid was in high demand, so it was simpler for the sisters to help one another.

Juliana watched through the mirror on her dressing table as Cordelia crossed the two braided lengths of hair and then coiled the braids around the bun at the back of her head. Cordelia held the ends in place with one hand as she accepted several hairpins from Juliana and tucked them into place.

"There. Oh, how lovely you look!" her sister said, fussing with the curls around Juliana's face. "Lord Sinclair will be enchanted by your beauty. I would not be surprised if he tries to steal a kiss this evening."

Juliana let her gaze fall away from her reflection. It seemed prudent not to respond to Cordelia's enthusiastic prediction.

"I refuse to remain longer than it takes to pay my respects to my mother and sister," Vane said, moving his shoulders as if he was attempting to scratch an itch.

"I do not seem to recall demanding that you join me."

Alexius would have preferred to have not encountered any of his friends this evening. He had accepted Thornhill's invitation because he had learned Juliana would be attending.

It had been simply by chance that he had encountered Vane and Frost in the front hall of Lord Thornhill's town house. The rumor floating around the clubs was that the earl had gambled away a substantial portion of his inheritance and was currently searching for an heiress. If this was true, then the gentleman probably viewed the cost of the ball as a worthwhile investment.

The trio greeted their host and moved on to the ballroom. Alexius searched the ballroom. It appeared that Lady Duncombe and her daughters had not arrived. He was not disappointed. Their late arrival gave him the opportunity to discourage his friends from lingering.

"Is Lady Gredell attending?"

Alexius looked at Vane. "I did not ask." In fact, Alexius had not spoken to his sister since the evening he had encountered her at Lord and Lady Kempe's ball.

"Lady Lettlecott is to the north," Vane muttered under his breath.

It was a complication, but it was one that Alexius could avoid. "If Lord Lettlecott is present, she will behave herself."

Frost placed his hand on Alexius's shoulder. "And Lady Lawrie is holding court to the west. Oh, and twenty paces to the right, is that not the brown-eyed chit you tumbled two months past?"

Vane cocked his head to get a better look at the lady. "Is that the one who stuttered?"

"However, I will wager none of them interest you this evening. Nor are they the one you seek," Frost drawled.

There was a nasty edge to his inflection that made Alexius look at his friend sharply. "Tell me, Frost, since when did you take up fortune-telling?"

The topic of women always seemed to awaken Vane's baser instincts. "Who is the lady, Sin?"

"No one," Alexius snapped, unwilling to discuss Juliana with his friends.

"There is a woman." Vane grinned as Alexius cursed. "Frost, what do you know about this mysterious lady?"

"What I know does not matter," the earl replied enigmatically. "I am more interested in hearing what Sin has to say about the wench."

It suddenly dawned on Alexius that Frost had met Lady Juliana. The bastard had been kissing her when the pair had stumbled into the Kempes' parlor. There was a possibility that he knew that his friend had been quietly pursuing the lady.

It would explain why Frost was behaving like an arse.

Coming to a decision, Alexius said, "Her name is Lady Juliana Ivers. This goes no further, however. My sister asked me to approach her. Belle is worried about the lady's friendship with a certain gentleman. I am merely providing a slight distraction."

By telling Frost the truth Alexius hoped to bank the fires of competitiveness that occasionally flared between them.

Just then, Juliana and her sisters were announced. Both Vane and Frost, like many other gentlemen in the ballroom, noted the ladies' entrance.

While both Lady Cordelia and Lady Lucilla were quietly attractive, it was Juliana's beauty that tightened Alexius's chest and stirred more than his lust. She wore a frock of spring green crepe over white satin, with silk roses adorning the short puffed sleeves. Her blond tresses had been braided and arranged into an artful coil. A slender pearl bandeau rested like a crown on her head, and she was wearing his pearls around her throat.

Frost's lips thinned in displeasure. He had also noticed the string of pearls around her neck. Both he and Vane understood the significance of the necklace better than its owner.

Alexius gave each of his lovers a pearl necklace.

It was a blatant declaration of his intentions.

"Is that what you are doing?" Frost asked, then walked off.

Vane nodded at Frost. "What is wrong with him?"

"The list is endless," Alexius replied, hoping that they could change the subject. "Is that your mother?"

"Damn me, it is," Vane said, resigned that he was not getting out of his duties. "I will see you later this evening at Nox."

Vane gave his coat a tug and marched over to greet his mother.

Alexius frowned as he watched Lord Kyd approach Juliana and her sisters. Juliana clasped the gentleman's hand enthusiastically and parted from her sisters. Belle had reason to worry about her lover. Alexius was worried about the baron, too, because the man was beginning to annoy him.

In her excitement, Juliana forgot to release Lord Kyd's hand as they strolled away from her sisters. She promptly corrected her oversight and softened her actions by giving him a winning smile.

"Pray forgive my impatience, my lord," she began,

once she was assured her sisters could not overhear their conversation. "Nevertheless, your note implied that you have news about our business venture. I daresay my heart has been pounding in my chest since I read your cryptic words."

The baron's handsome face sobered at her confession. He brought his fist to his chin and nodded. "Alas, I regret in my haste that I might have cast your expectations in the wrong direction. I must beg your forgiveness, Lady Juliana."

She shut her eyes to gain a measure of control and dismissed his apology with an abrupt wave of her hand. "We are business partners, my lord. We can speak plainly without offense. What is your news?"

Lord Kyd crossed his wrists behind his back as they walked the length of the room. "I fear the news I bring is discouraging. My meeting with the publisher—"

"Simpson?" Juliana interjected.

Her companion nodded. "Yes. The unyielding, visionless simpleton!" The baron's eyes hardened as he recalled their conversation.

From his cold expression, Juliana sensed that the meeting had been disastrous. She brought her gloved hand to her bodice and let it hover over her heart. "Simpson hated the compositions," she said, dreading that her private fears were about to become realized.

"Those were not the precise words that he used," Lord Kyd protested.

"You do not have to spare my feelings, my lord. Exactly what did Simpson have to say about my music?"

The baron stopped and studied her face, judging for himself whether or not she was capable of hearing the truth. "Lady Juliana, forgive me. Simpson saw little value in your work. He thought the compositions charming and quite appropriate for the family drawing room. However, in terms of an investment—"

Her hand moved from her heart to her right temple. "He will not publish my work because I am a woman."

It took everything within her not to scream at the injustice.

Juliana flinched as she felt Lord Kyd's hand on her elbow.

"Have you considered taking a male pseudonym? You would not be the first lady who—"

"I appreciate your honesty, my lord," she said, her voice rising as she fought back her anger and tears. "Thank you for visiting Simpson on my behalf. You were correct in calling the man a simpleton. I heartily agree."

"Lady Juliana."

She glanced away, unable to bear the compassion she glimpsed in Lord Kyd's solemn gaze. If she remained, Juliana feared she would further disgrace herself by giving in to the tears that burned in her eyes. "No. Not now. With your permission, I will leave you to your evening. Good night, my lord."

Juliana turned away from the baron and began to walk away from him.

"Do not despair, my lady," Lord Kyd called out before she could escape. "Simpson is not the only publisher in town."

Fifteen minutes later, Juliana stepped out onto one of the upper balconies to get some fresh air. Her mother had ensconced herself within the walls of Lord Thornhill's card room, and neither Juliana nor her sisters were likely to see the marchioness for hours.

Juliana idly wrapped the pearl strand around her finger as she stared blindly into the night. Lord Kyd's news had been distressing indeed. The publisher Simpson could not be bothered with a lady composer. Were her beautiful pieces only suitable for the family's drawing room, as the publisher had told the baron?

"Well, well," Lady Gredell said, joining Juliana at the railing. "This is a surprise. I had not expected to see you here at Thornhill's."

"Good evening, Lady Gredell," Juliana murmured, wondering if it would be unseemly to fling herself from the balcony. It was a kinder choice than remaining.

"Rumor has it that the gentleman is seeking an heiress." Lady Gredell's look was condescending as she scrutinized Juliana's evening dress. "You and your sisters would hardly qualify."

The countess struck with the instinctive accuracy of an asp.

Juliana curled her fingers around the iron railing as if she could draw strength from it. "Neither would you, it would appear. If Lord Thornhill is truly seeking an heiress, he will require someone young and capable of giving him heirs. How many husbands have you buried, my lady? Now if you will excuse me, my sister is waiting."

Eyes wide, Juliana sauntered off, belatedly horrified that she had lowered herself to Lady Gredell's level. Juliana could not feel her legs as she crossed the room. When Sin's large body filled the doorway, she almost wept in relief.

"Lord Sinclair, this is most fortuitous," Juliana said, believing that his presence would prevent the countess from pursuing their altercation. She silently willed him to step back so that she could make good on her escape.

Sin's hazel gaze shifted from Juliana to Lady Gredell, who shrewdly watched them from the balcony. "Have I interrupted something?"

"Nothing that cannot be put aside for another time," the countess assured him. She smiled broadly at the marquess. "I miss your visits, Sinclair. When you are free, I pray that you will remember your old friend."

Lady Gredell had the nerve to wink at Sin.

Juliana had seen enough. She pushed by the marquess and strode down the hallway.

"Lady Juliana—wait!"

Sin caught her halfway down the staircase. "What did she say to you?"

Juliana tried to pull her arm from the marquess's hold, but he refused to let her go. "Is Lady Gredell your mistress?"

"What?" Juliana's question had surprised him. "Is that what she told you?"

She glanced away, refusing to meet his angry gaze. "It is a reasonable question, Sinclair. After all, there seems to be so *many* of them in town."

Juliana attempted to leave, but Sin would not allow it. "You have to release my arm, my lord," she pleaded, her eyes tearing in frustration. "You are drawing attention to us."

"Let them stare!" Sin snarled, and then cursed when he noticed her tears. "Lady Gredell is not my mistress. Nor will she ever be."

He cupped Juliana's cheek and rubbed away her tears with the soft pad of his thumb.

"Now tell me what she said to you that upset you so much?"

Juliana shook her head. Sin thought Lady Gredell was the reason for her tears. Since she had no intention of revealing her business arrangement with Lord Kyd to Sin or anyone else, it was simpler to let him believe the countess was to blame.

Perhaps Lady Gredell was not his mistress. Still, it was apparent that they were friends. "Nothing." She inhaled deeply. "It is not important as long as I can avoid the countess the rest of the evening."

And, if she was fortunate, the remaining weeks her family planned to stay in London.

Sin startled her by nudging her down the staircase. "If you will trust me, I believe I can assist you in your noble endeavor."

Chapter Ten

"WHERE ARE WE?"

Alexius chuckled at the wealth of suspicion in Juliana's voice. It had been a calculated risk to bring her here. She did not wholly trust him, and rightfully so. He had designs on her luscious body. If fortune favored him this evening, he planned to taste every inch of her.

"I promised you an evening without Lady Gredell nipping at your heels. As for where we are . . . The house belongs to me," he said, the pride of owning such a magnificent house evident.

Entwining his fingers with Juliana's, he extended the lantern the coachman had supplied to lead his reluctant guest to one of the back garden gates.

"Sinclair, this is highly inappropriate," she said, deliberately slowing down her stride in an attempt to halt their progress. "I should have never agreed to leave

Lord Thornhill's town house. Even with a chaperone, visiting your residence would cause speculation that my family cannot afford."

Her argument was not unexpected. Although she was attracted to him, she seemed disinclined to indulge her passionate nature. It was a stance that often puzzled him. Why would anyone deny themselves pleasure? Rules be damned. Alexius preferred bending them to suit his needs.

"This is a gate," he said, releasing her so he could unlatch it. "There is nothing shocking about you walking through it."

He opened the gate. Feigning indifference, he waited for Lady Juliana to sum up the courage he credited her with to enter his gardens.

"Why should I?" she said tartly.

"If you do not, I will shove you against the stone wall and thoroughly ravish you until your knees give way," Alexius threatened, warming to the notion. Christ, he almost hoped that she would refuse. "Then I will carry you upstairs to my bed, where I will indulge all of my wicked fantasies."

There was a faint clicking sound as Lady Juliana swallowed.

"And the alternative?"

"You trust me to find an acceptable compromise to both our needs."

Alexius held his breath. If Lady Juliana walked back to the coach, the polite thing to do was to let her go. He was not one to be swayed by propriety. Impulsive, explosive, and prone to selfishness, he was taught from the cradle to take what he wanted. It was difficult for him to not give in to the unruly nature that was bred into the Sinclair line.

"Very well."

With her head held high, she walked through the gate and waited for him to latch it. Alexius encircled her waist with his free hand and tugged her up against his chest.

"You are a maddening creature, my lady." He stole a quick kiss from her lips before releasing her. "Unpredictable, too."

Together they strolled off the gardens' pebbled path toward the house. His diligent staff had prepared for their arrival. The soft glow of strategically placed lanterns lit their way to the terrace.

Alexius grinned at Lady Juliana's soft gasp of surprise as she noticed his butler Hembry standing expectantly beside the small, round table that had been hauled out of the drawing room for this special occasion. The servant had covered the mahogany surface with a pressed tablecloth and the Sinclair plate and silver. Dozens of candles flickered cozily on the night's light breeze.

"Sinclair, what have you done?"

"A compromise," he murmured in her ear. "Share supper with me."

Hembry bowed formally. "Good evening, milord. My lady. Everything has been prepared as you ordered, Lord Sinclair. Shall I see to the first course?"

"Lady Juliana?" Alexius cocked his head, his hazel green eyes coaxing her to accept his invitation. He extended his hand. "Share supper with me. The stars and Hembry will be our chaperones. What say you?"

She nodded.

Her expression revealed her private doubts about the wisdom of her decision. Alexius, on the other hand, was confident that the evening would conclude in a very rewarding manner.

Alexius Braverton, Marquess of Sinclair, was a high-handed, albeit charming and resourceful, gentleman. He also believed that he had deduced the convoluted workings of her feminine mind. The man had guessed that she would not enter his town house, even under the innocuous guise of a late supper after an evening of dancing. So he had their supper brought outdoors. The results were sweetly romantic, and she privately conceded that she was touched by his gesture.

He was courting her.

And, good grief, it was working.

"How is the quail?"

Juliana removed the tines of the fork from her mouth as she chewed the succulent meat. She paused, waiting for the marquess to drink from his glass. "Since it has been roasted and placed onto my plate, I would guess that it is doing rather poorly."

Sinclair nearly choked on his wine. His laugh was low and full of genuine amusement as he used his finger to carelessly wipe a drop of Madeira from the corner of his mouth.

He raised his glass to honor her. "Well done, my lady. You delivered your quip with the skill of a stage performer."

She acknowledged his praise with a nod. "I have two

older sisters, my lord. Tricks and dramatics have always been part of our merry household."

Or had been. She picked up her glass of wine and took a contemplative sip. Much had changed after their father had died.

"Are you enjoying yourself?"

"Yes. Very much," she said, realizing that she spoke the truth.

For an informal affair, Lord Sinclair had not shirked on enticing her appetite. Over the past hour, Hembry had served them several courses that included: fried oysters, Mazarine of Salmon, roasted quail with bacon and watercress and buttered spinach.

When Hembry removed their plates and returned with fresh fruit and D'Artois of Apricot, Juliana groaned. "I beg of you to show mercy on your visitor, my lord. I could not eat another mouthful."

"No?" Sinclair casually plucked a grape from the bowl, popped it into his mouth, and chewed. "We shall put aside the dessert course for now."

Rising from his chair, Sinclair invited her to do the same by extending his hand. Juliana placed her hand within his. She shivered in anticipation as his fingers folded over hers. There was little doubt that she was over her head with a gentleman such as Lord Sinclair. Still, she could not resist flirting with impropriety when he was near.

Sinclair captured both her hands and circled her about. "To dance beneath the stars seems appropriate, do you not agree? Regrettably I did not think to hire musicians for the evening." He pulled her closer and retreated.

Whether it was the glass of Madeira or the slow dance, Juliana's head was spinning. Or mayhap it was Sinclair's proximity. It was a pleasant sensation.

"I could play for you," she said impulsively. "It is the least I could do to repay you for a delightful evening."

He reversed their direction as he seriously contemplated her offer. "You are most generous, my lady. However, I feel I must point out that if I accept, then we would have to adjourn to the music room."

Juliana brought her heels together, ending their dance. "You have proved yourself honorable, Sinclair, and worthy of the risk."

"Now you insult me."

Before she could take her next breath, the marquess overwhelmed her with a swift, forceful kiss. There was a smugness glimmering in his hazel green eyes at her bemused expression.

"Hembry," he said, not lifting his gaze from Juliana's. "We will retire to the music room. Lady Juliana wishes to play with me."

She laughed at his outrageous statement as the butler disappeared to light the lamps in the music room. "Play *for* you, you rogue. Music. Nothing else."

"Hmm . . . ," he enigmatically replied.

Sinclair allowed her to put her own interpretation on his intentions as they entered the house.

Lady Juliana let her fingertips lightly dance across the keys of the pianoforte before she sat down. Alexius had taken quiet pleasure in her initial pleasure as they had entered the music room. Neither Alexius nor his sister had been blessed with the skill or patience to adequately appreciate the musical instruments on display. The room connected to the main drawing room and had been rarely used in recent years.

"There must be a collection of music books somewhere," he muttered, frowning at the oversight. "Mayhap Hembry—"

Juliana brushed the suggestion aside with her hand. "There is no need to bother your servant. I have committed several musical compositions to memory."

She began playing Haydn's *Deutscher Walzer*. Alexius was instantly struck by Lady Juliana's concise, almost aggressive execution. With a half smile on his lips, he sat down on the sofa to the right of the pianoforte so he could admire her profile.

Alexius enjoyed watching her play. Although she was wholly focused on her performance, the distraction gave him the opportunity to study the lady who had entranced him from the beginning. She looked resplendent in her pale green evening dress. The cut of the bodice was less daring than he would have preferred. The oval neck meticulously covered her firm, well-defined breasts while giving him a teasing hint of bare shoulders.

Lost in her music, Lady Juliana switched from Haydn to Beethoven.

"You clearly practiced your lessons more than my sister did," Alexius said, and was rewarded with a smile.

"You have a sister?"

"When I choose to claim her," Sin said nonchalantly. "Your elegance makes her playing seem ham-fisted."

She flashed another radiant smile in his direction.

"You are too generous with your praise. Did you

know that Beethoven dedicated this sonata to Haydn, who had once been his teacher?"

"No. My father did not deem musical instruction an important aspect to becoming Marquess of Sinclair." Music was too civilized for the elder Sinclair. He respected a man who could use his fists, his wits, and his cock.

"A pity." Lady Juliana frowned at the chord her fingers had just struck. "My father insisted that all of his daughters learn to play the pianoforte."

She stopped playing and gave Alexius a rueful look when he placed his hands on her bare shoulders. "At the risk of lowering your high opinion of me, I must confess that I cannot recall the rest of the piece."

"No matter, my beautiful *lybbestre*," Alexius said, placing a small, chaste kiss on the top of her head. "There is no need to impress me. Play whatever amuses you."

The confidence Lady Juliana exuded when she played the pianoforte faded when she glanced demurely at him for reassurance. If it were a coquettish game, the lady was an expert, because he wanted to soothe her. Alexius squeezed her shoulder, encouraging her to continue.

"Very well."

Her gaze returned to the keys.

The next chords that she played vibrated from her fingertips, up her arms, and tickled the palms of his hands. Darker than the other two pieces that she had played, this one was designed to stir the senses. As Alexius watched her fingers dance across the keys, he marveled at the passion she poured into her efforts.

"Haydn, again?"

"No, this one is mine," she said proudly.

Alexius arched his brow at her declaration. She played with her eyes closed, a faint smile on her lips as the music flowed through her into him. Lady Juliana was an enigma to him. Hidden beneath her shy demeanor was a woman of deep passions. The music she coaxed and pounded from the ivory keys told its own tale of endless nights and unspoken desires.

His knuckle trailed down the center of her neck. Lady Juliana stiffened but continued to play, the notes and chords so much a part of her that her fingers moved effortlessly.

Alexius had sought the woman out on behalf of his sister. His orders were to seduce Juliana, distract her from her pursuit of Lord Kyd. Alexius hooked the string of pearls around her neck with his finger and pulled lightly until the length draped down her back. Bedding Lady Juliana would not be a hardship. He could make certain that they both enjoyed it. His body heated at the thought of her directing all that hidden passion at him.

"I like seeing my gift around your neck," he murmured, kissing the tiny indentation at the nape of her neck.

Lady Juliana shivered.

"Your gift has piqued my mother's curios-s-sity," she said, drawing out the last word when he flicked his tongue over the sensitive spot.

"I can bear a little scrutiny."

Alexius nibbled lightly on her neck. Lady Juliana tilted her head to the side to give him better access. "That is well and good; however, I should warn you. My mother brought me and my sisters to London in hopes of finding us suitable husbands."

He lifted his lips from her neck. Perhaps his sister's concerns were not jealous ravings, after all. "Are you hunting for a husband?"

Without missing a note, Lady Juliana shrugged him off. "Good heavens, no! That is my mother's wish, not mine. Still, my sisters have attracted a few devoted suitors, so perhaps Maman will partially succeed in her endeavors."

Something did not quite ring true in the lady's renouncement of marriage, for he thought all females craved to ensnare their admirers. "I am relieved to hear that, my lady. For I would make a dreadful husband."

Instead of being offended, Lady Juliana surprised him by lifting her hands from the keys and laughing at his confession. "I think Maman disagrees, my lord." She looped her finger around the pearls. "When a certain gentleman bestows upon the lady's youngest daughter an expensive gift, the mother can only assume the gentleman desires an intimate friendship."

Alexius pivoted the narrow bench Lady Juliana was sitting upon around so that she was facing him. "Intimacy and pleasure go hand in hand."

Her cheeks flushed as she recalled how he had brazenly presented his gift. "I have no intention of discussing this further."

"If you would permit me, I would give you more."

Lady Juliana became flustered by the intensity of his expression. "Jewelry? No, I could not accept. I should not have encouraged you by keeping the pearl necklace."

He fell to his knees. His blood rushed through his veins and arteries as she stared at him with a fascinating contradiction of wariness and anticipation. "I was not speaking of jewelry, my lady."

Alexius captured Lady Juliana's hips and gently pulled her onto his lap. Yards of pale green silk pooled around them. He had to tread carefully. His lovely *lybbestre* might desire him, but seducing her into surrendering to her passions would take all his skills.

"Kiss me, Juliana."

She giggled at his quiet request. "I feel ridiculous sitting like this. What if Hembry enters the room?"

Alexius cupped her face with his right hand and rubbed her lower lip with his thumb. "Hembry is paid very well for his discretion. No doubt he has retired to his quarters for the evening."

She started to rise. "Then I should leave—"

Alexius pulled her back down. "I disagree. You have yet to give me my kiss."

"Oh, very well," she said, rolling her eyes heavenward even as she leaned in to carry out his demand.

She thought only to lay her lips against his. However, Alexius had something else in mind. His mouth swallowed her exclamation as he neatly rolled her onto her back.

"Sinclair!" she gasped.

"Call me Sin," he countered, caging her with his arms. "For I am about to do something very wicked."

Without asking for her permission, he flipped up her skirts, revealing layers of petticoats and an elegant pair of legs. She squeaked when he kissed each knee. "It is a pity to hide such lovely limbs under yards of muslin and silk."

Lady Juliana—no, Juliana, for Alexius was beginning to think it was time to put aside formalities—attempted to sit up and straighten her skirts. He gently pressed her shoulder until it touched the floor.

"I vow this will not hurt," he teased. The lady was panicking, so he would have to linger over her delightful legs later. Now was the time to stake his claim. "I asked you for a kiss. Allow me to return the favor."

Without warning he parted her knees. His hands speared through the remaining yards of fabric to the hidden prize at the apex of her thighs.

"Sinclair—Sin!"

Alexius could smell the subtle spice of her arousal, even though Juliana was fighting him and herself. He used his thumbs to part the soft folds of her womanly cleft and kissed her.

Juliana reared up, her fingers grasping his hair. If she thought to distract him from his goal, she had sadly underestimated his determination. He had the lady exactly where he wanted her. She was on her back and her legs were parted. Alexius would not be appeased until he had buried his cock into her.

Indeed, he could satisfy both his needs and his sister's with one decisive thrust.

Juliana sucked in her breath as Alexius licked the tender bud of flesh within the folds. "It appears I want dessert, after all." He suckled her, feeling the small bud swell against his tongue. Within his trousers, his cock responded in kind, lengthening and straining to be free.

"So sweet," he murmured, teasing her womanly core with his finger. The dew of her arousal coated his fingers, and he could not resist pushing deeper.

Juliana moaned and arched her back.

Thankfully, she had lost interest in tearing the hair from his head. Her fingers clenched, her hands had fallen at her sides as he continued to pleasure her with his mouth.

Alexius reveled in the heady taste of her arousal. She wanted him. Her desire coated his tongue, his lips, and his fingers. His cock craved to measure the hidden depths of her hot, slick core. Confident that Juliana would not deny him his pleasure, he used his thumb to stroke the diameter of her core as he applied his talented tongue across the swollen sensitive flesh.

Suddenly a high keening sound exploded from Juliana's lips. She lifted her hips as if begging him to take more. Alexius happily complied. He dipped his thumb into her core, relishing the rhythmic pulse of her inner muscles as she collapsed in mindless pleasure.

He sat up on his knees and wiped the dampness from his chin by using his coat sleeve as he admired Juliana's blissful repose.

Alexius slipped out of his frock coat and tossed the garment on the sofa. With a calmness he did not feel, he untied his cravat and unfastened the buttons at his throat. The scent of her filled his nostrils, making him restless and hungry to sate his own needs.

He unbuttoned his trousers and his cock sprang upward as he pushed the fabric lower, exposing his muscular buttocks. Their first joining would be swift and frenzied, because he had waited long enough for this moment. Later, he would take the time to undress her and discover all the enchanting curves that her dress concealed.

Alexius moved over her body and positioned himself between her legs.

Juliana smiled up at him, her eyes still glazed from the passion he had wrung from her body. "You are sinful."

He grinned at the awe in her husky voice. "And you, my sultry *lybbestre*, are too tempting for me to resist. I must have you."

Alexius used the head of his cock to part the swollen folds of her cleft. He groaned and closed his eyes as her moisture and sleek flesh enclosed over his rigid, demanding length.

"Christ!"

Juliana's tight, welcoming core would be his undoing if he did not take charge. Desperate to fill her, he thrust deeply, his weight and lust driving his cock into the heart of her.

Juliana cried out. "What are you doing?"

Alexius pressed his face into her shoulder, quivering and accepting her weak blows from her fists to pull out. His mind was still spinning from his discovery: the physical confirmation his instincts had sensed from their first meeting. The passionate woman beneath him had been a virgin. Lord Kyd was not her lover.

Belle wanted me to take Juliana's maidenhead, Alexius grimly reminded himself.

His sister had just interjected enough doubt about the lady's maidenly state to smooth over his initial reluctance.

Belatedly Alexius understood the source of Belle's fears.

Virginity was the one precious gift his sister could never bestow upon Lord Kyd, so she had looked upon Juliana's innocence as a threat that needed to be removed.

Alexius pressed a kiss to her shoulder. Although he had claimed Juliana's innocence, he damn well had not done it for his sister!

"Sin," Juliana said, pushing against his shoulders.

The inner muscles of her core flexed, squeezing his cock. He groaned as he tried not to move. "Hush. Stop fighting me, Juliana. Your body will accept me if you can settle down."

"It hurts."

Regret flashed in his eyes. The pain in her pale green eyes almost made him relent, but the damage had been done. It was up to him to show her that she could find pleasure in their union.

"I know." He kissed the tears on her cheeks. "I was too rough. Forgive me for my eagerness."

The hidden passion he had always sensed within Juliana was merely unrealized. He recalled the game he had played with the pearl necklace and how she had thrashed beneath him when he had tasted the essence between her legs. His testicles tightened with the knowledge that no other man had touched her.

Juliana was his.

She inhaled sharply when Alexius tentatively retreated only to reclaim the lost inches. "We should stop."

"Perhaps. Though it seems a tad cruel to leave me in this shameful predicament." He slowly moved his hips against hers. In spite of her initial pain, her core was wet and accepting of his intrusion.

"Cruel?" She glared up at him. "I am cruel?"

Momentarily forgetting her fear and discomfort as he had planned, Alexius lazily stroked her with his cock. "Not intentionally," he amended. "Just as I had not set out to hurt you. Do you recall the pleasure you felt when I put my mouth on you?"

Her hands fluttered to her breasts. Although they were concealed within her bodice, Alexius wondered if her nipples ached and itched beneath her corset. He longed to rip open her bodice and nuzzle the soft bounty.

"Yes."

He slipped his hand under her buttock and hitched the head of his cock so deep inside her that they both moaned. "I can improve upon that pleasure. I vow you will cry out my name when I have finished."

There was a flash of disbelief in her guileless expression, and truthfully he could not condemn her for it. Nevertheless, her body remembered the pleasure he had evoked. Her tight sheath gave way as the walls anointed his cock from tip to base.

Alexius sealed her lips with his own as he quickened the tempo of his thrusts. He teased her mouth with his tongue. Allowing his free hand to wander, he followed the outline of her hip, along her waist, before cupping her breast. He broke away from her mouth and tenderly nipped the covered breast.

"Sin."

This time when she said his name, there was a question in her inflection. Ruthless in his determination, Alexius's hand returned to her buttock. He held her firmly against him as his cock pounded into her core. She was so wet, he did not bother sparing her the frenzied pace he craved.

Juliana cried out.

Blind with need, Alexius silently rejoiced as her hips instinctively met his to deepen their connection. His testicles tightened in response to her feminine cry, and the blunt head of his cock swelled. His hoarse shout heralded his release as his hot seed burst from him, pulsing against her womb.

It was only when he had collapsed against her, his rigid cock still buried deep within her sheath, he realized that the angry promise he had made to Juliana had come to pass.

In the reckless throes of passion, it was his name that Juliana had cried as she blindly clung to him.

If Alexius had had the strength, he might have roared in delight.

Chapter Eleven

DAYS PASSED INTO weeks as Juliana blissfully savored the private joy of being Sin's lover. It was a secret that she had vowed not to share with her sisters. They would never understand, or worse, they might tell their mother. A marquess, even a roguish one, was too tempting a prize for the marchioness. If Lady Duncombe dared to press Sin into making a formal declaration for Juliana's hand, she feared that she might never see him again.

While Sin seemed to enjoy their friendship, she could not imagine him falling onto his knees and swearing fealty and love to her. He had no more interest in marriage than Juliana did, and she was honest enough to accept that once her family returned to their cottage in the country Sin would fade from her life.

It was unavoidable.

Like spring maturing into summer.

Not everything was idyllic in the Ivers household,

however. Love could not blind her from her mother's increasing melancholy. Their cousin, Lord Duncombe, had arrived in London. His visit to their rented town house had been extremely unpleasant. The marchioness had sent her daughters out of the room and borne the brunt of his wrath.

Afterward, Juliana's mother seemed to find little pleasure in London. Oh, the marchioness always ardently denied that something was troubling her when her three daughters questioned her. However, she was lying.

The previous evening, Juliana had stumbled across her mother and Lord Gomfrey in a vestibule. Juliana had encountered the earl on several occasions, but she did not know him well enough to offer an opinion on his character. That was until she caught him threatening her mother. Juliana regrettably had been too far away to overhear their conversation. Nevertheless, the gentleman's demeanor had been accusatory and rather menacing.

Juliana planned to get the truth out of her mother even if she had to do a little threatening of her own.

"No more evasions, Maman," Juliana said, waiting until after breakfast so she could catch her mother alone. "What is this business between you and Lord Gomfrey?"

Lady Duncombe's lower lip quivered at her youngest daughter's harsh tone. Juliana had always tried to treat her mother with the proper respect that she deserved but had grown weary of the subterfuge between them.

"The truth, Maman."

Lady Duncombe placed a trembling hand to her

lips and cleared her throat. "Do you recall my prideful assurances that my luck has improved at the card tables?"

Juliana pulled them both down so they were sitting on the sofa. "Yes. I know you spoke truthfully on the matter. A little more than a week ago, I overheard you as you faced your creditors and paid their bills."

Tears filled the marchioness's eyes. "Well, I did experience some good fortune. Enough to satisfy those merchants. That is, however, until the night Lord Gomfrey joined the table."

Juliana pried open her reticule and retrieved her lace handkerchief. "Here." She dabbed gently at the wetness on her mother's face and pressed the linen into her hand. "I assume the evening did not end well."

Lady Duncombe brought the handkerchief up to her nose and sniffed. "We seemed evenly matched. I won. He won. The conversation between us was lively and, dare I say, flirtatious."

"Then you began to lose."

"Dreadfully. Oh, the evening was a complete disaster! I sustained heavy losses. Naturally, Lord Gomfrey was sympathetic about my humiliating predicament. He generously offered me a stake so I could—"

Juliana dug her fingers into her temples to allay the pain. "Oh, Maman, how could you—"

The marchioness's expression hardened as she thought about that night. "And the more I tried to regain my balance—"

"The higher the debt accrued."

Lady Duncombe clasped her hands together. "It was silly of me to have accepted Lord Gomfrey's stake.

I should have realized his intentions, but I was shaken by the losses. I was so desperate."

The anger Juliana had felt earlier softened into pity. This was not the first time the family had faced financial adversity, and she doubted it would be the last. The marchioness was clever at cards, but even a skilled player could be defeated by a competent adversary. Juliana embraced her mother. "Not to worry, Maman. We will figure out a way to pay Lord Gomfrey. Your debt of honor will be satisfied."

The marchioness's spirit seemed to crumple at Juliana's words of assurance. As Lady Duncombe buried her face against her daughter's shoulder, the older woman's entire body shook while she sobbed.

Puzzled, Juliana rubbed her mother's back in a comforting gesture. "There, there. . . . It must have been a terrible burden keeping this secret."

Lady Duncombe hiccupped and shuddered.

Juliana pressed her nose into her mother's shoulder. The familiar floral scent had always been a source of love and comfort to Juliana. This was a chance to return her mother's gift. She could be strong enough for both of them.

Ten minutes had passed before the marchioness pulled away. Her mother wiped her cheeks and blew her nose as she struggled to compose herself. She tried to smile, but it was a poor imitation of a genuine effort.

"Oh, my darling Juliana," Lady Duncombe said, her voice cracking with emotion. "My burden lies not with keeping secrets from you, Cordelia, and Lucilla but rather with Lord Gomfrey's appalling terms."

"Terms?"

Juliana's mother straightened her spine. It seemed to take all her strength to meet her daughter's curious gaze. "Lord Gomfrey demands payment immediately, or he will reveal my disgraceful predicament to the *ton*."

"Beast," Juliana hissed.

Lady Duncombe laid her hand on the right side of Juliana's cheek. "More than you know, Daughter. He knows our family cannot withstand the scandal. And poor Cordelia and Lucilla! Any hope that Lord Fisken or Mr. Stepkins might offer for your sisters' hands in marriage will be soundly dashed once the rumors reach their ears. Not only will we be utterly ruined; your sisters' hearts will be irrevocably broken."

Sin's handsome face shimmered in Juliana's mind. She had never encountered a gentleman who seemed so irreverent to polite society's rules. Oh, how she envied his freedom and reckless nature. It also made him rather unpredictable. When he learned of her family's awkward circumstances, how would he react? Would he offer his assistance or simply walk away?

Perhaps it was unfair of her to speculate. In spite of her innocence, she had understood that Sin viewed their friendship as he would any other amusement. He loved her body and her wit, but he was categorically a rogue at heart. When she returned to the country, there would be another lady who would stand at his side and dally in his bed. Next spring, Sin would not even be able to recall her name.

Juliana tensed as the painful thought washed over her. This was not the moment for regrets. There was no use denying that she had been drawn to Sin from the very beginning. While one might argue that the experienced marquess had seduced her, she had done little to avoid the outcome. It had been her choice.

Her single act of defiance had been exhilarating and liberating.

No one, not even Sin, could take that away from her.

"Maman, you mentioned terms. This means Lord Gomfrey wants something other than money. What is it?"

"You."

Juliana did not recall standing or moving toward the hearth. The coals were unlit, though she doubted anything could penetrate the coldness that she felt in her bones.

With her back to her mother, Juliana said, "You refused him, I presume." When her mother remained silent, Juliana turned around and laughed. "How could you possibly entertain the notion that I would marry such a man?"

"The offer was not precisely one of marriage."

Juliana gasped as if struck.

Lady Duncombe rushed to her daughter's side, placed a supportive arm around Juliana and led her back to the sofa. It was not until they were seated again that Juliana found her voice.

"He desires for me to be his mistress?"

"The role of a mistress implies that your future prospects are, shall we say, limited, and too harsh to describe the arrangement the earl has proposed. I believe Lord Gomfrey hopes that you will look upon the arrangement as a courtship of sorts." Her mother seemed to age before Juliana's withering gaze. "He is willing to forgive the debt and return the promissory note that he forced me to sign if you agree to place him above all others."

Her mother was doing her best to rationalize that the

earl's arrangement was nothing more than a forced courtship. For Juliana, it seemed like Lord Gomfrey desired a mistress more than a wife.

"For how long?" Juliana choked out the words, fighting back the scream that was clawing its way out of her throat.

Wary of Juliana's control, her mother said, "Till summer's end."

"So little time?"

It seemed like a thousand years to Juliana.

Lady Duncombe glanced away. "L-Lord Gomfrey wanted me to tell you that he prays that you will not view your time with him as a punishment. He is rather taken with you and hopes that you will return his affection once you have spent some time with him. He made it quite clear that he is willing to set a date at summer's end if all goes well."

"Does he? Would that not assuage everyone's guilt in the matter?"

"Juliana!"

Juliana's vision blurred as she jumped to her feet. She wanted to flee the drawing room. If she could, she would leave the house and keep running until she collapsed from exhaustion.

"Do not touch me!" she exclaimed, pulling her arm out of her mother's reach. "How could you? If Lord Gomfrey had approached Papa with such a crude offer, Papa would have put a bullet into him. He . . ." Panting, Juliana tugged on the edge of her bodice. She could not catch her breath. "Papa would have never sold me to pay off a debt!"

With a muffled sob, she sank to the floor as her vision grayed.

Ignoring her faint protests, the marchioness wrapped her arms around Juliana, and they both settled onto the carpet. "Your beloved papa is dead," her mother said fiercely. "He has been lost to us these past five years, and what trials we face are ours alone."

She laid her cheek against Juliana's shoulder. "This world belongs to men. We live by their whims and laws. If I could spare you this fate, know that I would."

Juliana swiped at the tears rolling down her cheeks. "Refuse his offer, Maman."

"And then what?" She seized Juliana's chin, forcing her to accept the unpleasant truth that gleamed in her mother's angry gaze. "Scandal . . . the chance for you and your sisters to marry well is lost . . . debtors' prison? You alone have the ability to save this family. Is it really too much to ask?"

Yes.

Juliana closed her eyes, attempting to shut out the truth in her mother's words. "What if we appeal to Lord Duncombe? I know he is angry at you for bringing us to London. Nevertheless, he might pay off Lord Gomfrey in order to avoid the scandal."

"No, he will not." Lady Duncombe sighed, the sound heavy with regret. "You are correct; Oliver is angry with me. As far as he is concerned, my casual defiance of his authority has hardened his heart toward us. He will leave us to our grim fate and rejoice."

"So I am to be the sacrifice," Juliana said dully.

The marchioness stiffened as if slapped. "What exactly are you sacrificing, Daughter? Sinclair has already taken your innocence. Did you think you could hide something like that from your mother? I know you too well."

"Maman, please."

"You are fortunate that the *ton* is not speculating whether you are his mistress in name only or in deed. While I like the gentleman, I suspect you will wait in vain for a respectable offer from Sinclair. Lord Gomfrey, on the other hand, is offering a means to save our family."

She could not believe it. Her mother knew that Juliana and Sin were lovers. The realization made her physically ill. "Release . . . me," she said, struggling out of her mother's embrace. Juliana's legs became entangled in her skirts and she landed flat on her face.

Her cheek burned as her flesh connected with the carpet, but she welcomed the pain. Gritting her teeth, she unsteadily climbed to her feet and headed for the door.

"Juliana, be reasonable," the marchioness pleaded, using the sofa to aid her as she stood. "I did not mention Sinclair to shame you. A mother just knows when her daughter is in love. Your face brightened whenever Sinclair was close. Worse, I saw how he watched you as you moved about the ballroom. He wanted you, and considering his reputation, the conclusion was inevitable."

Juliana brought her hand up to her face. She had no illusions about Sin's reputation with the ladies of the *ton*. However, she refused to allow her mother to sully the tender moments she had shared with him. "Now I understand, Maman. You assume that since I was willing to play at being one man's whore, why not another's when it benefits the family?"

"No!" her mother shouted, her face reddened from exertions or belated shame. "You twist my words and it is cruel of you. I have failed you. I know this and

I deserve your hate. However, I beg you to consider Lord Gomfrey's offer. If not for me, for your sisters."

Juliana did not glance back at her mother until she had opened the door. The marchioness's face was a mess. Her nose was swollen and red, and tears leaked down her cheeks even though she did not make a sound. She looked as miserable as Juliana felt. If Lady Duncombe desired her daughter's forgiveness, she would have to give Juliana time.

Juliana was numb. "I will give you my answer this afternoon." She nodded her head. "Now if you will excuse me." Juliana turned away.

"Wait. Where are you going?"

Her mother took a step closer, but one look from Juliana forced Lady Duncombe to reconsider such a foolish action.

"I thought to take some air. Do not worry. I shall be quite safe in a carriage. You will have your answer in a few hours."

"There is one more thing that I have not mentioned," Lady Duncombe said before Juliana could close the door. "Lord Gomfrey has several terms that we must adhere to. The first: we cannot speak of the arrangement to anyone. The *ton* must believe that you are at the earl's side because you desire it."

"And the second?"

"You must end your friendship with Sinclair." The marchioness's eyes softened at Juliana's soft gasp. "Forgive me, Daughter, if this causes you pain. Nevertheless, Lord Gomfrey was most specific."

—

Two hours later, Juliana arrived by carriage at her cousin's town house. She had been unaware of her final destination when she had left her mother. With their argument ringing in Juliana's ears, she had ordered her coachman to drive through London. The carriage ambled up and down the streets for a good part of an hour before she noticed where she was. When the refined façade of Nox came into view, she almost begged the coachman to halt.

Since most gentlemen spent more time within their clubs than their own private residences, Juliana suspected Sin was behind those exclusive doors, laughing with his friends and discussing matters that were best not pondered by her.

In the end, she held her breath as her carriage slowly rumbled past the club, desperately wishing she had had the courage to tell him that she needed him. However, it was unfair to involve him, and more to the point, she was ashamed of the trouble her mother's gambling had wrought.

After all, a lady had her pride.

No, whether Juliana liked it or not, her cousin was the gentleman in the position to assist her. Besides, it was in his best interest to keep the matter within the family.

Juliana approached the front door of the town house with a dispassionate expression on her face. The residence had once belonged to her family. Whenever her parents had traveled to London, Juliana and her sisters had remained at Ivers Hall. The grand residence did not hold a place in her heart as Ivers Hall once had. It belonged to her cousin now, and he was entitled to it.

"Wait here," she told the footman as he helped her step down from the carriage. "I will not be long."

The servant had already knocked on her cousin's door to inquire if the marquess was at home. The butler had told him that Lord Duncombe would be receiving callers in the afternoon. Her calling card assured her an early audience.

As she stepped into the dim entrance hall, her cousin was descending the stairs. Juliana did not take this informality as a good sign. Why would he go to the trouble of greeting her when all he had to do was simply wait for his butler to announce her in the drawing room?

"Cousin," Juliana said, curtsying as he approached. "You look well."

Lord Duncombe raised his brows at the compliment. Dismissing the butler, the marquess clasped his hands around his back as he circled around her. "You, to be perfectly blunt, do not, Cousin. What brings you to my door at this early hour?"

He was far from welcoming. If they had been close, he would have escorted her to the drawing room or even his library. Instead, she was standing in the front hall like an unwanted guest. Perhaps she should count herself fortunate that he would see her at all.

"Well?"

Be forthright, she privately counseled herself. Her cousin would not respect a meandering approach.

"Maman is in trouble."

He snorted. "Gambling trouble, I assume."

Juliana lifted her chin at his derisive tone. "Yes. I am told Lord Gomfrey holds her promissory note and the debt is considerable."

The marquess chuckled softly. "I am certain it is. Lord Gomfrey is not one to trifle with at the card table. Your mother was aware of his reputation."

"My lord, be that as it may, we have need of your assistance."

"No."

The simple monosyllable wiped away Juliana's prepared appeal. Momentarily speechless, she stared at him as she attempted to gather her scattered thoughts. She glanced longingly at the chairs positioned along the left wall. Since Lord Duncombe had not deigned to offer her the small courtesy, it bordered on rudeness to simply sit down.

"I do not think you understand the severity of the situation," she said, her hands gripping her reticule so tightly that the tips of her fingers tingled. "Lord Gomfrey expects the note to be paid off by dusk."

Lord Duncombe frowned and then straightened the sleeve of his coat with a firm tug at the cuff. "Terms, I assume, your mother agreed upon."

Her cousin was so cold. She wondered if he had ever cared for anyone other than himself. He had showed more concern about the proper alignment of his sleeves rather than her mother's predicament. "Yes."

He lifted his head, his cool gray eyes pinning Juliana in place. "Then it is up to your mother to face her obligations."

Juliana's stomach roiled in protest at his callousness. "M-Maman is unable to meet these obligations without your assistance. You and I both know this to be true. How can you be so cruel as to turn your back on your family?"

"Family?" Lord Duncombe stalked toward her, causing her to retreat until her back was pressed against the door. "Is that a declaration of love, Cousin?"

He stood so close, Juliana could feel the heat radiating from his body. If his purpose was to intimidate her, he was succeeding. Her reaction only made him laugh.

"Our connection is merely an accident of birth, Lady Juliana. Your affection for me is as meager as your mother's purse."

Juliana loathed that he was correct. It mattered little that he had done nothing to earn the respect and affection of the Ivers women. She would not be standing in Lord Duncombe's front hall if she did not need his wealth to save her mother.

Juliana took a fortifying breath and deliberately looked him in the eye. "If Lord Gomfrey pursues this in the courts, there will be a scandal. The family's name—"

"The family's name?" He scratched his left brow. "Is that the best you can do? You are such a clever young lady. I expected more logic and less emotion from you."

"As head of our family—," she began.

"Now you will lecture me on my duty!" The marquess moved away from her and gestured broadly to the empty chairs in the hall. "I will tell you about duty, my lady. It is my duty to bear the Duncombe title with honor, nurture the wealth and lands in my stewardship, and marry well so that my seed will one day inherit everything I have protected. I understand my duty."

"This will ruin Maman," Juliana said softly.

"Mayhap then she will learn her place," Lord Duncombe thundered back. "Your mother has gained an unpleasant reputation for not honoring her promises. I cannot say that I am surprised, considering my own dealings with the woman."

Anger sparked in Juliana's green eyes. "What promises? Maman always meets her obligations."

Eventually.

"Always with my assistance, Lady Juliana!" he shouted, his words echoing. "Are you aware of how many occasions your mother has written me about my duty to you and your sisters? No? Did your mother also forget to tell you that I sent money every time it was asked, no, dare I say, demanded?"

Juliana blinked back the sting of her tears, refusing to cry in front of Lord Duncombe. She would never give him the satisfaction.

"I was unaware of the loans that you made to my mother."

"Indeed. Then I can assume that you were unaware of the promise that I demanded from your mother six months ago when she once again begged for my assistance."

"What promise?"

He sneered, believing Juliana was feigning ignorance. "I was willing to pay off your mother's debt with one stipulation: she was not to bring you and your sisters to London."

"Maman mentioned that you would be vexed when word reached you that we were residing in London for the season, but she did not explain the reasons for it." Juliana gave him a sullen glance. "Besides, everything about Maman seems to vex you. No doubt, she believed you could think worse of her."

"Your mother was wrong," Lord Duncombe snapped. Ignoring Juliana's gasp, he reached behind her and opened the door. "Good day, Cousin. If you wish, you may send my condolences to your mother. It is all that she will receive from me."

Juliana stepped through the doorway and into the bright sunshine. Lord Duncombe shut the door firmly behind her. She shielded her eyes as she made her way to the carriage. How silly of her to have forgotten her parasol. The sun was almost blinding.

As she settled into the carriage, Juliana desperately wanted to despise the marquess for his indifference. She had not known about all the loans Maman had begged from him. Lord Duncombe was a patronizing prig, but he had yet to prove himself to be a liar. Why had Maman not told her about the money and her promise not to travel to London?

The marquess suspected it was the rich purses that had lured her into town. Juliana disagreed. In spite of all Lady Duncombe's faults, she loved her daughters. She wanted to see her daughters settled into their own households, not locked away in their rented cottage in the country. A season in London would have been viewed as crucial to the marchioness's plans, even if it meant defying Lord Duncombe's dictates.

"Oh, Maman," Juliana sighed, oblivious to street activity rolling by as she returned to the town house.

Her dark thoughts eventually led her back to Sin. Juliana was tempted to order the coachman to take her to the Sinclair residence. If he was not at home, she could wait for him. How would the unrepentant rogue react if Juliana, upon his arrival, collapsed hysterically into his arms? She chuckled softly. If the man possessed an ounce of sense, he would drag her to her carriage, toss her in, and send her on her way.

Perhaps she was being unkind. Sin was a good man. He was just incapable of offering more than a temporary diversion. Had he not warned her of his flaws from the very beginning? It was unfair to turn to a gentleman who diligently strived to avoid all entanglements.

Now I am lying to myself!

Those were not the real reasons why she was reluctant to involve Sin in her family's problems. Juliana feared that Sin would challenge Lord Gomfrey once he heard the gentleman's terms. Sin would feel obligated to defend her good name. She refused to risk his life over a gambling debt.

Not for her.

Juliana would have to be the one to end their affair.

Her stomach burned at the thought.

How does one go about discarding a lover? One misstep and she still might provoke her jilted lover into challenging Lord Gomfrey.

If something happened to Sin, my heart would shatter—

She blinked and straightened at the silent admission. Love.

Did she love Sin? No. No-no-no! She stomped the floorboards of the carriage to punctuate her denial.

Cordelia and Lucilla were the ones who fell in love whenever a gentleman glanced in their direction.

Would her quandary amuse Sin if he were sitting beside her? Or would he pity her? He had warned her not to confuse passion with love, and she had assured him that she was aware of the difference.

She had warned herself not to fall in love with him.

Juliana buried her face into her gloved hands and groaned. She and her mother had something in common. Neither of them seemed capable of keeping her word.

The depressing revelation clung to Juliana like an oily shadow as she disembarked from the carriage and entered the town house. She found her mother in the study with the housekeeper. They had been discussing the menu for the week when Juliana hesitated at the threshold.

"How was your walk?" the marchioness inquired after she dismissed the servant.

"Most unrewarding."

The marchioness wearily nodded. For the first time, Juliana wondered if her mother had guessed the true reason why she had left the house.

"I have come to a decision." She clutched the door frame for support. "Since Lord Gomfrey is calling in your promissory note, I see no alternative but to accept his vile terms. I will agree to this courtship."

"Juliana." Her mother opened her arms and moved forward to embrace her.

"Please." She held up her hand, halting her mother's approach. "I feel so fragile I might shatter. I need to be strong. For me. For all of us."

Her mother bowed her head. "If there was any other way . . ."

Juliana slowly turned and began to walk away. "Send word to Lord Gomfrey. He shall have his pound of flesh."

Chapter Twelve

"TWO IMPERIAL SUMMONSES in one week," Hunter teased Alexius as they entered the lobby of the theater with Saint, Reign, and Dare lagging behind them. "What have you done lately to upset the ice queen?"

Alexius gave his friend a pained look. "I would appreciate it if you would cease referring to my sister as the ice queen. If word gets back to her, she will most likely insist that I do something to silence you."

A hand clamped affectionately on Alexius's shoulder. "If you need assistance, I would be happy to volunteer," Dare offered. "Silence from Hunter would be worth bloodying my knuckles."

"And upset Lady Allegra?" Hunter placed his hand over his heart and fluttered his lashes in a feminine manner. "Heaven forbid. Perhaps if you plead on bended knee she will tend your manly wounds."

With the body build of a pugilist, Dare took an intimidating step toward the duke.

Saint blocked Dare's slow, deliberate stalk with his arm. "Think of where we are. Save the bloodshed for later."

Alexius grimly nodded. "It took a substantial bribe to convince the manager not to ban us because of our last unfortunate brawl in one of the private boxes." He glared pointedly at Hunter.

The Duke of Huntsley bristled at the accusation. "Blame Vane and Frost. They were the ones who foolishly asked Lady Wodgen if she had plumped her breasts by tucking rags into her corset. Both had bedded the silly wench before her marriage to the Earl of Wodgen, and neither could recall fondling such a generous bounty."

"Christ," Alexius muttered under his breath. Wodgen had been out for blood that night. Perhaps it had been wise to ask his friends to join him as he satisfied his sister's curiosity about why his affair with Juliana had continued in spite of Belinda's continual demands that he carry out her plan and cast the lady aside. "I have no plans to linger in my sister's private box."

Once he had suffered Belinda's displeasure, he intended to seek out the lady who was the focus of his sister's ire. In the afternoon, one of the Ivers footmen had delivered to his residence a rather odd note from Juliana. She had written of the need to meet with him, but the missive lacked the warmth he usually associated with the lady.

Alexius sensed something was amiss in the Ivers household.

Whatever the problem, he would fix it. He was an expert at soothing hurt feelings and imagined slights.

"I trust all of you can control your baser instincts for an hour."

Dare looked at him incredulously. "Settle for half that time. Frost and Vane are unfettered and lurking somewhere."

Lord Gomfrey held on to Juliana's elbow until she was seated. A casual observer might consider his actions solicitous. Juliana suspected the gentleman was worried that his newly bought companion would slip away.

The earl was astute.

As her unwanted suitor settled in next to her, Juliana was half-tempted to fling herself off the balcony. While such an attempt would be highly dramatic, it was doubtful that the fall would kill her. Besides, she had made a promise. Summer's end was scarcely three months away.

"Are you comfortable, Lady Juliana?"

Only when you keep your hands to yourself.

Her lips quivered as she forced the soft flesh to curve into a faint smile. "Yes. It is kind of you to inquire."

Encouraged by her politeness, the earl leaned closer. "My dear, forgive me for not including your sisters on our first outing. I realized their presence would have eased your nerves. Nevertheless, this evening is a public declaration of our courtship. I hope you will indulge me."

"Courtship?" she said derisively.

"Merely a polite deception, my dear, to satisfy the *ton*," he explained, patting her hand. "After all, your sisters still hope to marry well. There is no reason to ruin their noble ambitions with a scandal as long as I am pleased with your performance. Besides, as I told your mother, I could do worse for a bride."

The orchestra had begun to play the first music, though no one, above or below, would likely pay attention until they played the overture. The boxes all around Juliana were brimming with their elegantly dressed patrons as they mulled about paying their respects to friends, enemies, and the curious.

Juliana squirmed in her seat, sensing that she had just fallen into the latter category. She was Lord Gomfrey's silken prize, and he was silently displaying her for all and sundry.

Where was Sin?

She had yet to tell him that she could no longer see him.

Gomfrey had never doubted that Juliana would accept his offer, and arrangements had been made while she had been at her cousin's residence begging for his assistance.

Juliana had sent one of the footmen to Sin's residence in hopes of summoning him to her house. However, as each hour passed, there had been no sign of Sin. Any chance of telling him that their affair had come to its fated conclusion waned as daylight blurred into twilight.

When her mother voiced her concern about Sin, Juliana burst into tears and locked herself into her bedchamber.

This was not the way she wanted Sin to learn about her sudden interest in the earl. Neither would a note have sufficed. Tomorrow she vowed to go to his residence and confront him. If he was not at home, then she would go to Nox. His friends would know where she could find him.

Sin never attends the theater.

The realization gave her comfort. Had he not told her on several occasions that he abhorred the theater? Juliana imagined that Sin was spending his evening at Nox or he was roaming London with his friends.

There was still time.

Tomorrow she would say farewell to Sin, and he might very well tell her to go to the devil.

It seemed appropriate, since Juliana was already in the devil's clutches and there was no chance of escape.

Lady Gredell was holding court in her private box when Alexius arrived with his friends. She looked resplendent in her silver evening dress. It must have taken her maid hours to curl his sister's waist-length sleek midnight-colored tresses and then artfully arrange them so the curls brushed her bared shoulders. Diamonds glittered from her throat, wrists, and gloved fingers.

He wondered which of the five gentlemen vying for his sister's attention had given her those fancy baubles and what the gent had received in return for his generosity. If Alexius knew his sister at all, she had wheedled expensive gifts from all of them.

Where the devil was Lord Kyd?

If Alexius had been in the baron's place, he would

not have tolerated Belinda's flirtations. His sister needed a firm hand to her backside.

Noting Alexius's shrewd regard, Belinda gave him a sly answering smile. She held out her hand to him. "Alexius, it was so good of you to accept my invitation."

Her brown gaze glowed with pleasure as Saint, Dare, Reign, and Hunter shouldered their way into the crowded box. Belinda's sycophants were not pleased by what they had perceived as potential rivals. Alexius could have assured them that none of his friends were foolish enough to cross him by seducing his sister. The Lords of Vice followed few dictates; however, seducing a fellow member's sibling would have only resulted in bloodshed.

"Oh good, you have brought some of your friends. How utterly mischievous of you!" Belinda winked at him and nodded to the seat to her left. The gentleman currently sitting in the seat, understanding that he was being dismissed, swiftly scrambled out of Alexius's way.

"We will not be staying, Belle." Alexius's narrowed gaze swept across the theater without any true interest. It would be better for all of them if he collected Frost and Vane and departed before a challenge was issued. "Why have you summoned me?"

"Oh pooh!" His sister dismissed his curtness with a flutter of her silver and ivory fan. "Of late, your manners border on insulting."

Alexius kissed his sister's cheek. "Press me further, Belle, and I shall exceed your expectations."

Slightly taken aback by his threat, Belinda fanned herself as her calculating brown eyes measured him for a funerary shroud. His demeanor was far from the repentant brother she had summoned before her.

"I have done nothing to deserve this surly tone from you, Alexius."

Out of habit, Alexius sought out his friends. Dare was standing in the back engaged in a conversation with Reign and two other gentlemen. Saint and Hunter were in the front corner flirting with several ladies sitting in the next box. No one seemed to be paying attention to the siblings as they argued.

"Why have you summoned me, Belle?"

Her eyes widened at his deliberate dim-wittedness. "You know very well why. I have sent you messages. Dozens of them, all with the same question: why have you failed me?"

Alexius refused to be swayed by the emotional quiver in his sister's voice. "Failed you? How so?"

Belinda snapped her fan closed. A faint blush colored her cheeks. "You were supposed to seduce the chit and discard her."

His annoyance flared at the reminder that his pursuit of Lady Juliana had not been initiated as a pleasurable indulgence but rather by a less palatable objective. "I have done what you have asked of me," he said, glowering at her.

He had bedded Juliana. The deed had been done many times over, and the lady had reveled in the thoroughness of his seduction. Nonetheless, he would be damned to offer the particulars to his own sister.

Belinda expelled a breath of exasperation. "Of that I had little doubt. I noticed the lovely pearls that adorn her neck. The necklace came from you, did it not? A shameless indication that your virile cock has forged an intimate claim. My dear brother, you do love your carnal games." She laughed at his telling silence. "The little fool has no inkling of the meaning behind your gift, does she?"

The muscles in his throat constricted to such a painful degree his molars ached. Damn him! He should have never given Juliana those bloody pearls. At the time, the notion of pleasuring her with the pearl necklace had seemed irresistible. The rainy afternoon he had held her in his arms and teased her nether regions with his gift, Alexius had not known how much Juliana would come to mean to him.

She was unlike any other lady he had bedded, and yet he had treated her like all the others before her.

At the request of his ruthless sister.

Alexius frowned at his sibling. "I have no desire to share the intimate details of my life, Belle. Or have you grown so dead inside that it takes something wholly depraved, like the notion of me bedding other women, to arouse you?"

Belinda tilted her head to the side; her face glowed in triumph. "Yes. Lady Juliana is ignorant of your wicked games. I wonder how she would react if she knew that half the ladies of the *ton* are very well aware of your naughty predilection for pearls. Are you in a betting mood? If I were to use my opera glass to search the boxes, how many ladies do you think I might find who are boldly wearing your gift around their necks right under their husbands' noses? Two? Seven? A dozen?"

Alexius was aware that his sister was goading him. The knowledge did not stem the temptation to strangle her in front of witnesses. He seized her wrist when Belinda brought her opera glass to her eye. "Do not behave so predictably, darling. Why would I mention past history to a lady who was already skittish of me? I was supposed to gain the lady's trust."

"Forgive me, Alexius. You were so brave, so loyal, to sacrifice your body and your malleable principles on my behalf."

"So kind of you to notice," he muttered under his breath.

"Then tell me, brother mine, why have you not completed the lady's humiliation by publicly discarding her?" Belinda twisted her wrist free from his grip and lifted the opera glass to her eye.

If she was searching ladies' necks for his bloody pearls to prove her point, Alexius was not going to be accountable for his violent response. Why did it seem as if the women in his life were all conspiring to drive him mad?

Belinda wanted him to hurt Juliana. If Juliana learned of his duplicity, Alexius sensed that she would not so readily forgive him. His sister's undisguised animosity toward the lady would seal his fate. He owed his loyalty and love to one and greatly admired and desired the other. What had begun as a lark had become complicated ever since he had allowed his growing affection for Juliana to sway him. He doubted anyone, himself included, would be satisfied once Belle's game of deceit had been played out.

He stared at his sister's elegant profile as she scrutinized the audience for friends, rivals, and potential lovers. There were few ladies who overshadowed Belinda in beauty. It was a pity that she could not be content with her blessings.

"I have my reasons," Alexius said, hoping his answer would appease her.

It did not.

Belinda made a disapproving sound. "Come now, brother; you can do better."

Alexius weighed his limited options. He could simply refuse to answer, leaving his sister to speculate on his affection for Juliana. However, the outcome was unpredictable, since Belinda had a nasty habit of taking matters into her own hands without thought to the consequences. It was one of the reasons why he had agreed to her small favor in the first place.

It gave him a modicum of control that allowed him to protect both ladies if necessary.

Even if it meant spinning pretty lies.

Alexius clasped his hands together and braced his elbows on his knees. His sister seemed fixated on a certain box, but he knew she was listening. Lowering his voice, he said, "Why settle for mere seduction? Bedding Lady Juliana provided little challenge for me."

It was a lie, of course. His reluctant lover had led him on a merry chase, but such a confession did not suit his purposes.

Never in his life had he experienced such hunger for a woman. When Juliana finally had surrendered in his arms, triumph and need had ruled him as he had pummeled his hips against hers. His sister and her petty revenge had not intruded until much later.

Belinda pulled her eye away from the opera glass. "What do you propose?"

"A seduction of both the heart and body," Alexius replied easily.

Too easily.

It was a reminder of how little value he usually placed on both. "The lady has already lost her innocence to me. Permit me to lay siege to her tender heart and win her love. It is a slight that Lady Juliana will never forgive."

If he willfully carried out his sister's plans, he would lose Juliana forever. The very thought made him want to rend and break the seats and people around him.

The cold, arrogant man he had once been ceased to exist once Juliana entered into his life.

Alexius needed to find Juliana and confess some unpleasant truths. It was a formidable task, and there was always the risk that she would not forgive him. He ignored the jab of pain in his chest. Juliana would come to forgive him.

Eventually.

For now, he just had to convince his sister that his fealty still belonged to her.

Belinda's high trill of laughter reminded Alexius of a bird singing out to the dawn. "Dearest Sin," my handsome instrument of revenge, are you certain you are capable of such a feat?"

His answering smile was cruel as much as it was beautiful. "Lady Juliana will love me."

Belinda closed her right eye and peered with her left through the opera glass. Whatever had captivated her eye caused humor to bubble through her slender body like a fountain. "It appears time is your enemy, dear brother."

She handed him the opera glass.

Impatient and irritated by her misplaced humor, Alexius held the opera glass to his eye. What he beheld brought him to his feet, grayed his vision as his fury took hold of him.

"Time, Alexius, is the least of your troubles," Belinda said, unmoved by this threatening stance. "It appears you have been replaced."

Chapter Thirteen

"GOMFREY, HOW THE devil did you steal this beautiful creature away from Sinclair? I thought he was courting her?"

Juliana cringed at Lord Ripley's crass question. The gentleman was positively ogling her, which was disrespectful not only to her but also to his female companion. Was this a sign that Juliana's position in society had plummeted? How many encounters such as this would she be forced to endure?

If not for Lord Gomfrey's fingers digging into her arm, she might have bolted. The pain radiating up her arm was a warning to behave. Her family's fate depended on her ability to convince the *ton* that she had rejected Sin for Lord Gomfrey.

The earl was enjoying himself, basking in his enviable position. "I credit Lady Juliana's discernible taste for recognizing the better man. Is that no so, my love?"

The pressure on her arm increased. With her teeth

clenched together, she smiled. "I would not dare challenge the eloquence of your words, my lord."

Everyone around them laughed, though she noticed Lord Gomfrey's brow furrowed in puzzlement as if he was debating whether she was mocking him. Lord Ripley changed the subject, and she was ignored.

Nitwit. Sin and a dozen others would have recognized her sarcasm for what it was. If Lord Gomfrey expected her to speak plainly, he was going to be vastly disappointed. She was his prisoner until he considered Lady Duncombe's debt repaid. Defiance was the only weapon Juliana could wield.

Below them, the orchestra had played the first and second music and the opening strains of the overture had commenced. Juliana looked about the theater. No one seemed interested in finding their seats. She longed to lose herself in the music, but she could barely hear it over the din of conversation. There would be no respite in her torment.

Her eyes burned. Tears? Juliana turned her head away from Lord Gomfrey. No, this was not the place to indulge her tears. She was supposed to be enjoying her new suitor. If the earl noticed the slight, she was certain to face his wrath later.

As she furiously blinked away the evidence of her brief slip, she realized someone in the next box was observing her. Outrage fortified her as if someone had slapped her across the face. Oh, the impertinence of some people! Juliana prepared to deliver her most scathing glance to the rude gentleman, but her hand fluttered to her throat in horror as she recognized the man.

Lord Chillingsworth.

Juliana wanted to scream at the injustice. Of all of Sin's friends, this gentleman seemed to dislike her the most, although she could not exactly fault his words or actions if she overlooked the evening he had kissed her. Nevertheless, there were odd moments when she would sense him watching her, his light blue eyes blazing with undeniable hostility. She could not fathom what she had done to offend him.

His slow smile filled her with alarm.

She read the triumph and satisfaction on his handsome face. Chance had chosen him to be the dark messenger, the one to tell Sin of her betrayal, and the tale would not be flattering.

Neither was the truth.

"Where are you going?"

The cutting annoyance in Lord Gomfrey's tone shattered the nonverbal exchange between Juliana and Lord Chillingsworth. Without thinking, she had attempted to rise from her seat before she was unceremoniously dragged back down by Lord Gomfrey. His firm hand had not strayed from her arm.

She might as well have been wearing a lead rope around her neck like a horse or a dancing bear.

"I feel indisposed," Juliana lied, twisting her arm in a small attempt to free herself. Her fingers were growing numb from his fierce grip. "I require a few minutes in the anteroom."

He gestured with his unfettered hand toward his friends. "You are among friends. There is no reason why you may not use your vinaigrette here."

Lord Gomfrey had yet to glance at her.

Juliana leaned forward and whispered in his ear,

"My lord, there are other reasons why a lady feels indisposed. Some are of a private nature." She glanced pointedly at her arm. "Nor require your assistance."

The earl hesitated.

Did he think she would flee the theater if she left his side? Or perhaps Lord Gomfrey was worried that she might tell others of the devil's bargain he had brokered with her mother? If he and Juliana had been alone, she could have told him that he worried needlessly. She would honor her mother's debt.

"Good heavens, let the poor girl go settle her nerves in private," Lord Ripley's female companion chided.

It was apparent that Lord Gomfrey suspected that Juliana was lying about the reasons why she needed some privacy, but her polite request was not unreasonable. He did not want to appear like a tyrant in front of his friends.

He nodded, releasing her arm. "The anteroom. No farther." He patted the bruises hidden by her long gloves. "I will join you if you are unable to return to us."

His threat was as clear as the icy annoyance in his gaze.

If she did not return to her seat, he would find her and drag her back. Juliana acknowledged him with a shaky nod of her head.

She straightened and then made a small choking sound.

Sin was blocking her escape, his demeanor positively murderous.

Dear god, it was worse than she could have ever imagined.

Sin's barely restrained fury was about to be unleashed. Juliana feared she was the likely target.

Chapter Fourteen

BETRAYAL BURNED IN his gut as Alexius glared at Juliana.

"Unless you plan to leap from the balcony, you are fleeing in the wrong direction."

The fear he saw in Juliana's eyes damned her as well as her futile attempt to distance herself from him. A day earlier, no, even an hour earlier, Alexius would have struck down anyone who dared to question the lady's honor. Even now, with the proof in front of him, he struggled to find a plausible excuse that placed Juliana in Lord Gomfrey's hands.

Alexius extended his hand. "Come with me."

Juliana's skittish gaze shifted from him to Lord Gomfrey, who had moved up to stand behind her. Alexius's upper lip curled. *Sniveling poltroon. A real gentleman would never hide behind a woman.*

"Lady Juliana has tired of your company, Sinclair,"

the earl said, drawing his shoulders back and puffing his chest like a bullfinch. All that was missing was the soft call of *whib, whib, whib.* "Do not embarrass the lady or yourself by tarrying where you are not wanted."

With his gaze narrowed on Juliana, Alexius silenced Gomfrey with a slicing gesture of his hand. "Is this true? Have you gone to this braying ass willingly?"

Juliana glanced everywhere but at Alexius's face. "I-I needed to speak with you. I tried—I sent a footman with a note."

"Your note explained none of this!" he shouted, causing her to wince.

They had garnered a captivated audience and the attention was clearly making her uncomfortable. Unfortunately for her, Alexius did not give a damn about her discomfort and he was devious enough to use it to his advantage.

"Well?"

Her gaze snapped up to his face. Alexius expected to see tears in her magnificent green eyes, a potent weapon most women would have used to battle a man's fury. He would not have thought less of her if she had succumbed to using such a ploy. Juliana's eyes, however, were dry.

"If you understood me at all, Lord Sinclair, you would already have the answer," she said tonelessly.

It was exactly the sort of cryptic reply that he would expect the exasperating woman to deliver just to annoy him. He took a step toward her. Gomfrey placed his hand on Juliana's shoulder in a gesture of support or possession.

The reasons were of little consequence to Alexius.

The fact that Gomfrey was touching Juliana in such a proprietary manner, and that she stood there stiffly, just accepting his claim without protest, spurred Alexius's tongue and temper.

"Lady Juliana, I must confess that I have never understood you at all. Although my words might appear cruel and personal in their criticism, pray do not take them so. I rarely ponder the workings of a lady's mind when all I desire from her is a thorough fucking."

The implication was unmistakable.

Juliana inhaled sharply, as if Alexius had slapped her. The ladies and gentlemen in the box with them murmured comments of surprise and dismay.

Alexius deliberately kept his face impassive. He refused to react to the flash of pain Juliana could not hide from him.

Her blond curls bobbed riotously as she nodded in agreement. "And I have always understood you all too well, Lord Sinclair."

"Have you?"

"Yes!" She tossed her head back in a defiant manner. "Nevertheless, do not be concerned about my tender feelings. If you had been capable of offering me something of a personal nature, I would have mourned the loss for years."

Her confession staggered Alexius. The little fool was casting aside what little pride she had left and risking public mockery. "Juliana—," he said warningly.

"I am not quite finished," she said, her voice thick with emotion. "I might have mourned you, if you had taken something of value from me. You have not. So you are free, Lord Sinclair." She spared a scathing glance at Frost, who had one foot braced on the balcony as if he had been prepared to leap to Alexius's defense. "Free to return to your friends . . . your greedy mistresses and your coldhearted life . . . and spare me your condemnation on who I choose to share my evening with!"

Gomfrey trailed the side of one finger down Juliana's cheek. "Well said, my dear." He grinned evilly at Alexius. "Your courage does you justice."

Juliana tore her gaze away from Alexius's impassive face and sent the earl an impatient look. "How so?"

"Very few individuals defy Sinclair and his sister."

Alexius froze. His stomach seethed as his hot, angry gaze sought out his friends, Dare to his right and Saint and Hunter to his left. Who had betrayed his confidence? Few had been privy to the details of Belle's small favor. Whoever had told Gomfrey would in due course feel the full measure of Alexius's wrath.

"His sister?" Juliana echoed, the color bleaching from her complexion. "Lord Sinclair only mentioned her once in passing. I was not aware she was in town."

"How strange, since Lady Gredell has been very aware of you, my lady," Gomfrey revealed with relish. "Pray, forgive me—did no one tell you that they are brother and sister?"

Stunned by the revelation, Juliana shook her head.

Gomfrey shook his head chidingly as Alexius's hands curled into fists. The earl was enjoying himself.

"Who told you?" Alexius demanded.

The earl ignored him, concentrating on Juliana. "A tragic misstep, though I doubt anyone could have anticipated the siblings' malice toward an innocent."

In dawning horror, Juliana's lips parted as if to speak, but the question she wanted to ask the earl was caught in her throat.

Lord Gomfrey, the slimy piece of chicken excrement, had no such difficulties. "Sinclair's affection for you was counterfeit. A close confidant of Lady Gredell told me that the marquess approached you at his sister's request with the purpose of stealing your innocence. I have no doubt that he succeeded."

Juliana swayed dangerously, causing several nearby gentlemen to step forward in case she fainted.

"I am fine," she said tersely, brushing aside the hands of those who wanted to help her.

Although he sensed Juliana would fight him, Alexius longed to sweep Juliana into his arms and carry her out of the private theater box, away from their captivated audience. In the distance he could hear his sister's distinct laughter. With Gomfrey's assistance, Alexius in a jealous tirade had publicly shamed Juliana in a manner that most likely exceeded Belle's expectations.

Once again, he had lived up to the Sinclair name.

His father would be so proud of Alexius's latest mischief.

Since the earl had managed to proclaim Juliana as his and ruthlessly crush any tender feelings the lady might have harbored for her former lover in one decisive stroke, Gomfrey could not resist gloating. "I have often wondered, Sinclair, how can you tolerate being your sister's whore?"

Alexius's response hit Gomfrey like a lightning strike. One second Alexius was staring at Juliana's drawn face, and the next he was burying his fist into the earl's insolent mug. Pain exploded as Alexius's knuckles scraped Gomfrey's sharp teeth. The man staggered backward and landed on his ass. There was blood. A lot of it. Fortunately, most of it belonged to Gomfrey.

The earl bared his bloodied teeth. "Filthy bastard!" He wildly launched himself at Alexius.

Dare grabbed Juliana and dragged her out of harm's way. No one in the box seemed to know what to do as both men crashed into several empty seats and sent several others skittering. Alexius grunted as Gomfrey landed a solid punch into his stomach. They rolled, causing several of the ladies in the box to scream and flutter. Behind them, he could hear men shouting. Suddenly, unyielding hands clamped onto his upper arms in an attempt to separate him from Gomfrey. Alexius used the opportunity to plant his heel in the earl's testicles. As Alexius struggled against the hands that held him, it was satisfying to watch as Gomfrey turned over onto his side and retched.

Alexius was prepared to pummel his captors until he realized it was Frost and Hunter who held him. He shook off their hands and wiped the corner of his mouth with his sleeve. "How the devil did you get here? Sprout wings and fly?"

Frost slapped the palm of his hand against Alexius's bruised back. "If I had tarried, I would have missed all the fun."

"So much for worrying about Vane and Frost instigating a fight," Saint murmured. He and Reign released the gentlemen they had been restraining so they could attend to their friend.

Alexius eyed Gomfrey. He could barely stand even with the assistance of his friends. "Where is Vane?"

No one bothered to speculate.

"With this many witnesses, the managers will probably ban us for life," Reign added cheerfully.

"We could always offer them a sizeable bribe." Frost shrugged at Alexius's scowl, opened his arms, and gestured at the boxes surrounding them. "At the very least, they should be paying us for such an entertaining performance!"

Juliana.

She stood silently beside Dare. Thankfully, she seemed untouched by the violence.

Ignoring the growing stiffness in his lower back, Alexius limped past his friends and moved toward her. "Come with me."

The moment he touched her on the arm, Juliana seemed to recover from her shock. She struggled against Alexius's side as he escorted her out of the box.

"Sin, release me at once!"

Gomfrey shoved his friends away. "She is mine, Sinclair. You cannot have her." He moved to prevent Alexius and Juliana from leaving.

"Help Gomfrey clean up his face." Alexius called out over his shoulder, knowing his friends would make certain that no one followed him and Juliana. "I want to have a brief chat with Lady Juliana before I take my leave."

Chapter Fifteen

SIN SWEPT THE crimson velvet drapery aside with his arm and marched them through the narrow opening. He was taking her to the small anteroom where she had planned to escape Lord Gomfrey's insufferable company. That had been before Sin had arrived with his friends.

"Unhand me," Juliana ordered through clenched teeth. "I have nothing to say to you!"

"Liar."

Sin pressed her back against the wall and held her in place with the length of his body. If she could have extended her arm, the door would have been within reach.

"After that amusing bit of drama for the *ton*, I suspect we both have a few things to say to each other."

Juliana's face crumpled at the reminder. Between Sin and Gomfrey, she had been completely humiliated in front of the entire theater. Her position did not give her much leverage, but it did not stop her from striking Sin's shoulders with her fists. "That dreadful woman Lady Gredell is your sister?"

"Half," he replied succinctly. "Different mothers." Sin gave Juliana a little shake. "Quit fighting me. You are only hurting yourself."

"No, I think we can both agree that *you* are responsible for my pain!" she yelled back, renewing her efforts to free herself from his grasp.

Unmoved by her efforts, Sin held her in place until her strength left her. Blast it all, she could not even claw at his face with her fingernails. Bothersome gloves! Tired, she sagged against the wall.

"For reasons I could never fathom, Lady Gredell took an instant dislike to me." Juliana turned her face away from his, her burning gaze narrowed on his coat sleeve. It hurt too much to look at Sin, knowing he had betrayed her. "She seemed determined to ruin my stay in London, and you have been helping her all along!"

"Not as much as you might think," he shouted back. "Belle has often accused that my loyalties were divided where you were concerned."

Juliana's eyes widened as she rapped the back of her head against the wall in outrage. "You discussed what we did together with *her*? Oh, this is too much to bear! The first time that I saw you in the Lettlecotts' gardens, I thought you were an untrustworthy rogue."

Sin's hazel eyes glittered dangerously. "Did you? That knowledge did not keep me from putting my hands on you. I do not recall you resisting overly much when I—"

"Stop." In her mind, she thought about those early

encounters. The stolen kisses they had shared. The rainy afternoon in the coach. The pearls. Oh god! She had been such a naïve fool. "Was Lord Gomfrey telling the truth? Did your sister order you to seduce me?"

His silence was damning. Juliana watched as the muscles in Sin's throat constricted. "She viewed her request as a favor," he said eventually.

"How could you? I thought you—" She broke off, no longer believing in the caring, loving man she had welcomed into her life.

Sin glowered down at her. "What? Loved you?"

Juliana winced at his scathing mockery of her feelings and his lies.

"In the Lettlecotts' gardens, you witnessed firsthand the sort of man I was. An untrustworthy rogue, you called me. Juliana, do you truly believe my sister would demand from me a task that I would not have willingly pursued on my own with countless other women? Did you think you were different from my other conquests?"

His questions, as he had intended, cut Juliana to the quick. "I did not know Lady Gredell was your sister. Had I known . . ."

The tight constriction of her corset would be her undoing. She took several rapid breaths to keep from fainting. Juliana met his heated gaze. "Had I known, I would have avoided you at every turn. I would not have dared to breathe the air around you."

Sin laughed, his warm brandy-laced breath washing over her. She could not resist inhaling, taking a small part of him into her lungs. "My poor lovely *lybbestre*. How it must chafe your pride, knowing that you took more than my breath into your body."

If regret was a dark, fathomless lake, she would have drowned in it.

Juliana pushed against his upper chest. The man was made of granite and would not yield. "It more than chafes, Lord Sinclair. It disgusts me!"

"Really? You wound me, Juliana. Unfortunately for you, I am in the mood to prove that you are just as much of a liar as I am."

Before she could react, Sin fused his mouth to hers. The kiss was demanding and thorough. Desire licked her flesh like a gentle flame, reminding her that Sin possessed her body and soul. Juliana moaned in despair. What they had shared had been based on a cruel deception. If he was pressed into choosing between her and his beloved sister, Sin's loyalties unquestionably belonged to his family.

It was difficult to blame him, since she would have done the same.

Still, he had hurt her.

Sin lingered, biting lightly at her lower lip before he ended the kiss. "Tell me why Gomfrey thinks he has the right to put his hands on you?"

Befuddled by Sin's kiss, Juliana just blinked at him. His grip on her upper arms gentled as he tasted her mouth again. "Tell me. Give me a reason why I should not march back into the box and challenge him."

Color suffused her neck and face as she caught onto Sin's game. "Let go of me this instant!" She bit his lower lip when he tried to placate her again with a kiss.

"Christ! Bloodthirsty witch!" Sin released her and brought his fingers to his lips to check for blood. He stabbed his finger at her. "You liked my hands on you just fine. Do not even try to deny it."

There was no point in denying the obvious. "Try to kiss me again and you will need a surgeon to fix the damage," she threatened, rubbing her arms to put some blood back into her limbs.

"Gomfrey—," he began.

Juliana gaped at him in disbelief. Sin's arrogance and tenacity had no boundaries. "Is not your concern." She paused, tilting her head back defiantly. "Neither am I, for that matter. After what you have done, you no longer have the right to question with whom or where I spend my evenings."

Sin scrubbed his face with his hand. He looked uncomfortable, as if what he had done had not set well with him. *Good!* Juliana refused to soften her heart toward him. The man could suffer for a thousand years and it still would not be enough to make up for his misdeeds.

He moved closer, crowding her until she felt the wall at her back. "Can you answer one question? Why him? Why Gomfrey?"

This was not concern, Juliana had to tell herself. Sin was outraged that she had discarded him for another gentleman. Thank goodness she had not been foolish enough to run to Sin with her family's problems. He and his sister would have laughed merrily at her appalling predicament. By morning, the entire *ton* would have learned that Lady Duncombe had sold her youngest daughter to Lord Gomfrey to settle a gambling debt.

Oh, she wished that she could turn back the hands of the clock and return to earlier in the day. Instead of driving past Sin's club, she would have ordered her coachman to stop. She would have marched up Nox's front steps and demanded that Sin show himself. It would have given her immense pleasure to end their affair and ruin his plans.

It might have allowed her to hold on to the tattered scraps of her pride.

Juliana crossed her arms. "You have asked three questions, and I have no interest in addressing any of them. Now if you will excuse me, Lord Gomfrey is waiting for me."

Dread swelled in her breast at the thought of Lord Gomfrey. Juliana did not want to return to him or the curious speculation of the *ton*. If given a choice, she would have gladly walked away from both gentlemen for using her for their pleasures.

Sin caught her by the arm. "We have not settled things between us."

"Settled what, Sin?" she asked, her throat aching with grief. "What do you want from me? Tears? Do you wish to see me beg? Lay broken at your feet?"

"Christ, no!" He seemed sincerely revolted by the suggestion. "Juliana," he sighed, his usual charm and wit eluding him for once. "Do not return to Gomfrey. You have not heard the rumors about him. He is not . . . gentle with his lovers. You are too innocent to comprehend the deviant appetites of some gentlemen."

Unlike Sin and his friends.

It was not astonishing that Sin and his ilk congregated in clubs where they drank themselves into a stupor, regaled one another with debased tales of conquest, and placed bets on their next victims.

Juliana wondered if her name currently graced one of those betting books. It was a depressing thought.

Misunderstanding her silence, Sin turned her so that she faced him. "Listen, you do not have to prove anything to my sister, Gomfrey, or the damn *ton*. I already know that you possess the courage of a dozen men. Allow me to return you to your family."

He pitied her, and rightly so. Juliana longed to move closer and bury her face into his chest. She had always felt so safe, so cherished, when he had held her.

Instead she brushed away his hands and his offer. "That is very generous of you, Lord Sinclair, considering the unscrupulous part that you played in this debacle."

Sin's brows lifted. "Did I call you brave? 'Dim-witted' is apt, since I planted my fist into the face of the last man who insulted me."

"Go ahead; strike me down." Her arms opened, daring him to hit her. "The pain could not be worse than the realization that I fell in love with a lie."

His hazel eyes dulled with shock and then narrowed with suspicion. "You are not in love with me," he said flatly.

"Not anymore. Hate has stifled it." She gestured toward the outer hall. "You have had your victory. Take it and leave."

"And Gomfrey?"

She knew Sin well enough to aim a spiteful verbal barb with accuracy. "The better man."

Sin closed his eyes and nodded. "Very well." He walked by her and tore open the curtain separating them from the private theater box. "Let us depart," he told his friends.

The curtain dropped back into place as he turned to face her. Juliana braced for his next words, because they would be his last. After this bitter parting, she did not expect to see him again.

Sin reached into his coat and retrieved something from the inner pocket of his waistcoat. To her surprise, he removed a small white plume.

"I never understood why I kept it," he said, his voice thick with emotion. "I have been carrying it around since that first night." He laughed softly at his foolishness. "Well, it no longer matters."

He blew on the downy feather. Both of them watched as the feather caught the invisible current of air. It floated gently downward until it alighted on top of her left slipper.

Juliana crouched down to pick up the feather.

Is this . . . ?

She peered at the insignificant piece of fluff.

Yes, this was the blasted feather that had betrayed her to Sin all those weeks ago when she had been caught in the Lettlecotts' hazel tree.

Why had he kept it?

Juliana was so distracted by his unexpected revelation that she had not realized Sin had moved away from her until he spoke again.

"One more thing," he said tersely. "What if you are with child?"

The question managed to startle her. She automatically brought her palm to her stomach and worried. "I-I am not—at least, I do not believe I am."

"Be certain," he said abruptly. "And let me be clear.

It will not bode well for either you or your family if you try to foist Gomfrey's bastard on me."

His threat delivered, Sin turned on his heel and headed for the outer hall.

Juliana slapped a shaking hand over her mouth at the time the crimson drapery parted and Lord Hugh, the one Sin affectionately called Dare, Lord Rainecourt, and the Duke of Huntsley walked into the anteroom. She backed away from the threshold and nonchalantly curled her hand under her chin as she studied a poor rendering of the port in Hastings.

One by one, she felt each of the noblemen's gazes as they lingered thoughtfully on her profile before they followed Sin into the night. Juliana was not fooling anyone. She spun around and leaned against the wall. There was a good chance everyone in the private box had overheard the heated exchange between her and Sin.

Lord Sainthill cleared his throat, alerting her to his presence as he moved toward the open door. "Lady Juliana," he murmured respectfully. He paused at the threshold. "During the confusion, Sinclair might have been remiss in his manners, so if I may speak in his stead and offer the following. If you need anything from him or the Lords of Vice, please do not hesitate to send a message to the club. I will make certain Sin receives it."

He disappeared and his footfalls could be heard as he made his way down the hallway.

Juliana's vision blurred at Lord Sainthill's unexpected kindness. It was also her undoing. One sob escaped from her throat and then another. She covered her mouth and sagged lower until she was practically sitting on the floor.

"What the devil are you doing?"

She dropped her hand onto her lap at the sharp lash of Lord Gomfrey's question. "N-nothing."

He marched over and hauled her onto her feet. The blood was gone from his face. His lower lip was swollen and split from Sin's fist, and his cheeks were mottled with colorful bruises. The earl's disposition was as rotten as his moral principles, and he was looking for a fight that he could win. "If I wanted a sniveling girl at my side, I could have picked one off the street for a shilling. You, on the other hand, cost me a great deal more."

Lord Gomfrey took out his handkerchief and threw it at her. "Clean up your face. Fix your hair. You have an audience awaiting your return, and you will not disappoint them."

Juliana dabbed at her eyes. She turned away from the earl and delicately blew her nose before she slipped the soiled handkerchief into her reticule. She opened her clenched fist and stared somberly at the feather Sin had discarded. Impulsively she shook it into her reticule and gave the strings of her reticule a vicious tug.

Upon straightening, she noticed the narrow rectangular mirror on the opposite wall. It gave her an excuse to distance herself from Lord Gomfrey while she smoothed her hair.

She frowned at her reflection. The woman staring back at her looked like she had been thoroughly kissed by her lover. Her lips were red and slightly puffy from Sin's demanding lips. During their brief passionate struggle, he had loosened some of the pins in her hair.

Juliana dutifully gathered up her errant blond strands and tucked them into place.

"Did you tell Sinclair anything about our bargain?"

Juliana glared at his reflection as he stood behind her. "No. What would have been the point? I think I have endured enough humiliation for one evening."

"Not quite," he said, tracing the curve of her neck down to her bare shoulder. "Why did you let him kiss you?"

"I did not," she said tightly.

Lord Gomfrey shoved her hard against the wall. Her right cheek connected with the gilt frame of the mirror so swiftly Juliana did not have a chance to cry out. He seized the back of her neck and jerked her backward. The mirror plummeted to the floor, shattering at their feet.

"Never lie to me again, Lady Juliana." The earl smoothed the rigid muscles in her neck with his hand. "You will not enjoy the consequences."

From the corner of her eye, Juliana noticed Lord Chillingsworth standing in the anteroom, one section of the drapery still clenched in his fist. How much had he seen? It really did not matter. While Lord Sainthill had offered her kindness, his friend Lord Chillingsworth was more likely to applaud Lord Gomfrey's abuse.

Juliana met Lord Chillingsworth's insolent smile with a level stare.

"Forgive me for interrupting," he said politely. "I was just leaving. It was impressed upon me that I should return to my seat in, let us just say, a conventional manner."

"Come, my lady," Lord Gomfrey said, taking her by the elbow. "We should also return to our seats."

He nodded to the nobleman. "Chillingsworth, give Sinclair my compliments on his refined tastes." Lord Gomfrey leered at Juliana as he escorted her through the parted curtain. "Tell him that I look forward to savoring every carnal delight imaginable and I have him to thank for my good fortune."

"Oh, I will," Lord Chillingsworth softly replied.

Juliana glanced back at him. He let the curtain fall back into place and left her to her fate.

Chapter Sixteen

HOURS LATER, LORD Gomfrey contemplated his new acquisition as his coachman drove them back to his town house. That was how Juliana was beginning to view herself. Somehow she had become a pawn, one to be used and discarded. First her mother had thought to barter Juliana and her sisters into marriage for the sake of the family, then Sin had sought her out and seduced her at the whim of his spiteful half sister, and now Juliana was the prize for another selfish gentleman.

She stared blankly through the small window and glimpsed the future. It appeared as bleak and shadowed as the London streets.

"It was a fine evening," Lord Gomfrey gloated. He had positioned himself on the opposite bench, his long legs stretched out so that his dirty shoes bumped against her left hip.

"You did not seem pleased when Lord Sinclair bloodied your nose with his fist."

Unconsciously Lord Gomfrey gingerly touched his nose as he frowned at her. "It might not bode well for you if you keep mentioning Sinclair. If you are not worried about your lovely neck, think of your mother and sisters."

As much as Juliana loathed admitting it, the earl was correct. It was foolish of her to provoke him. "I do not mean to offend, my lord. I was stating a simple fact. I cannot fathom why Lord Sinclair's attack would please you."

Her quiet apology mollified him. She saw the white of his teeth flash at her in the dim interior of the coach. He even leaned forward and patted her knee.

"Sinclair may have been doing Lady Gredell's bidding. Nevertheless, the man was enjoying himself tremendously. He was not quite finished with you, and it galled him that I stole you away." The earl practically hummed with delight. "The insidious blow I struck against him was worth a little spilt blood."

Juliana leaned back and allowed the darkness to swallow her. Any hope that the earl might have returned her to her family this evening was dashed when she had overheard him order the coachman to return to Lord Gomfrey's town house.

He had quietly amended the terms of the bargain he had brokered with the marchioness, and the gentleman did not seem repentant about it.

Still furious with Sin, the earl planned to take his revenge by bedding Juliana. The thought of taking something away from the marquess seemed to give Lord Gomfrey immense satisfaction.

She allowed her eyelids to droop as she studied the passing street activity through a heavy veil of thick eyelashes. Sin had been the only man who had touched her intimately. She had initially feared the responses he had seemed to effortlessly evoke from her body. Later, she had reveled in their love play.

Were all lovers the same?

Would Lord Gomfrey be able to touch her and make her burn as Sin had? Would the earl make her forget the salty taste of Sin's flesh as she flicked her tongue over his nipple, the scent of his arousal, and the low growl of pleasure that rumbled in his throat when his seed burst from his manhood? Her chest still ached when she thought of Sin's betrayal, of the hateful words they had said to each other.

Had anything they had shared meant anything to Sin, or was it all a game to him?

Juliana would have sold her soul to learn the truth.

"You fell asleep." Lord Gomfrey's hand on her arm was possessive and yet oddly tender. "We are home, my lady."

As she descended from the coach, he covered her shoulders with her cloak and led her to the front door.

"It does not trouble you?" She bit her lower lip, instantly regretting the question.

"Does what trouble me?" The earl opened the door and nudged her into the front hall. "You sound half-asleep and make little sense. Are you still dreaming, my dear?"

"No. Not anymore."

She stood shivering in the darkness as she listened to Lord Gomfrey close the door. He moved past her, she assumed to light a candle or a lamp.

"If you have a question, ask it."

There was a scratching sound, and the light from a candle flared to life.

Her eyes focused on the flicking flame. "It does not bother you that Sin had me first?"

Lord Gomfrey brought his fist to his mouth and chuckled. He picked up the silver candlestick and walked toward her. The earl was still smiling when he bathed her in candlelight. "Your naïveté is rather charming, Lady Juliana. Is it feigned or did you actually manage to hold on to your innocence in spite of all the wicked things Sinclair did to your delectable body?"

The earl took her by the arm and pressed a kiss into her temple. "To answer your question, no, it does not bother me that Sinclair bedded you first. The fact that the rogue still wants you, and cannot have you, will make each fucking more pleasurable."

"You are wrong. Sin does not want me."

The earl stared at her in amazement. "Utterly charming. I look forward to our summer together, Lady Juliana."

He led her to the staircase.

"Who knows, once you have settled your mother's debt, you might beg to remain in my bed."

Never, she thought, but did not speak the word aloud.

"I usually tire of my lovers after a few weeks," he remarked casually, confident in his prowess and power over his lovers. "However, if you please me, I might be tempted to keep you."

Alexius slammed the empty bottle of brandy down on the card table. "I'm finished," he said, slurring his words as he staggered to his feet.

After he and his friends had left the theater, they had crammed themselves into a coach and headed for Nox. He had announced that they were celebrating his liberation from both his sister and the tantalizing wiles of Lady Juliana.

His friends had applauded him for his cavalier dismissal of the lady who had managed to tangle his cock and heart into dense complicated knots, and cheerfully poured a bottle of the club's finest brandy down his throat before they settled earnestly into gambling away a small fortune.

Frost stared blurrily at Alexius. "Nonsense. That was only our fifth bottle."

"When did you develop such a weak stomach?" Vane teased. With a plump brown-haired wench on his lap, he was handling his cards and brandy better than his companions.

"Not the brandy." Alexius sneered at the insult. "I'm done with this game. I have no head for cards this evening."

"I wish you would stay," Hunter grumbled. "I would have won your town house and favorite horse by morning."

Reign leaned back to swipe a bottle of brandy from a nearby table. He used his teeth to remove the cork. "I thought you were going to let me win Sin's horse." His friends laughed as Reign refilled several of the empty glasses on the table.

Alexius braced both palms on the table to steady himself. "And you call yourselves my friends. All the more reason to quit."

"Coward," Frost called out as Alexius staggered away from the table.

He responded with a rude gesture that everyone who noticed thought was uproariously humorous.

In spite of the late hour, Nox was crowded. Alexius maneuvered the room by bumping from one individual to the next. It was the only reason why he was still standing. Dare and Saint caught him by both arms before he reached the doorway.

"Where are you going, Sin?" Dare shouted into Alexius's face.

"I am looking for more brandy." If he kept drinking, he would eventually drown out Juliana's voice in his head.

Saint laughed while he shoved Alexius into Dare's arms. "I will find you another bottle. Try to keep him from throwing himself down the stairs."

"Do you want to go upstairs?" Dare asked.

Alexius shook his head. "Chair," he said succinctly.

"Christ, you are heavy."

With Dare's help, Alexius landed on a table and flowed into a chair that gave him a view of the activity in the room. "Just make sure I get home. If I'm going to die, I want to die in my own damn bed."

Dare stared down at him. "If you say so. Do you want me to stay?"

Alexius scrubbed his face, trying to ignore the pity he saw on his friend's face. Dare was intimately acquainted with losing the lady whom he loved.

Love? Alexius frowned at the notion. He was not in love with Juliana. He was just mourning the loss of her warm, willing body. Her laughter. The way she bit into his shoulder when she shuddered in his arms.

Saint returned with a bottle and a glass.

Alexius grimaced as he grabbed the bottle. "No. Go away."

Saint glared at Dare. "What did you say to him?"

"Nothing. He is drunk and surly." Dare watched as Alexius missed the glass and poured the brandy onto the table. "Here. If I may." Dare filled the glass and slammed the bottle down. "He will pass out before he finishes that bottle."

"I disagree. A hundred pounds says he will finish it and drink another before he goes under," Saint countered.

"Agreed."

The two men shook on the wager and left Alexius to his brandy.

He was content to be left alone. No one was paying attention to him. As he drank his brandy, he listened to the bawdy song several men were singing across the room. It mingled with the laughter of the whores flirting with the patrons, the angry shouts from the sore losers, and the hoots of glee from the winners.

It was halfway through the second bottle Dare had not anticipated that Alexius abandoned the bottle and chair so he could relieve himself out back in the yard. He could not recall the journey outside, but his body was happy. The cool air was pleasant, too. It revived him enough that he was willing to go back to the table and finish his bottle.

It took him several minutes to shut the door properly, and when he turned around one of Madam V's girls was standing between him and his brandy.

"G'evening, Lord Sin."

Alexius squinted at her. He had seen her with Frost and several of Nox's patrons. "I know you." At the moment her name escaped him.

"Aye. They call me Rose."

She slowly approached him, uncertain of her welcome. He did not brush her hand away when she laid it on his chest or rebuke her when she wrapped her arm around his back. "Ye look like ye could use some company. A little unsteady on yer feet this night."

"Dizzy," Alexius mumbled, burying his nose into her red hair. The scent was not unpleasant. She was a pretty wench, with long limbs, pale skin, and large deep blue eyes. If he believed Frost's recommendation, she was one of Madam V's handpicked favorites and quite inventive in bed.

Together Rose and Alexius took a step forward. It was a disaster. He laughed as his weight caused them both to whirl and collapse against the wall. He used his back to keep himself upright as she propped him up with her palms on his chest.

"Yer a big beast," she cooed appreciatively. "Why haven't I had ye? Do ye find me pretty?"

"As a rose," he said, pleased that he could jest in his current condition. Alexius placed his hands on her hips and pulled her closer.

There was nothing about Rose that reminded him of Juliana.

Alexius thought that was Rose's best quality as he

roughly covered her mouth. With his head swimming in brandy, he squeezed her breasts and lowered his head to nip the exposed flesh.

Rose did not seem to mind his drunken fumbling. She wriggled against him and managed to undo several buttons on his trousers. Alexius hissed as her fingernails scraped the underside of his testicles.

"Better than an elixir." He was breathing heavily as he kissed her neck.

Alexius was too drunk to feel much of anything. Blindly he reached for Rose and turned her around. He could not think of a single reason why he should not bury his cock in this willing female.

What he had with Juliana had ended. She had chosen Gomfrey. The faithless bitch was probably in the earl's bed, begging and squirming under him.

Alexius abruptly pushed Rose down on all fours; he fell on top of her and fumbled with her skirts. He would not be a gentle or tender lover. All he wanted to do was forget. . . .

Chapter Seventeen

"WAKE UP, MY darling Alexius!"

With his face buried into a pillow and the bottle and a half of brandy he drank last evening still churning in his gut, Alexius moaned. So this was what death felt like. Utter hell. He could not decide which hurt worse, his head or his stomach.

Someone grabbed him by the arm and shook him. Alexius could actually hear the brandy in his stomach slosh from side to side. To his sensitive ears, it sounded like he had swallowed the bloody ocean.

"Go away!"

Where the devil was he? It smelled and felt like his bed, but he had no recollection of returning to his town house, let alone crawling into his bed.

"Oh, you were always a beast in the morning!"

The word "beast" triggered a faint memory, but it escaped him. Disorientated and still half-drunk, Alexius tried to identify the voice of the annoying wench in his bed. His last tangible memory was of returning to the club with his friends. The rest of the evening was a torrential river of brandy. He must have been a man possessed to have summoned the lust of Eros neither his body nor head could recall.

He carefully rolled onto his back. The movement made Alexius dizzy, and he had not even bothered to open his eyes. "I am not in the right mind for companionship. Be a good girl and go away before I smother you with this pillow."

Alexius was lying. He did not have the strength for murder. All he could do was lie there and suffer.

"Alexius?" The cruel harpy pressed her thumbs to his bruised eyelids and forced them open. The filtered sunlight burned like hot pokers. "Are you awake?"

He yelped in pain and impatiently batted the woman's hands away. "Christ, woman, cannot a man perish in peace?" he roared, and his stomach roiled.

Damp with perspiration, Alexius pressed his hand over his eyes and fought back the nausea. When he felt like he had triumphed over his overindulgence, he glared at the woman who was rubbing his stomach.

He blinked rapidly as his sister's beautiful face and dark hair came into focus. "Belle? What are you doing here?" he asked, his voice rough.

His question seemed to surprise her. Belinda tipped her head to the side. "Who did you think—?" Her lips parted in a wordless O as she realized that her brother had not recognized her. She brought her hand to her mouth and giggled. "Oh, poor Alexius. How often do you wake up to an unfamiliar lady in your bed?"

"If I felt better, I would say not often enough," he grumbled, and was rewarded with another giggle.

Since Belinda had no intention of letting him dismiss her, Alexius opened his eyes and realized he was naked. Someone, probably his valet, had undressed him. A tangled sheet covered him from the waist down. It still did not stop him from grabbing the blanket he had kicked aside in his sleep and dragging it over his bared torso.

"What time is it?" he asked, bracing himself up on his elbows.

"Eleven o'clock, I believe."

Alexius yawned. "It is a tad early for a morning call, Belle. I thought you had a rule about leaving your bed before eleven?"

Suddenly recalling the reason for her visit, Belinda climbed up onto his bed. Her eyes sparkled with childish eagerness. "I could not wait. This little visit could have been avoided altogether if you had returned to my theater box after your confrontation with Lady Juliana and Lord Gomfrey."

The indulgent expression on Alexius's face vanished as the previous evening's misdeeds flooded back.

Thoughts of Juliana.

"I told you that I had no intention of staying."

His sister was blithely ignorant of Alexius's mercurial mood and the distance his explanation had placed between them. She wiggled closer, and he shifted his legs to the left to make room for her.

"True." Belinda pouted. "Nevertheless, after your brazen confrontation last evening, I had hoped that we might celebrate."

She leaned over and kissed him on the cheek. Belinda wrinkled her nose as the stale odor of sweat and brandy filled her nostrils. "However, you, my foul-smelling brother, had no trouble celebrating without me."

Alexius scowled at her through narrowed eyelids. "What do want from me, Belle?"

"Tut-tut," Belinda chided. "You are in a devil of a mood. And here I came to apologize."

"Apologize for what exactly?" he asked warily, though he suspected he knew the reason for his sister's cheeriness.

"Why, for ever doubting you, my love!" She practically crawled into his lap as she hugged him. "Now, do not give me that look. I know you have never broken your word to me. However, Lady Juliana was a cunning rival. After she stole Lord Kyd's affections from me, I feared that you, too, had fallen under her spell. Can you believe I almost accused you of falling in love with the silly chit?"

The pounding behind his eyes worsened. Alexius shut his eyes as he pressed his fingers to his eyelids to stem the pain. "Your fears were unwarranted, Belle. Falling in love with Lady Juliana would have been very foolish on my part."

And suicidal.

"I have often wondered, Sinclair, how can you tolerate being your sister's whore?" Gomfrey's snide question echoed in Alexius's head.

Juliana despised him. He had made certain of it.

His sister pulled his hand away from his eyes and tenderly kissed each finger. "Oh, you were simply brilliant. And most unpredictable! No one could guess your intentions when you went charging over to Lord Gomfrey's box in a jealous rage. Like everyone else, I sat agog wondering if you were going to toss Gomfrey off the balcony or merely bloody his face."

"If given the chance, I would have happily done both."

Alexius hated leaving Juliana in the earl's disreputable hands. Unfortunately, Juliana was too angry at him to be reasonable. She would not even explain why she had agreed to attend the theater with Gomfrey.

A shadow of concern passed over Belinda's face. "For claiming Lady Juliana?"

"No," Alexius said, annoyed by the reminder that Juliana had returned to the earl for comfort. "My unfavorable opinion of Gomfrey was set long ago when he solicited the Lords of Vice for membership to the club."

Belinda clasped her hands together and brought them to her lips. "You blackballed him."

Alexius shrugged dismissively. "The vote was unanimous. Gomfrey is a simpering ass. Even if he had fit our membership requirements, I would have blackballed him on principle."

Belinda laid her cheek and palm against Alexius's bare chest. "Then it is fitting that he gets your cast-off mistress. You did well, my brother. I had my opera glass trained on Lady Juliana's face when you publicly rejected her. The despair and anger I glimpsed revealed more than any words could have conveyed. I daresay the lady was in love with you."

Not any longer.

Alexius had killed Juliana's affection as ruthlessly as he had claimed her innocence. He abruptly sat up, keeping his sister at arm's length. "Then you must be well pleased with your mischief, Belle." He seized the blanket and wrapped it around his waist. He climbed down from the bed, needing to separate himself from his sister.

Belinda nodded. "Indeed. After you and your friends left, Lord Kyd paid his respects and remained at my side the rest of the night."

"And Lady Juliana?" Alexius could have bitten off his tongue for curiosity. He did not want to renew his sister's animosity toward Juliana. His family had done enough. "Did she and Gomfrey remain?"

Alexius padded over to the far wall and tugged on the bell rope. If he could not go back to sleep, he wanted a bath. He would let his valet bully Belinda from his bedchamber. If he was lucky, perhaps, she would not remain for breakfast.

Belinda seemed content to remain on the bed. She stretched out, reminding him of a spoiled cat. "They remained for most of the play. Needless to say, it was apparent to everyone that Lady Juliana longed to flee her humiliating predicament. One of my companions wagered she would be in tears after her private discussion with you. But, alas, that cost me ten pounds."

"I will cover your losses," Alexius said absently as he retrieved his blue silk banyan from a chair.

Belinda's friends were a cold, callous lot to think a lady's tears made good sport. With the sheet knotted around his waist, he slipped one arm and then the other into the sleeves of the banyan. He turned his back to his sister and dropped the sheet. Alexius thought as he buttoned the front of his banyan that he could have told his sister that Juliana had more courage than most gentlemen.

However, any defense of the lady Belinda viewed as her rival would have only fueled his sister's hatred. For Juliana's sake, Alexius held his tongue. It was the least he could do.

Belinda idly wrapped an errant curl around her finger as she admired his back. "So tell me, what did you and Lady Juliana discuss in the anteroom? Gomfrey practically had to hold her up as they returned to their seats. I want all the delicious details."

Alexius's gaze collided with his reflection in the mirror before he hastily looked away. He was not particularly fond of the arrogant bastard glaring back at him.

"Belle, my head hurts and I feel like I spent the night licking the plaster from the walls." He ignored her outburst of giggling. "I have no further interest in discussing Lady Juliana with you or anyone else."

His valet's timely knock at the door spared Alexius from the argument that he and his sister were likely to have if she persisted. He walked over to the door.

"You have had your pound of flesh, my dearest sister. Be content with your victory."

Alexius opened the door, successfully ending their unpleasant conversation.

Chapter Eighteen

WHEN A MAN could not find peace in his own house, he usually sought out his club. Once he had bathed and dressed, Alexius slipped out of the house through the servants' entrance and hired a hackney coach, leaving Belinda waiting impatiently for him in the breakfast room.

He could not decide which one was more unpalatable: his sister's gloating about Lady Juliana's humiliation or the notion of adding food to his already unsteady stomach. If he had remained, he would have likely disgraced himself. The jostling drive to his club had done little to improve his weakened condition. Before he had reached Nox, he sharply ordered the coachman to halt. Alexius climbed down from the coach, deciding that he would feel better if he walked.

That was until he noticed Lord Kyd approaching him

from the opposite direction. The gentleman touched the brim of his hat and bowed.

"Good day to you, Sinclair. It is a fine day for a walk," Lord Kyd said with undisguised enthusiasm.

"Kyd."

It was not the first time that Alexius had wondered why his sister craved this man's good opinion above all others'. He was not the most handsome or the richest man Alexius's sister had lured into her bed. In temperament, she and Kyd were complete opposites. The baron's self-effacing nature was oftentimes grating, and he seemed too tenderhearted for Belinda's ruthlessness. Nor did he seem worthy of the pain Alexius and his sister had caused Juliana.

The realization outraged Alexius. He was half-tempted to punch mild-mannered Lord Kyd in the face. What kept Alexius from physically taking his ire out on Kyd was the fact that the gentleman was blissfully unaware of what his fickleness had caused.

Alexius was, regrettably, not so fortunate.

"May I be so bold as to join you on your walk?" Kyd said, gesturing for Alexius to continue his journey to the club. "I have longed to speak privately with you for some time."

He nodded. "I suppose you wish to discuss my sister," Alexius said after a few minutes of silence.

The baron fussed with the alignment of his cravat. "Well, actually, I had hoped to speak to you about Lady Juliana."

Alexius almost stumbled at the mention of Juliana's name. Without thinking, he stopped and grabbed the other man by the upper arm. "I would not credit you for being a reckless man, Kyd. I planted my fist into the face of the last gentleman who wished to discuss Lady Juliana with me."

"Ah, well," Lord Kyd said, his face reddening with the realization that he was treading into dangerous territory. "You speak of Lord Gomfrey. I heard of what transpired between the two of you in the theater."

And of the cruel exchange between you and Juliana.

The admission was unspoken, but the knowledge was visible on Lord Kyd's handsome face. There would have been talk at the theater. Later, when the baron had paid his respects to Belinda, she would have naturally shared her amusement over Juliana's humiliation without revealing that Alexius had initially approached the lady on his sister's behalf. Alexius knew her well. Whether he was dubbed the hero or the villain by the *ton*, Belinda was content to let him bear the notoriety alone.

Alexius let his hand drop to his side. He resumed his casual stride, assuming that Kyd would follow. The gentleman caught up to him seconds later.

"Have you come to chastise me for striking Gomfrey?"

The thirty-five-year-old baron seemed taken aback by the question. "Goodness, no! The man is a scoundrel. It is the very reason why I wished to speak with you. Several people told me that Lady Juliana had arrived with Lord Gomfrey, and that was what prompted your heated exchange with him."

"Among other things."

Kyd sent Alexius an inscrutable look. "Forgive my impertinence, Sinclair. I was under the impression that you harbored a certain affection for Lady Juliana."

Alexius's throat tightened. "I did."

"Then why the devil did you permit her to leave in the custody of Lord Gomfrey?" the baron demanded.

Alexius's body jerked as if he had taken a stroke from a lash. It was the thought of Juliana in Gomfrey's bed that had impelled Alexius to drink an ocean of brandy. "Although it is not any of your business, Kyd, no one coerced Lady Juliana to spend the evening with Gomfrey. She chose to remain with the bastard, even after I offered to escort her home to her family."

The baron frowned and shook his head in denial at Alexius's allegations. "No, I do not believe it."

Neither had Alexius. His gaze narrowed on Kyd's flushed, angry face. The gentleman looked almost as bad as Alexius felt. "You seem a trifle upset. Did you think that she would turn to you once her infatuation with me waned?"

Such news might even provoke Belinda into committing murder.

Lord Kyd blinked in response to the dangerously soft accusation. "Of course not! I consider Lady Juliana a good friend. Nothing more. My loyalties and affection belong to your sister, and have for some time."

The baron's indignation was genuine. It quelled Alexius's jealousy as effectively as water on a fire. He certainly could not condemn the man for laying his allegiance at Belinda's feet. Had not Alexius done the same?

"I am in love with your sister, Sinclair," Kyd confessed, shooting several wary glances in Alexius's direction as if attempting to assess his companion's reaction to the declaration. "If you think to issue a challenge, it is unwarranted. I am not seeking your blessing, or Belinda's hand in marriage. After Gredell's heavy hand, your sister is content to remain unfettered."

Alexius merely lifted his brows. Very few people knew of Gredell's abuse toward his wife, and all of them would have feared retribution for turning Belinda's torment into casual gossip. The only way the baron might have learned the truth about the details of her disastrous marriage would have been from Belinda.

"You understand Belle better than most."

"It is my goal that one day I might change her mind, and that she will have me," Kyd confided, "though I would consider it a personal favor if you did not share my aspirations with your sister."

"And where does Lady Juliana fit in your aspirations?"

The baron cleared his throat, clearly stalling as he pondered how to answer Alexius's question. "Before I reply, I must beg another favor of you."

"Have a care, Kyd," Alexius warned. "I have a nasty habit of calling in such favors."

"I asked not only for myself, but for Lady Juliana as well. I am breaking a confidence, and it does not set well with me." The baron removed his hat and threaded his hand through his hair. He settled the hat back in place. "Last evening, Belinda was vague about what transpired between you and Lady Juliana. I can only assume that Lady Juliana's decision to remain as Lord Gomfrey's companion for the evening means that she has cut her ties with you."

"If you are asking me, did we argue about Gomfrey?" Alexius's exhalation was a bark of laughter. "I can assure you that we did in a very public manner. As you know, my family is not known for their discretion."

Kyd halted abruptly and stared at him. "Then perhaps it would be best if I said nothing more about Lady Juliana. I admire her. Respect her. I would not want to be responsible for hurting her or adding to her burdens."

"Lady Juliana is fond of you, too. To be honest, I have had the devil of a time wondering about the secrets between the two of you."

How could he tell Kyd that his quiet friendship with Juliana had driven Belinda into a jealous rage? Instead of confronting her lover, she had simply turned to her protective brother and begged him to help her gain her revenge against her rival.

Kyd was too compassionate to appreciate Alexius's and Belinda's ruthless nature that had been honed by their father. It was one of the reasons why Alexius thought the man was all wrong for his sister. The man was too sensitive and often appeared weak. Alexius doubted the man would be honored by his lover's cruelty toward a lady he viewed simply as a friend. No, if the baron learned the truth, it might be the one thing to drive the man away from Belinda.

Several months ago, Alexius might have relished doing just that under the guise of protecting his sister.

Not today.

Perhaps Belinda deserved to be punished for her selfishness and her cruelty toward Juliana. However, Alexius did not have the heart to hurt her when his sins were much worse. He had never been one to dwell on his mistakes or feel guilt or regret. At five and twenty, he was becoming intimately acquainted with the dour sentiments.

Alexius shifted his gaze to a passing wagon filled with barrels of ale. "In spite of last evening's debacle, I have no desire to hurt Lady Juliana." He shrugged. "Well, any more than I have."

The baron took a deep breath as he silently debated whether or not Alexius was trustworthy. If this discussion had occurred a week earlier, he would have been insulted by his companion's reluctance.

"This is not common knowledge; however, since her arrival, Lady Juliana has been discreetly seeking a publisher for her musical compositions," the baron explained, keeping his voice low. "She asked for my assistance, and regretfully, I have not had much success."

Alexius did not deserve the relief that loosened the knots in his gut. Juliana had tried to explain what music meant to her. He, on the other hand, had been too busy tempting her into an affair to truly listen to her. "She once played one of her compositions for me."

And then I took her innocence.

"She's remarkably talented. I had hoped my bookseller connections would prove fruitful, but alas, a lady composer does not instill the confidence and respect of her male counterparts."

"Indeed."

"Nor is her family encouraging her to seek out a profession. Lady Duncombe would rather see her daughters married according to their position."

"Lady Juliana had mentioned her mother's aspirations." And yet Juliana had been deliberately silent about her private dreams, Alexius grimly mused, realizing he was angry again. It did not take much deduction to find the source. She had not trusted him to keep her secrets. He tucked his tongue between his teeth as the revelation found its mark. It stung, but the lady had excellent instincts.

"In spite of these obstacles, I am not discouraged," the baron continued, oblivious to his companion's dark thoughts. "In fact, I have considered approaching Lady Juliana with a business proposition of my own. I have been entertaining the notion of getting into the publishing business."

Alexius glanced at the gentleman with new respect. "You want to publish Lady Juliana's musical compositions?"

"Why not? I think it would be a profitable endeavor for both of us. However—" Kyd sighed heavily. "Your sister would not approve, which is why I must ask that you keep what I have told you in the strictest confidence. Belinda is already skittish of marriage. I doubt my aspirations to dabble in a trade would secure her affection."

Juliana's friendship with Lord Kyd had not been of a romantic nature. Like his sister, Alexius had been a jealous fool.

"You were afraid that Belinda would reject your offer of marriage if you became a publisher."

Kyd sheepishly looked up at Alexius. "I love your sister, Sinclair, but I am not blind to her faults. She might seduce a man that she considered beneath her, but she would not willingly marry him!"

Chapter Nineteen

NOT LONG AFTER his enlightening conversation with Lord Kyd, Alexius was pounding his fist against Lady Duncombe's front door. He had stopped at Nox only long enough to borrow Hunter's phaeton. Thankfully he had not delayed Alexius by asking questions he had not been prepared to answer. He had not been as fortunate with Frost.

For reasons he had never quite fathomed, the earl had disliked Alexius's relationship with Juliana. The night Frost and Juliana had literally stumbled upon Alexius and Nell in the Kempes' parlor his friend had been trying to kiss the lady. Alexius had been so surprised to see Juliana, he had dismissed the incident. What had transpired before the couple had entered the room? Had Frost secretly coveted Juliana and his efforts had been spurned? Unscrupulous bastard! The notion of Frost putting his hands on Juliana had been enough to ignite Alexius's temper.

"*What do you want from me, Frost?*"

"*Did you enjoy yourself last evening?*"

There was something about his friend's casual question that prickled the hairs on the back of Alexius's neck. "*As much as any other gent, I suppose. I cannot recall much once we sat down to play cards. How much did I lose?*"

"*Then you do not remember Rose?*"

"*Rose?*" *The name summoned the image of an attractive whore with a wealth of red hair.* "*Is she not one of Madam V's girls?*"

"*Since you shooed Dare and Saint away, I sent Rose over to your table to save you from your suicidal attempt to drink yourself to death.*"

Alexius rubbed the back of his neck as he tried to piece together the fragments of the evening. He vaguely recalled laughing with the pretty red-haired woman. She had tried to help him back to the table. There was a good chance that he had tried to kiss her.

"*You sent Rose to me.*" *It unnerved him that he did not remember what he and Rose did together.* "*Why?*"

"*Why not?*" *Frost argued back.* "*I thought you deserved someone who would desire nothing more from you than a playful fucking.*"

Tantalizing images flickered in his brain. His mouth on a woman's breast. A woman's hand stroking his cock. Covering a woman and pushing up her skirts.

Had he bedded the wench?

"*You had no right, Frost,*" *Alexius said, suddenly furious that he had been manipulated into bedding the* whore. "Damn you! You knew Juliana was the woman I wanted. I was in no condition to—"

"I know. I would want to forget the details, too, if I had been caught in such an embarrassing predicament."

Alexius could only gape at his friend. "What?"

"You shoved Rose to the floor and passed out on top of her." Frost shook his head in disgust. "We found you with your trousers unbuttoned, so I can only assume that you at least knew what to do with a willing female. Rose told me later that she was disappointed, too."

"Oh, for Christ's sake!"

It was ridiculous, but bedding another woman seemed abhorrent to Alexius. It seemed like a betrayal of Juliana, which made little sense, since she despised him and had chosen to remain with Gomfrey.

"You actually look relieved nothing happened." Frost sounded surprised and vaguely disapproving. "Dare told us that you wanted to die in your bed, so we scraped you off the floor and dumped you in a coach."

He was going to end up killing Frost if he remained. "We will discuss your helpfulness later, you selfish bastard. Lucky for you, I have to go."

Frost followed Alexius down the stairs and blocked his way before he could head out to the stables. "My dear Sin, you know, you are ignoring all good sense by chasing after that fancy bit of skirt."

"Do not talk to me about good sense when you sent an eager whore to take advantage of my stupidity. Oh, and another thing: Lady Juliana was never a fancy bit of skirt, as you so charmingly put it. My sister was wrong about her." He stared starkly at his friend. "So was I, which means you were wrong about her, too!"

Alexius turned away.

"And what about Gomfrey?" Frost called after Alexius as he tried to make good on his escape. "Chances are, your precious Lady Juliana spent the night with Gomfrey pumping himself betwixt her luscious thighs."

Alexius closed his eyes, hating the thought of Juliana in anyone's arms except his own. Frost seemed to know it as well and was taking perverse pleasure in Alexius's discomfort. He glanced back at his friend. "Then it is no more than I deserve for leaving her with the bastard."

Alexius managed to clear four steps before the earl spoke again.

"One more thing, Sin. Something that I forgot to tell you last evening that you might find of interest," Frost drawled; his nasty inflection had Alexius spinning back with a snarl on his lips.

"What?"

The earl was just itching for a fight, and if he persisted, Alexius was prepared to accommodate his friend.

Frost trailed a fine vertical crack on the plaster wall. "After your departure from the anteroom, Gomfrey was rather persistent in finding out what you and your lady discussed. Lacking your natural finesse with ladies, he was reduced to using his brutish strength to gain the answers he craved. I fear Lady Juliana's face might have been slightly bruised by his persistence."

"Damn him! I will kill him with my bare hands if I find a mark on her." He took several shallow breaths. "Why did you not mention this sooner?"

"You seemed willing to let Lady Juliana go." Frost

*crossed his arms and shrugged. "Why would I dis-
suade you from being sensible for once?"*

Alexius raised his fist and pounded on the Ivers door
again. He was still angry at Frost for not telling him
about what he had witnessed between Gomfrey and
Juliana. And then there was that business with Rose.
Perhaps it was not in the earl's nature to interfere in
matters that were none of his concern; nonetheless, if
he had told Alexius, he would have done something
about it. Instead he and his friends had returned to Nox
for a night of drinking and gambling.

His heart stuttered every time he dwelled on Juliana's
evening with the sadistic lord.

No, Frost was wrong. Juliana had been hurt and furious, but she would have never done anything so fool-
hardy as to remain with Gomfrey. Such petty revenge
for Alexius's slights would have been beneath Juliana.
After he had departed with his friends, she would have
insisted that the earl return her to her family.

The door opened and Alexius was greeted by the
Iverses' butler.

"Good afternoon, milord."

The servant was polite, but he was not particularly
friendly. Alexius did not consider the man's cool manner toward him as a personal slight. A person could
end up with a house full of unwanted visitors if one's
butler was too affable.

"Tell Lady Juliana that Lord Sinclair requires an
audience with her."

The butler did not step aside. "My apologies, Lord
Sinclair. Lady Juliana is not at home."

"To just me, or all of London?" he demanded belligerently. He had had some experience with confronting tetchy females.

"Lady Juliana and Lady Duncombe are out of the house, milord."

Alexius caught himself before he sagged against the threshold. Juliana was with her mother. At least he did not have to worry that she was in Gomfrey's hands. "And Lady Juliana's sisters?"

"I have been given strict orders that Lady Cordelia and Lady Lucilla are not receiving visitors this afternoon."

There was no doubt that Juliana had told her family about Alexius's connection and his true reason for seeking her out. Her sisters would not be pleased to see him. However, he could never resist a challenge. "I will wager you five pounds that the ladies will receive me."

It was apparent that no one had ever tried to wager their way into the Iverses' household. The very suggestion seemed to perplex the butler. "Lord Sinclair!"

"Tell them I have come to see their sister," Alexius said, willing to take advantage of the breach in the servant's composure. "If I am wrong, then you will have the pleasure of taking my five pounds and tossing me out onto the street."

The butler measured him from head to toe. He still looked doubtful of Alexius's reasons for confronting the sisters. "You will go peacefully if Lady Cordelia and Lady Lucilla refuse to see you?"

He placed his hand over his heart. "Lady Juliana is

the one I want," Alexius said, his voice ringing with sincerity. "I am merely concerned about the lady's welfare, and hope her sisters can assure me that she is faring well."

The butler seemed satisfied with Alexius's answer. "Very well. I cannot invite you into the front hall, so you will have to make do with the front step."

The door was firmly shut in his face.

Five minutes had passed when it occurred to him that he might have been duped by the butler. Alexius glanced up at the windows, wondering if the Ivers women were having a hearty laugh at his expense. If they were watching him, they were being very discreet. Alexius could not detect any movement at the windows.

The door abruptly opened again, and the butler stepped aside. "Lady Cordelia and Lady Lucilla will see you in the drawing room, Lord Sinclair," the manservant said formally.

Alexius stepped into the hall, his gaze drifting to the upper landing of the staircase. It was empty. He buried the disappointment that he felt. It was ridiculous of him to think Juliana might have been waiting for him.

"I owe you five pounds, milord," the butler said gruffly.

Alexius had no desire to relieve the man of his five pounds. The wager had been simply a desperate ruse to get into the house. "I will consider the debt honored if you answer my question truthfully. Is Lady Juliana at home?"

The servant shook his head. "I spoke the truth earlier

when I said that Lady Juliana was not at home." The butler hesitated at the large double doors to the drawing room. "The family is worried about her."

Without giving Alexius an opportunity to respond, the man opened the door and announced him.

Juliana's sisters were already standing, awaiting his arrival. The taller one was attired in a yellow morning dress, while the other sister complemented her sibling in light blue. Although their blond hair and fair complexions resembled Juliana's superficially, neither lady could compete with her younger sibling's grace and beauty. He bowed his head politely as he greeted each sister. "Good afternoon, Lady Cordelia. Lady Lucilla. Pardon my intrusion."

Both ladies curtsied. It was Lady Cordelia who beckoned him to sit on the green sofa. "Pray be seated, Lord Sinclair," she said crisply.

Her good manners were a poor disguise for the open hostility shimmering in the lady's pale blue eyes.

"Shall I bring tea, my lady?"

"That will not be necessary, Gilbert," Lady Lucilla replied, settling down in the chair across from Alexius. There was no warmth in her gaze or smile. "Lord Sinclair's visit will be exceedingly brief."

No one spoke until the butler had closed the doors to give them privacy.

Alexius sat on the edge of the cushion, half-expecting to be attacked by Juliana's sisters. "Where is your Juliana?"

Lady Cordelia stood behind her sister; the pair of them were united in their dislike for him. "Precisely where you abandoned her, Lord Sinclair."

He braced his palms above his knees. "It is a tad early for the theater."

Lady Lucilla sat stiffly in her chair. Her hands were clasped together so tightly it should have been painful. "Let us put aside formality and pretenses, my lord. Word of your humiliating exchange with our beloved sister has reached our ears."

"I have little doubt that Juliana told you what happened, and that you both view me as the vilest of villains," he said, injecting the proper amount of contriteness. "However, there are certain details that I was not aware—"

"We have not seen Juliana since she ascended Lord Gomfrey's coach last evening," Lady Lucilla blurted out the startling news.

Lady Cordelia's mouth curled into a thin, unpleasant smile. "Unfortunately, we have not lacked for visitors this morning. The first one arrived before we had finished our breakfast. Needless to say, we had lost interest in finishing our meal once we had learned of your intimate connection to Lady Gredell and what you had done to poor Juliana."

"Gomfrey did not escort Juliana home?" Alexius did not give a damn about their lost appetites or their dismay over learning that Belinda was his half sister. He wanted to know why Juliana had not returned home to her family.

"Poor Juliana." Lady Lucilla removed the lace handkerchief she had tucked into the cuff at her wrist and dabbed her eyes. "And to think that she fancied herself in love with you."

"Now, now, Lucilla," Lady Cordelia said soothingly

as she touched her sister on one shoulder in a gesture of comfort. "Lord Sinclair made fools out of us all. Juliana was too innocent to understand evil has many disguises and some can be quite handsome and very charming."

Alexius knew he was being baited, and he refused to lose his temper. "I will happily tender my apologies to your sister if you will tell me where she is."

"She will not believe you."

"Neither do we," Lady Lucilla added defiantly.

"Gomfrey has Juliana," Alexius said flatly. He glowered at both of them. "Why the devil did your mother not summon a constable to search the bastard's house when your sister did not return from the theater?"

The silence in the drawing room was oppressive.

"It was one of the conditions."

"Cordelia, we were not supposed to speak of it. Maman said so."

"What conditions?" Alexius said through clenched teeth.

The sisters stared at each other wordlessly, debating whether they should tell him the truth.

"Tell me!"

Lady Cordelia bit down on her lower lip. She sighed. "It all started with Maman's gambling debt to Lord Gomfrey."

Alexius pinched the bridge of his nose. Although gambling was not his passion, he had experienced unpleasant nights when the cards had not favored him. "I take it her losses were heavy."

"More than she could pay," Lady Lucilla sadly interjected.

Her sister nodded in agreement. "Lord Gomfrey insisted that she settle her debt immediately."

"Your mother surrendered Juliana to pay her debt to Gomfrey." Alexius swore and jumped to his feet. He began pacing the room. "Bloody hell! And you both think I am the devil for trying to protect my sister."

Lady Lucilla lifted her head; her pale green eyes were clouded with confusion. "Why would—"

"Not now," he snapped, causing both of the ladies to cringe. "What was the bargain struck between Gomfrey and your mother? And why the hell was Juliana chosen instead of one of you?"

Lady Cordelia gripped the back of the chair she was using as a shield. "Do you think that we are so cruel as to sacrifice our own sister? We love her. Lord Gomfrey chose Juliana. He told Maman that if she could not pay off the debt, then he would take Juliana as his mistress."

"He will consider the debt satisfied at summer's end." Lady Lucilla sniffed into her soggy handkerchief.

Alexius froze as he recalled the sense of betrayal he had felt when he had confronted Juliana about Lord Gomfrey.

"Is this true? Have you gone to this braying ass willingly?"

"If you understood me at all, Lord Sinclair, you would already have the answer."

Her calm reply had seemed cryptic last evening, and that had only spurred his temper. Now Alexius understood what she had been trying to tell him. If he had trusted her at all, he would have instinctively known that she would not have sought out the earl willingly.

"Oh, Juliana. Why did you not come to me?"

Alexius had not realized he had spoken the question aloud until Lady Cordelia replied, "We were forbidden to speak of the bargain to anyone. It was one of the conditions. Everyone had to believe that Juliana cast you aside for Lord Gomfrey. According to Maman, the earl was most insistent on that particular point. If we failed, he threatened to reveal Maman's gambling habits to the *ton*. He knew our family would have been ruined by the scandal. Any hope of marrying—"

Lady Cordelia looked away.

Alexius sneered. He had never slapped a lady, but his fingers itched to strike the haughty blonde for putting her marriage prospects above her sister's welfare. "So it was best for the family to sacrifice one daughter, rather than all three, eh?"

"Either way, it was a devil's bargain," Lady Lucilla said in a reasonable tone. "That is why Maman left to see Lord Gomfrey."

Alexius muttered an oath. The Ivers women needed a keeper if they truly believed they were capable of handling a blackmailing scoundrel such as Gomfrey. Alexius growled his farewell and strode briskly toward the closed doors.

"What are you going to do?"

He scowled at Lady Cordelia. "What should have been done last evening. I am going to Gomfrey's town house to collect your mother and your sister."

Alexius seized the latches and pushed open the double doors.

Once he had dealt with Gomfrey and Juliana was

safely home, Alexius planned to drag the furious lady upstairs to paddle her sweet backside for not trusting him enough to keep her secrets.

Then he would apologize for his own dastardly misdeeds.

Chapter Twenty

ALEXIUS WAS NOT in the mood to be polite or reasonable by the time he reached Lord Gomfrey's town house. When the earl's manservant opened the door, Alexius surprised him by kicking the door with his booted foot. As the door swung open wide, the startled servant instinctively stepped aside to grasp the door.

"My lord!"

Alexius did not bother with explanations or apologies. He stepped inside and swiftly studied the layout of the town house.

"Leave at once. You cannot just enter Lord Gomfrey's residence without a direct invitation." The butler seemed at a loss on the proper way to eject the noble intruder without getting sacked by his master.

"Where is the blackguard?" Alexius glanced upstairs. "Still in bed?"

His face hardened with murderous intent at the

thought of Juliana curled around Gomfrey as they slept together in the bed. The servant also noticed the dangerous stance and stepped back.

"Lord Gomfrey is not at home." The man wrung his hands and fluttered to the staircase when Alexius took a threatening step in that direction. "If you refuse to leave, I will be forced to summon a constable."

"Your loyalty is admirable, but misplaced." Alexius noticed the closed door to his far left and deduced it was the earl's library. "Summon a constable. Let Gomfrey explain to the magistrate why he kept Lady Juliana Ivers against her will."

"Are you drunk or simply mad? Lord Gomfrey is a gentleman," the servant said, convincingly affronted by the charge.

Alexius backed the butler up against the balustrade. His grin was hardly reassuring as he placed his hands on the servant's shoulders. "I have sobered up, so you may assume that you are dealing with the unpredictability of a madman. Where is Gomfrey? I vow, if he has violated her, and it can be proved that you were aware of your lord's nefarious deeds, I will see to it that the magistrate charges you as well."

The butler's throat audibly clicked as he swallowed. Without speaking, he used his bulging eyes to direct Alexius to the closed door across the hall.

He patted the butler on the shoulder. "Good man." Alexius released the servant and pivoted. He marched toward the door with deliberate purpose.

"The door is unlocked."

Without turning back, Alexius raised his hand to let the man know that he heard him. Only the butler would be worried about the bloody door. Alexius twisted the doorknob and pushed open the door. The servant had not been lying. Gomfrey stood in the middle of the library with his back to the door. At his side he clutched an empty glass. If he had heard the commotion in the outer hall, the earl did not seem particularly concerned about Alexius's arrival.

There was no sign of Juliana or her mother. Perhaps Juliana's sisters had been wrong.

"Where is she?"

Alexius's first inclination was to rush into the room and tackle Gomfrey to the floor. With the man's teeth firmly buried in his fine rug, Alexius could take his pick which body part of the earl's he wanted to pummel first.

"Sinclair," Gomfrey drawled as he brought the glass up to his lips. He frowned when he realized it was empty. "Somehow I am not surprised to see you. I hope you did not have to throttle my butler to gain entry into my house. He is not the bravest soul, but he is loyal."

The earl walked over to his desk to retrieve the small bottle. "I am being rude. Would you like some port?"

Alexius's stomach protested at the offer. "I have not come for a drink, Gomfrey."

"No?" The earl offered his back while he filled his own glass. "This particular bottle comes from the Douro region and the quality is exceptional."

"Where is Juliana?"

Gomfrey held up his glass and admired the port's deep red color in the sunlight filtering in through the windows. He sighed and leaned against the edge of his desk. "Lady Juliana. 'Quality' and 'exceptional' are words that apply to her as well."

Alexius stalked toward him. "She is not a bottle of fine port, Gomfrey. Nor is she just another possession to collect."

"Such righteous passion! One might believe that you are in love with the lady." He took a sip of the port and stared at Alexius over the rim of the glass. The earl wagged his little finger chidingly at him. "However, we both know that your ambitions for Lady Juliana were less honorable than mine. A remarkable feat considering I was blackmailing her."

Alexius had heard enough. Juliana's sister had told him that Gomfrey had claimed Juliana as payment for their mother's debt of honor. He had not expected the man to confess his deeds so readily. It took three long strides to reach the earl. Alexius knocked the small glass of port out of his hand and drove his fist into Gomfrey's stomach.

The earl doubled over and retched. The glass shattered against the window, splattering the bloodred port. It was easy enough for Alexius to imagine the liquid as his opponent's blood. Alexius was far from finished. He brought up his knee and drove it into the man's face. Gomfrey landed on his desk, sending everything on top scattering in all directions.

Alexius kicked away the bottle of wine as it collided with his boot. He seized Gomfrey by the edges of his coat. "My apologies for ruining your rug, but I am losing patience. Where is Juliana? Have you locked her in one of the bedchambers?"

"She isn't here, Sinclair."

"Liar!"

He pulled the earl up and slammed his fist into the man's jaw. Alexius's knuckles stung from the cuts and bruises he had collected from hitting Gomfrey the previous evening. He, on the other hand, looked worse. His broken nose was twice its normal size, and the mottled bruising was spreading. Alexius had managed to split the man's lower lip, too. Blood was seeping from the corner of Gomfrey's mouth and his right nostril.

Alexius crawled up on top of the desk and settled on the earl's chest. "I went to her town house. I spoke with her sisters. You did not escort her home."

Gomfrey bared his teeth. Blood morbidly outlined each tooth. "Get off me, you bastard," the earl hissed. His breathing was shallow because of the burden of Alexius's weight pressing on his chest. "I will tell you— everything!"

Alexius stared down at the earl dispassionately before he slowly climbed off the man.

Gomfrey shot up, gripping the edges of the desk for support. He was seething that the man he had always despised had slammed him onto his back as effortlessly as his cook might have done to a green turtle trying to escape the cooking pot. "I had every intention of fucking her, you know."

Instead of attacking him, Alexius bent down to retrieve his trampled hat. "To satisfy Lady Duncombe's debt of honor."

The earl gave him a quick reckless smile. Gomfrey winced and gingerly probed the bleeding wound on his lower lip. "In part. Then there was the additional enticement of stealing away your current mistress."

Gomfrey chuckled at Alexius's grim expression. "Your indignation that you had been publicly cast aside by your mistress was worth the broken nose. Oh, and then there was the delightful opportunity of satisfying every whim I had with Lady Juliana's albeit reluctant body." Gomfrey gave him an appraising glance. "Of course, you should know better than I."

Alexius could not believe Juliana had endured an evening in Gomfrey's custody and had escaped unscathed. "You did not bed her," he said, not hiding his disbelief.

Gomfrey parted his hands in a gesture of surrender. "It was not out of nobility, I assure you. I brought Lady Juliana here because I wanted to savor my victory and I knew she would submit to my demands for the sake of her family."

"What happened?"

"Do you want that drink now? I know I could use one." Gomfrey was feeling better, because he staggered over to the small cart along the wall and selected a crystal decanter. "This is not as good as the port, but it will suffice."

He poured himself a drink.

"I kissed her," the earl said, smiling at the memory. "She tasted better than wine. Her sleek tongue as potent and seductive as opium."

Alexius stood stiffly, his hands fisted at his sides. His pride and anger and Juliana's devotion to her mother had driven her into this man's arms. Alexius hated himself almost as much as he hated Gomfrey.

And the bastard knew it.

"I wanted her. Craved her, but I was a mess from our brawl at the theater, and Lady Juliana was skittish." He walked by Alexius and sat down in a large overstuffed chair. "I sent her into a bedchamber to prepare for me. I went into my bedchamber to undress, and I drank a small dose of laudanum to ease the throbbing in my nose. I followed the laudanum with several glasses of wine. I wanted nothing to distract me from enjoying my prize."

"Juliana ran away." Alexius could just imagine the brazen lady tossing several knotted sheets out the window and climbing down to flee her blackmailer.

"Nothing so theatrical, Sinclair." Gomfrey dug into his waistcoat pocket and pulled out a handkerchief. He blotted at the blood from his nose. "Regrettably, I misjudged the laudanum dose. I fell asleep in an uncomfortable chair, and did not awaken until my manservant knocked on the door this morning."

Alexius laughed, shaking his head at Juliana's good fortune.

"Yes, it was a rather amusing reprieve for Lady Juliana," Gomfrey said humorlessly. "Nonetheless, she still belonged to me. Now that I was fully recovered from my ordeal, you might have found me sampling the carnal delights of your former mistress had it not been for her mother and cousin's inopportune arrival."

"They took Juliana away?" Alexius arched his brow. "It is not like you to surrender your prey so easily."

"Well, I did try to keep her," he said, audacious and unapologetic until the end. "Lord Duncombe had originally refused to honor his cousin's gambling debts. He must have belatedly had a change of heart over the matter. They appeared at my door, insisting that I exchange Lady Juliana for the money, or else they would summon a constable."

Duncombe had known about Gomfrey's sordid bargain and had left the marchioness and her daughters to an uncertain fate? Before Alexius was finished with this business, he intended to pay a visit to the new Lord Duncombe and remind him about his duties to his family.

"So you see, Sinclair, your grand gesture to redeem yourself in Lady Juliana's eyes was for naught." Gomfrey dropped his soiled handkerchief and used his hand to push himself up from the chair. "Your lady has been returned to her family, and more importantly, she still despises you for your trickery. You have lost her."

"Perhaps." Alexius needed to see for himself that Juliana was safe. "However, you have enough troubles of your own to be concerned with my private affairs."

"How so?"

Alexius punched the earl hard, sending him flailing backward into the chair. "I cannot be placated with money. Consider yourself challenged, Gomfrey. My seconds will pay you a visit to set the day and hour."

He pulled out his handkerchief and tossed it at the earl. "I look forward to watching you bleed."

Alexius walked out of the library, leaving the manservant to tend to his lord.

Chapter Twenty-one

JULIANA WAS NOT at home.

After he had left Gomfrey, Alexius had returned to the Ivers town house. He had expected the butler to turn him away; however, the servant startled Alexius by opening the door and told him to wait in the hall until he was announced.

Although he was not Lady Cordelia's favorite person, she greeted him politely at the threshold of the drawing room and invited him to join her sister and mother. Without his help, they had rescued Juliana from Lord Gomfrey unscathed, and yet none of the women seemed pleased with their triumph.

Where was Juliana?

"I have come from Lord Gomfrey's. The earl will not bother you again," Alexius assured them, hoping to ease the tension in the room.

Lady Lucilla gave him a weak smile. "It was kind of you to confront the gentleman on our behalf."

"Our sister will be grateful when she learns of your kindness."

Bemused, Alexius stared at Lady Cordelia. "I doubt it. Your sister will likely make me crawl before she forgives me. If she were a man, she would call me out just for the pleasure of putting a bullet into me."

Lady Lucilla's eyes widened at his outrageous statement. "Juliana possesses the soul of an angel. She would never be so cruel!"

"Your sister is stubborn, prideful, and can be rather spiteful when she feels she has been wronged." Alexius held up his hand to silence her sisters' loyal protests. "I deserve her anger, and if she gives me a second chance, I hope to earn her forgiveness."

"Noble aspirations, Lord Sinclair," Lady Duncombe said wearily. One of her daughters had placed a damp cloth over the marchioness's eyes to ease the pain of a developing headache. "Nevertheless, you are too late."

"I mean no disrespect, Lady Duncombe," Alexius said carefully, still unhappy with her for her reckless play that had placed her youngest daughter in the hands of an unsavory gentleman. "However, I prefer to discuss this with Juliana privately."

The marchioness lifted the cloth and peeked at him. He had seduced her daughter, turned her into his mistress, and humiliated her in front of half the *ton*. Alexius should have been intimidated by the older woman, for she likely knew all the wickedly delightful things he had done with her daughter. It was difficult to feign repentance about those wonderful nights seducing Juliana. He did not regret them, and by god, he hoped Juliana had enjoyed them as much as he had.

If she did, he was determined to remind her of what they had shared before his sister and Juliana's mother's troubles had placed them on opposing sides.

"That might prove difficult." The marchioness covered her exposed eye with the cloth.

Alexius brazenly reached over and pulled the cloth away from the woman's face. "How so?"

"How dare you! Give it back!"

With the cloth dangling between his fingers, his gaze shifted from one sister to the other. He might not be able to intimidate the marchioness, but the daughters were weaker prey.

"Juliana is not upstairs, recovering from her frightful night with Lord Gomfrey. No, do not even try to lie," he said, silencing Lady Cordelia before she had a chance to utter a single word. "Gilbert would have told me when I inquired at the door. What have you done? Did you sell her to someone else?"

All three women gasped, their faces displaying various degrees of surprise and anger.

Lady Duncombe was the first to recover. "This is wholly your fault, Lord Sinclair."

Alexius slapped the cloth in his hand down on the table in front of them. He had spent most of the day chasing after Juliana, and his temper was honed to a deadly edge. "Mine?"

"Yes, it is yours," Lady Duncombe said crossly.

"Maman."

Lady Cordelia seemed equally perplexed by her mother's accusation. "You cannot blame Lord Sinclair for our troubles."

He assumed that Lady Cordelia was tiptoeing around the marchioness's heavy play at the gambling tables and her staggering losses to spare her feelings.

Alexius had no such qualms.

"It was your deep play with Gomfrey that placed Juliana in danger. Not I."

"I am aware of my part, Sinclair," the marchioness shouted back at him. "You clearly were not aware of yours, you stupid man. You were supposed to *save* us!"

Lady Duncombe might as well have slapped him. Her reasoning certainly left him dumbfounded. What made him feel better was that her daughters were also surprised.

Alexius rubbed the back of his neck. He had not eaten all day, and the lack of food was making him lightheaded. Or maybe he was trying too hard to make sense of Juliana's lunatic family. "Perhaps you might want to elaborate how I was to save you when I had no inkling of your financial difficulties."

The marchioness pointed at him, her eyes gleaming with triumph. "Exactly my point! If you had been a proper gentleman for my girl, Juliana would have run to you and told you of our problems. Instead, she went to our cousin."

"He turned her away." Alexius already despised the gentleman.

Lady Duncombe sadly nodded. "I could have told her that it was useless. Our cousin is not like us in temperament."

"He loves to lecture us," Lady Lucilla added. "The man could go on for hours."

Lady Cordelia clasped her sister's hand. "He does not approve of gambling. Our father supported our family with his winnings. He did not have a head for business, but he was sinfully good at the card table."

Alexius had heard talk of the elder Lord Duncombe and his luck at the gaming tables. However, Alexius had never encountered the gentleman.

Lady Lucilla leaned forward. "Maman is rather skillful at the tables, too."

"Until Lord Gomfrey," Lady Cordelia amended.

The marchioness sighed heavily. "Yes. Gomfrey bested me. I confess, I have never seen such luck. Not since your dear father."

Alexius held his tongue. He glanced at all three women in amazement. He was surrounded by a family of sharpers. "Does Juliana gamble, too?"

Lady Cordelia wrinkled her nose. "Papa taught all of us the basics. Nevertheless, for Juliana, it was her music. She played so beautifully and composed the love-liest musical compositions, so our father was happy to indulge her."

"And then, my husband died and in an act of desperation I brought my girls to London in hopes of them finding suitable husbands. When I heard that you were sniffing after my Juliana I was so pleased. She seemed to like you, too. It was a shame that you turned out to be a heartless rogue," the marchioness lamented.

So Lady Duncombe was back to blaming him again.

"If you had asked any member of the *ton*, they would have warned you to keep your daughters away from me and my friends," Alexius said gruffly before he could stop himself. Somehow the marchioness had twisted the conversation around so that he was insulting himself. "I was not looking for a bride," he said defensively.

"Indeed," Lady Cordelia crisply replied. "After your impromptu performance at the theater, now everyone knows that you were simply doing Lady Gredell's bidding."

Lady Lucilla shuddered. "I met her once. A dreadful woman." Belatedly she recalled that Alexius was the countess's half brother. "No offense."

Lady Duncombe tilted her head so that she could look down her nose. "You claim that you were not seeking a bride. How odd, since you had no misgivings about treating my Juliana as a man does his wife."

It was difficult not to cringe at the accusation. Agitated, he covered his mouth with his hand and stroked his chin. He did not care how open-minded these women were, he was not about to discuss the intimate details of his affair with Juliana.

The marchioness retrieved her discarded cloth and carefully refolded the damp fabric. "Well, there is no point castigating you for my mistakes."

Precisely.

"I should have studied you more thoroughly, and learned of your connection to Lady Gredell. If I had, I would have discouraged my daughter from seeing you and picked another gentleman to marry my Juliana." She placed the cloth over her eyes and sagged against the sofa.

Alexius snatched the cloth away. "You did not choose me for Juliana," he said flatly.

"If you say so." She held out her hand in anticipation of him returning her cloth.

He clutched the cloth tightly in his fist. "What was the plan? That I would marry Juliana and rescue her family from their impoverished circumstances?"

Lady Cordelia and Lady Lucilla would not meet his questioning gaze. The marchioness simply shrugged.

"Gomfrey muddled your plans with his demands. However, you were assuming Juliana would come to me for the money. You knew I would never allow her to become Gomfrey's mistress. It was not far-fetched to guess that I would pay off your debt and punish Gomfrey for his insulting bargain."

Lady Duncombe leaned back against the sofa and looked expectantly at him. "You confronted Lord Gomfrey this afternoon. What did you do?"

Alexius had wanted to kill the man for touching and frightening Juliana. "I ruined his pretty face by breaking his nose and jaw, and perhaps cracked a few of his ribs as well. I have also challenged him to a duel."

"Excellent," the marchioness said, her face softening with pride and smug satisfaction. "I knew I could count on you! Of course, Juliana has vowed never to forgive you over this business with your sister. However, I am older and rather practical when it comes to my daughters. I knew you would come to Juliana's aid if she needed you."

He had to credit the woman for her cleverness. He had been neatly outmaneuvered by an expert. Odder still, he did not seem to mind as long as he could see Juliana again.

"Where is she, Lady Duncombe?"

The marchioness smiled coyly at him. "Juliana is currently residing with her future husband."

Alexius lunged for the older woman, causing her daughters to shriek. He caged the marchioness with his arms and glowered at her. "When did you find the time to dig up another husband for her?" he raged.

Alexius could not believe it. Just when he had ripped Juliana out of the greedy grasp of one man, some other gent had absconded with her.

Lady Duncombe gave Alexius's arm a sympathetic pat. The woman was positively fearless. "It was our cousin's price for paying my gambling debts to Lord Gomfrey." She straightened her spine and matched his ire with a quelling glare. "I told you, my dear boy, that you were to blame for this mess. I had given up on you, and there was little I could do but accept Lord Duncombe's dreadful conditions."

"He will not let us see her," Lady Cordelia said, her eyes misting with tears. "Not until the wedding."

"Naturally the young marquess believes I cannot be trusted with his bride."

If Alexius had not caught onto the older woman's games, he might have believed that she was truly hurt and bewildered by her cousin's decree. What Lady Duncombe wanted was revenge, and she had already guessed Alexius would be her willing messenger to atone for what he had done to Juliana.

The marchioness was correct.

Alexius grinned at her. He was beginning to like this devious woman.

"What say you, Lord Sinclair?" she said, tossing her head back while her eyes twinkled challengingly. "Are you willing to assist me in meddling in my daughter's life just one more time?"

Chapter Twenty-two

"YOU ARE SO incredibly beautiful."

Juliana sat at the dressing table that once had belonged to her mother and studied her reflection in the small oval mirror. She was still attired in the white satin dress she had worn when she sat beside Lord Gomfrey in his private box. It was the same dress she had been wearing when she learned Sin had been conspiring against her with his half sister, Lady Gredell.

Juliana idly touched the glass beads decorating the bodice. This dress had witnessed humiliation, greed, violence, deceit, and hatred. All she wanted to do was tear the evening dress from her body and burn the ragged remnants.

"I do not feel beautiful, Cousin." She glanced away from the mirror and stared at Lord Duncombe. "I feel like your prisoner."

Hours earlier, she had been Lord Gomfrey's prize

before her cousin had paid off her mother's debt of honor and had stolen Juliana away. Days earlier, she had thought of herself as Sin's woman. Now all she craved was to be left alone.

She did not want any man.

"You are still upset about that business with Lord Gomfrey," the marquess said, his hands trembling as they hovered over the transparent gauze and lace that made up her puffed sleeves. He dug his fingers into his palms, resisting the urge to soothe her with his touch. "It was cruel of me to send you away, letting you believe that I would not assist your family. I beg your forgiveness."

The air behind her stirred as her cousin abruptly stepped away from her, his body as restless as his thoughts. "For many years, your mother has abused my benevolence. Once I had learned that she had once again ignored my dictates and harried you and your sisters to London, it seemed fitting to teach her a lesson. I needed someone to lure your mother into deep play, and Lord Gomfrey seemed the ideal opponent. My greatest mistake was underestimating the man's flexible morality and his hatred of Sinclair. If I had deduced that he would have been so brazen as to bring you to his town house, I would never have trusted the gentleman."

A lesson.

Juliana felt a bubble of laughter rise in her throat. She covered her mouth, muffling the misplaced amusement. Lord Duncombe had been attempting to teach her mother a lesson. Why was she the one paying the price?

To defend her mother was as natural to Juliana as

breathing. "My lord, Maman means well. I realize that she oftentimes seems reckless to you. Nevertheless, she thinks only to protect her family."

The marquess's face hardened. Juliana had always thought him quite rigid and cold. If the gentleman felt mercy, he spared none for her mother.

"Well, what matters most is that you are unharmed from your ordeal. Lord Gomfrey has been dealt with and Sinclair is no longer a problem. Furthermore, I am prepared to assume my duties toward you and your family."

He laid his hand on the nape of her neck. "I will be a good husband, Juliana. I swear it."

That was the problem, she thought despairingly. She did not want to marry her cousin. Whether she was Lord Gomfrey's mistress or the marquess's wife, both gentlemen had essentially bought her as if she were a possession to be bartered.

"My lord, this arrangement is impractical." Juliana gestured helplessly at the bedchamber that was once inhabited by her mother. "I do not even have a clean dress." She turned toward him, placing her hand on his wrist. "You do not have to fulfill your duty to our family by marrying me. I would make a dreadful wife. I belong with my mother and sisters. I beg of you, please take me home."

The marquess stepped back, and Juliana allowed her hand to fall into her lap. "I have been inconsiderate," he said brusquely. "You need food, a warm bath, and clean dresses. That dress is a hideous reminder of the ugly business with Lord Gomfrey. Remove it at once."

—

"You are not leaving without us, Sinclair!"

Alexius grimaced. He had escaped as far as the front hall before the marchioness's resounding declaration had him pivoting and striding back to the ladies, who were determined to vex him.

"You will only get in my way," he replied tersely.

Alexius suspected that the ladies would not approve of his method for returning Juliana. His plan was simple. He would kick in Duncombe's front door, trounce the self-righteous bastard for bullying his cousin into marriage, and then, whether she liked it or not, Juliana would have to deal with Alexius.

Something in his expression must have tipped the marchioness off about his violent intentions. She uttered a mild wordless sound of disapproval. "The young marquess has acted rather brashly, but I highly doubt he will hurt Juliana. After all, the man has offered her marriage."

Alexius muttered a vulgar oath.

"Need I remind you, Lady Duncombe that your cousin is blackmailing your daughter into marriage? Does that seem very honorable to you?"

The butler entered the hall, his arms laden with the ladies' cloaks.

"Thank you, Gilbert," Lady Cordelia said as she selected a dark gray cloak from the pile. She slipped the garment over her shoulders and looked Alexius in the eye. "You must be reasonable about this, my lord. The servants will open the door to us."

On any other occasion, he would have found their naïveté charming. "And if Duncombe has given them strict orders to turn you away?"

"We could always sneak into the house from the

servants' entrance at the back," Lady Lucilla chimed in, behaving as if they were embarking on some grand adventure.

He was half-tempted to lock them in the cellar and have Gilbert guard the key. "You are all remaining here," Alexius said in an uncompromising tone. "Let me handle your blackmailing cousin."

Lady Duncombe bowed her head so a maid could adjust her bonnet. "And how do you plan to handle my daughter?"

Alexius hesitated. He had not considered that Juliana might be a problem. If she had any sense, she should be grateful that someone was preparing to rescue her. However, this was Juliana. Stubbornness had been bred into her very bones.

He shrugged carelessly. "If the occasion calls for it, by tossing her over my shoulder."

All three ladies railed at him for his brutish response.

"Unacceptable!"

"Absurd."

"Insensitive swine!"

Gilbert, who stood off to the side, rolled his eyes upward.

"Perhaps we should send a note to Lord Fisken," Lady Cordelia said to her mother. "I realize you did not want to involve him in our private affairs until I had some assurance of his feelings. However, I think—"

"No."

Fortunately, the marchioness was not enthusiastic about her daughter's suggestion either. "I fear, Cordelia, that Lord Fisken may not be as sympathetic to our plight as you might hope. There is no reason why we should risk any misunderstanding."

Although he had no personal grievances toward the gentleman, Alexius thought Fisken's delicate nature would suffer greatly if thoroughly tested by the Ivers family. It took a sturdy constitution to engage these ladies. "Forget Lord Fisken. It would take too long to find him."

"I agree with Lord Sinclair."

Alexius rewarded Lady Lucilla with a dazzling smile. She sweetly preened under his perusal.

"Then it is agreed, all of you will remain here."

Lady Duncombe brushed past him and headed for the door. "Nonsense. You need us, Sinclair."

Gilbert rushed forward and opened the door.

She raised her finger to illustrate her position. "Lest you forget, my Juliana has not forgiven you as I have. With her family around her, my daughter will be more amenable to your presence. You have your work cut out for you, my boy. Indeed, you do."

With her daughters behind her, the marchioness walked out the front door.

Alexius had only one option. He surrendered gracefully.

"Stand up and give me your back," Lord Duncombe ordered. "The dress is wrinkled and filthy. You will feel better once it is removed."

Earlier, Juliana had had similar thoughts. She straightened her knees, rising from the small padded bench. "If you send in a maid, I will undress."

Impatience flashed in the marquess's stern gaze. "Your mother's defiance was what brought me to London. I had no plans to enjoy the season, and thus the house has not been properly staffed and prepared. I will remedy that on the morrow. For now, you will have to be satisfied with my clumsy attempts to play lady's maid."

Juliana edged away from the dressing table toward the door. "I have already slept in this dress. Another night will not matter."

"Rubbish! I only wish to see to your comfort." He moved in closer. "Since I shall be your husband soon, there is nothing improper about me seeing to the task."

She cringed at his first tentative touch. "My lord, truly—"

"Hold still." he commanded, setting to work on the neat line of glass buttons securing her dress. "Do you find the touch of all males offensive, or is your dislike reserved exclusively for me?"

Her reply would displease him, so she ignored the question. She had always felt awkward in his presence. Since he and her mother had collected her from Lord Gomfrey's, the marquess had taken charge of the situation. Heedless of the marchioness's protests, Lord Duncombe had ordered her from the family's coach with the stunning announcement that he would marry his errant distant cousin.

Juliana's reunion with her mother had been tearful and unacceptably brief.

The back of her dress parted. Without asking her permission, Lord Duncombe stripped the puffed sleeves from her bare arms and shoved the skirts to the floor. In spite of her corset, chemise, and petticoat covering her almost as sufficiently as her evening dress, Juliana felt exposed.

She had not thought her cousin capable of it, but his eyes softened and heated as he stared at her in her undergarments.

"Guileless and enchanting." He circled around her, his gaze devouring her. "That was my impression of you when I visited your family six years ago. It was summer. You were thirteen years old and you strolled about the gardens as if you were a queen."

He came up from behind and buried his nose in her hair. Juliana danced away when she felt his left hand on her hip. "I recall you visiting us on several occasions," she said, moving to the end of the bed. "You were heir to the title, and by then Maman had given up her dreams of delivering a son. Papa had once told me that it was important for you to be acquainted with the lands, to appreciate their beauty."

"And to understand my duty to the family."

Juliana sighed. "That, too." Her father loved his family. He would have wanted to gain the future marquess's promise that his family would be looked after.

She grasped the end post of the bed and pivoted so that she faced her cousin as something he had said prompted her curiosity. "Why does that particular summer linger in your mind? I do not recall anything unusual occurring."

The marquess leaned against the opposite post and crossed his arms. He seemed bemused by her question. "Your father did not tell you?"

"Tell me what?"

Lord Duncombe made a soft scoffing sound. "Of

course he did not tell you. Why would he?" He lifted his head so their gazes met. "That summer, I declared myself to your father and asked for your hand in marriage."

"I-I did not know."

He did not seem to hear her. "At first, he laughed. Your father thought it was a jest."

"I was thirteen."

He became incensed at the gentle reminder. "I would have waited until you were older. You saw me only as an annoying distant relation. There was enough time for you to grow and to learn to love me. I assured your father that I would be a good husband to you." He staggered backward as he threaded his fingers through his hair. "Your father rejected my offer. He had the audacity to tell me that I was a good man, but that I was not good enough for his precious daughter."

"You must have misunderstood." She licked her dry lips. "My father would have never been so cruel."

The marquess thumped his chest with his fist. His eyes burned with old frustration and rage. "Oh, there was no possible way to misconstrue your father's refusal. While you, my sweet Juliana, were off chasing butterflies in the pasture and composing silly songs to amuse your family, your father was in the library lecturing me about my unyielding character and how it conflicted with the temperament of his creative, vivacious youngest daughter. He proclaimed that such a marriage would be disastrous."

Her father had never mentioned the marquess's proposal of marriage. Perhaps he had hoped to spare the young man's feelings. It also explained why their cousin's visits had ceased. Then, a little more than a year later, her beloved papa was dead.

And the lecturing tyrant had inherited his title.

"How you must hate me." She blinked furiously. "My family."

He startled her by plucking her by her waist and pulling her into his arms. "Convince me otherwise."

His mouth descended and there was little Juliana could do to avoid his kiss. She tasted the faint bitterness of ale as he cradled her head in his hands and tried to convince both of them that her father had been wrong. Silently she despaired, knowing that her father had been right. Juliana felt nothing as the marquess nibbled and caressed her lips, demanding some kind of response from her.

Juliana shuddered against him.

All her cousin evoked was a terrible sadness.

And fear.

Lord Duncombe took her wordless response as acceptance.

"I have gone about this business all wrong," he murmured huskily. "I should have taken you as my bride the day your maid packed away your mourning clothes."

He groaned against her lips while his fingers found the pins in her hair and cast them aside. Her blond tresses fell around her face and shoulders. He pulled her body closer, letting her feel his arousal.

He wanted her.

Panicking, Juliana twisted in his arms. Good grief,

the man was strong! It was apparent the marquess was determined to anticipate his wedding night.

"No," she murmured against his mouth. She used the bed's post as leverage to shove him away. "This is wrong."

The marquess slapped her hard across the face. The momentum sent Juliana sprawling across the bed. Before she could push her hair from her face, Lord Duncombe seized the front of her corset and dragged her to him.

"Wrong?" He pinched her chin and kissed her roughly. "I wager you did not protest when Sinclair tossed up your skirts and mounted you." She cried out when Lord Duncombe tangled his fingers into her hair and jerked her head back.

Juliana tasted blood. It might have been his. She *hoped* it was his. "Are you mad? Let go of me!" she seethed, furious that she was too weak to fight him off.

He crawled on top of her, straddling her hips. She kicked and strained against him. He sharply bit the curve of her shoulder.

"Madness is learning that your future bride was hauled off to London by her reckless mother to find a proper husband." The marquess bent down to kiss Juliana, but she ruined his aim by turning her face away. He licked her cheek. "I tried to scare your mother by sending her letters—"

Juliana gasped. "*You* sent the blackmail letters?"

Those notes had terrified the family.

"It was merely an attempt to delay your ambitious mother until I could travel to London," he said, panting from exertion.

Juliana froze, letting his words sink in. "Those notes . . . you were still in the country and yet you knew specific details . . . ," she said, her voice giving out on her.

Her cousin grinned down at her. "I have kept my promise to your father. I hired someone to discreetly watch over you and your family. He was my eyes and ears until I could join you in London."

He forced her arms over her head. Juliana dug her fingernails into his wrists as he used his knee to part her legs. "I knew about Sinclair before your mother did. Of the naughty games you played with the man. Once I watched the two of you together. I heard you begging him like a greedy whore."

She and the marquess struggled silently for a few minutes as he locked her wrists together with one hand. He used his unencumbered hand to admire the string of pearls around her neck.

"These are a gift from Sinclair, are they not?"

Juliana did not bother replying to the question. The marquess had been spying on her and her family. He knew who had given her the pearl necklace.

"You let the man claim your innocence, and still, there were so many things you did not know about your lover." The marquess wrapped the pearls around his finger, tightening the circumference until the pearls pinched her neck. "He never told you that he was Lady Gredell's half brother. If he had told you the truth, you would have never let him touch you. Nor did he mention his fondness for pearls."

Juliana sucked in several quick breaths, wondering

if the marquess was planning to strangle her with Sin's gift. "My lord, you are hurting me."

"I was told that Sinclair gifts all his mistresses with a string of pearls," her cousin said, his keen gaze marveling at the perfection of each pearl. "He has a rather unique manner in which he bestows his expensive gift—"

The afternoon in the coach.

Juliana hiccupped and choked on the tears clogging her throat.

How many women had worn his string of pearls? A dozen? Fifty? Her mind feverishly thought back to all the compliments that she had received about the necklace. A few of the ladies had equally stunning pearl necklaces. Had they been gifts from Sin, too? Juliana groaned, recalling how she had returned the compliments. Oh, she had been such a fool. Everyone had guessed the wicked things she had done with Sin. The pearls around her neck had been a public declaration of Sin's carnal prowess.

Ashamed, she shut her eyes in defeat.

"Ah, yes, I see the rumors are true." Lord Duncombe freed his finger from the necklace, letting it fall against her collarbone. "I must confess that I am rather surprised by your conduct, Juliana."

He unshackled her other wrist. She did not bother trying to sit up.

He stroked her hair. "I was not prepared for Sinclair. My spy reported back to me that the man was pursuing you, but I could not fathom why. You were too innocent to appeal to a man of his amorous appetites. Until the confrontation in Gomfrey's private box, his motives puzzled me."

Juliana rolled onto her side.

"I can assume that Sinclair will no longer be a problem?"

She stiffened at the marquess's patronizing manner. Juliana opened her eyes and glared up at him. "If you are asking me if I detest Sin as much as I do you, my dear cousin, then my answer is 'yes'!"

Lord Duncombe bellowed with fury. He slammed his fists down on the mattress over and over. Juliana screamed, though she managed to avoid each thunderous blow.

"Enough!"

Sobbing, she battered his head with her hands and kicked as the marquess grabbed the hem of her petticoat. He ripped the fabric at the seam and proceeded to tear a long strip of cloth.

"No—no!" she screamed, fearing that he intended to strangle her.

Lord Duncombe appeared oblivious to her frantic struggles. He bound her wrists with the length of petticoat and dragged her to one of the bedposts. She cried out in pain when he pinned her tied wrists against the ornate wood.

"Hold still," he snarled, using the loose ends to secure her to the post. Unsatisfied with his efforts, he removed his cravat from his neck and wound the length around both her wrists and the bedpost several times before knotting the ends.

Juliana flexed her fingers. The tips tingled unpleasantly.

"You cannot keep me tied to this bed forever." She laughed hysterically. "Someone is bound to notice."

"The bindings are temporary. I cannot have you running off while I see to a few tasks," he said, visibly shaking.

The marquess bore her marks, she mused with savage pride. There were red welts on his neck from her fingernails, and a bruise was blooming on his left cheek from her elbow. He was sweating and his clothes were mussed.

He kissed her lightly on the mouth.

"We are on our own this evening," he confessed, stroking her knee affectionately. "So no one will hear you if you cry out. When I return, I plan to remove any doubt that you might have about my abilities to be a good husband."

Juliana bit her lip as she stared at the thickening bulge in his trousers. Hurting her had aroused him. She tugged on her bindings.

The knots held.

Chapter Twenty-three

IT WAS A shame his friends were not here to watch Alexius break into Duncombe's town house. They would have laughed themselves into a boneless puddle of mash as his female confederates armed with beaded reticules prepared to rescue their beloved Juliana.

Their endeavor had all the earmarks of a colossal disaster.

"Step aside," he ordered the three ladies as they approached the front door.

Lady Duncombe whirled about and used her arms and body to block the solid oak door. "You cannot kick it in."

Alexius was beginning to feel like a vicious dog that had been collared and tethered to a tree by a sly blond tabby cat. "Of course I can. Step aside and watch me."

"Sinclair, this house has been in the Ivers family for

fifty-five years. The workmanship alone deserves our respect."

"Why do you care?" he demanded. "The house belongs to Duncombe. Your family has been cast out."

Lady Duncombe was resolute. She braced herself for violence. "Nevertheless, it still means something to this family. You will have to find another way to get into the house."

Lady Cordelia shattered his stalemate with the marchioness by reaching past her mother and knocking on the door.

"There goes our element of surprise," he said with disgust. "A brilliant stroke of genius, my lady."

He lifted his hands in surrender and backed away from the ladies. With each passing minute, his respect for Juliana had increased. She seemed to be the only rational one out of the four women. "If Duncombe is willing to blackmail Juliana into marriage, do you honestly think the gent is so foolish as to invite you into the house?"

Lady Cordelia's mouth curled as she gave Alexius an exasperated glance. "Our cousin has servants to open the door. There is a good chance we might be able to talk our way into the residence."

"Where is the butler?" Lady Lucilla wondered aloud to no one in particular. "No one is answering the door."

"Shameful," the marchioness grumbled. "Simply shameful. Leave it to Oliver to hire staff as boorish as he is."

It was time to take charge of the situation. Alexius looped his arm through Lady Duncombe's and grabbed Lady Cordelia by the wrist before she knocked on the door again. He marched them down the steps toward the waiting coach.

"I insist the three of you sit in the coach. Someone is bound to alert a constable if we continue to brawl in front of Duncombe's magnificent fifty-five-year-old door."

Lady Lucilla trailed after them. "No one is brawling."

Alexius halted in his tracks, striving for patience. "I am tempted to start one if the three of you do not cease your prattle. Duncombe would have to be deaf not to hear all the commotion at his door."

"He might not have heard us. Perhaps he is upstairs with Juliana?"

It was exactly Alexius's fear.

Lady Duncombe and her daughters did not seem overly concerned about the marquess. They thought him too scholarly and rigid to succumb to his baser instincts.

Alexius privately disagreed.

In spite of his foppish manners and intellectual pursuits, Duncombe was a man, after all. He had gone to a lot of trouble to possess Juliana. Alexius doubted the gentleman's interests in his distant cousin were merely altruistic in nature.

"Stay," Alexius ordered, praying that the women would heed him. "I will climb over the wall and check the back entry. If no one detains me, I will open the front door for you."

"Can we assume you have some experience in these matters, Sinclair?"

Alexius's smile exposed plenty of sharp teeth. "Indeed you can, madam."

There were reasons why smart, ambitious mothers

with marriage on their minds kept their pretty daughters away from Alexius and his friends.

The marchioness opened her reticule and began digging. "Very well, if you insist on breaking into the house alone, then perhaps you might want to take my knife." Noting Alexius's openmouthed expression, she hastily amended, "Merely as a precaution, of course."

The blade was removed with an exaggerated flourish.

"Maman!" exclaimed her daughters, impressed that their mother had come prepared to commit mayhem.

Alexius bent down and retrieved the long, thin blade that was sheathed in the inner lining of his right boot. All three women gasped in surprise. "I appreciate your generous offer, madam. However, I prefer to use mine."

That did not prevent him from carefully relieving Lady Duncombe of her blade. The woman was unpredictable. In a panic, she was more than likely to stab him rather than someone who actually deserved being pricked by her ornate bauble. He tucked the blade into his boot.

He had little difficulty scaling the brick wall. As he landed on the other side, Alexius took note of his surroundings. The faint light of twilight was slowly retreating into darkness. There was enough light left for him to move confidently from window to window. The house was shut up tightly and eerily silent. Moving around to the back, he climbed the curved stairs up to what he assumed led to the library. There he found a small balcony and double doors.

Smirking a little, Alexius recalled the marchioness's earlier concerns about him marring the pristine workmanship of the doors. Out of respect, he quietly tested the lock on the doors. Metal rattled against the wood. The doors were locked.

With the handle of the blade clamped in his hand, he peered through one of the glass panes. In the dim light he could see that the furniture was still covered to protect the pieces from dust and vermin. If Duncombe was in residence, he had not bothered airing out the house.

Alexius grinned at his good fortune.

Perhaps the marquess had also neglected to hire a staff. Alexius flipped the knife over his fingers in a practiced movement and ran the edge of the blade against the connecting seam of the double doors. His skills with locks were not as polished as Frost's or Hunter's, but they were more than adequate. A few minutes later Alexius opened one of the doors and slipped through the narrow opening.

The interior of the house was darker. After his knee connected with the corner of a table, he was tempted to light a candle, but he could not shake the unease he felt as he moved from the library to the drawing room.

The house was empty.

Where had Duncombe taken Juliana? Alexius's ears were ringing as he strained to hear some small sound of life in the house.

Nothing.

He made his way down the stairs to the front hall. There was no reason not to let Lady Duncombe and her daughters search the house. When he opened the door, he was not surprised to see the three ladies standing on the other side.

"You were supposed to remain in the coach."

Lady Duncombe pushed by him. "You were gone long enough to cause some concern. We wanted to be nearby just in case you needed us, dear boy."

Juliana's sisters were content to linger closer to the door.

"Did you find Juliana?" asked Lady Cordelia.

Alexius shook his head as he shut the front door. "I have searched only a few rooms. From all appearances, the house is empty."

"That is not possible," protested the marchioness. "Oliver has been in town for a week."

The furniture in the front hall was uncovered. Someone had been in the house, but there was nothing to indicate who had been there or if they had intended to remain.

The marquess had lied to the widow.

Alexius leaned over and sheathed his knife in his boot. The impotence he felt as they stood in Duncombe's empty town house made Alexius want to break a few things. He was certain the marchioness would not approve.

"Perhaps Duncombe thought it too much trouble to open the house for the season. He could have rented a room somewhere."

"What do you do? Search all of London?" Lady Lucilla wailed.

"You there!" a masculine voice thundered overhead, the vaulted ceiling echoing the gentleman's indignation.

One of Juliana's sisters squealed in fright. Four pairs of eyes looked heavenward.

Although his face was cast in shadows, Alexius deduced that they had found the haughty Lord Duncombe.

"This is a private house," the man announced, not moving from his position on the upper landing. In his hand was a loaded pistol, which he had aimed at Alexius. "You are all trespassing. Leave this house or I will have you put in chains and dragged in front of the magistrate."

Lady Duncombe cocked her head to the side. "Oliver? Is that you?" She took several risky steps forward. "Where is Juliana?"

"Madam, please," Alexius hissed.

The realization that the trespassers were family did not diminish the marquess's hostile demeanor. "Juliana is resting upstairs. The physician gave her some laudanum to soothe her nerves. Come back tomorrow, and pay your respects at a proper hour. Now leave!"

"Of all the nerve—!" murmured Lady Cordelia. "We are family, you pompous twit!"

Duncombe fired the pistol. All three women screamed and scattered in opposite directions with their hands over their ears as the Dresden hand-painted urn, the centerpiece of the round table near the bottom of the staircase, exploded. Alexius charged up the stairs. The marquess had been aiming at Alexius's chest when he had pulled the trigger. However, distance and panic had caused the bullet to go awry.

Alexius was not going to give the man a second chance. As he raced up the stairs, Duncombe was attempting to reload the damn pistol. If he got off another shot, this one would be harder to avoid. With his heartbeat pounding in his ears, Alexius reached the top landing just as the marquess had finished loading his weapon.

"Sinclair!" the marchioness yelled from below.

Recognition flared in Duncombe's gray eyes and one side of his mouth curled into a sneer. Without issuing a warning, he aimed and fired the dueling pistol.

Bloody miserable bastard!

The .65-caliber bullet grazed Alexius's left shoulder. Christ, it stung! He lurched forward and collided into Duncombe. Both men fell to the floor. The empty pistol and copper flask skidded out of reach as the two men wrestled for dominance.

He cursed when the marquess landed a hard blow into Alexius's shoulder. Instead of pressing his advantage, Duncombe crawled away and stumbled to his feet. He ran for the stairs, hoping to reach the next landing.

Coward.

Panting heavily, Alexius trailed after his quarry. His shoulder burned, but the wound was not fatal. He grabbed the wood newel and propelled himself forward up the stairs. Duncombe had told them that Juliana was sleeping in one of the bedchambers. Was the man so pathetic that he planned to bargain his life for Juliana's?

"Duncombe!"

Alexius caught the man by the waist and threw him up against the closest wall. "Where is she?"

He seized the marquess by the back of his neck. On the landing below Alexius could hear Lady Duncombe and her daughters. He did not have much time before the older woman interfered.

Duncombe grunted as the side of his face collided with a closed door. Alexius spun the man around and

sent him careening into the bedchamber door across
the hall.

Alexius stalked over and pulled the man up by his
hair. He noted impassively that Duncombe's attire was
informal. The man wore wrinkled trousers and a linen
shirt. The shirt was smudged, several buttons had been
undone, and his cravat had been removed.

"How many bedchambers do you have in this house,
Duncombe?" Alexius whispered in the man's ear. "I
feel like counting them."

"No!" Duncombe managed to croak before his face
connected with another door.

He crouched down, staring up at Alexius as if he
were the devil himself. He probably looked like a murderous lunatic with his clothes disheveled, blood soaking into his coat sleeve, and his hazel eyes simmering
with the need for retribution.

"Juliana!"

The silence was maddening.

"Where is she?"

He pulled Duncombe up by the front of his shirt.
Two doors later, the man was babbling and crying in-
coherently. His nose and mouth were bleeding, and
there was a nasty gash on his forehead. He was a pitiful
sight.

"Last chance, my friend," Alexius said, literally
holding the man up. "If I run out of doors, I just may
toss you out the window."

The marquess spewed spittle and blood at Alexius.
"Go to—"

He did not give the man a chance to finish. His patience at an end, Alexius did not even bother aiming for

a door. Duncombe flew face-first into one of his sour-faced ancestors' portraits that lined the hallway. The marquess had already lost consciousness when the back of his head bounced against the hardwood flooring.

"I am here."

Alexius's head snapped up at Juliana's faint plea. "Where are you?" With Duncombe already forgotten, Alexius continued down the hallway, pounding on each door. He halted when he heard her voice again.

"Sin?"

The suspicion in her tone made him grin. Alexius sagged against the door. "Who else are you expecting?" He placed his hand on the latch and quickly realized it was locked.

"My cousin has the key."

The simple statement was very telling. Alexius glared at the unconscious Duncombe. Had he locked Juliana away to punish her or did he have something sinister in mind for his cousin? Alexius did not trust himself to touch the man again for fear that he would kill Duncombe.

"Stand back," Alexius ordered, pushing himself away from the door.

Lady Duncombe could berate him later.

It took three hard kicks to break the latch. He limped into the bedchamber and fell to his knees in shock. The marchioness had told him that Duncombe had planned to marry Juliana. Alexius had never dreamed that the man would be capable of torture.

Duncombe had tied Juliana to one of the bedposts at the end of the bed. He had stripped her of her dress, and her undergarments were in tatters.

"Juliana."

Alexius hastily crawled toward the bed and dug his fingers inside his boot to retrieve his knife. His hands were shaking as he gently sawed the blade through Duncombe's cravat.

Juliana cried out as Alexius lowered her arms to her lap. The long hours tied to the bedpost had strained her muscles. How many hours had she been alone with her cousin? What had he done to her?

Alexius brushed the blond strands of hair from her face. His jaw clenched when he noticed her swollen lip and the signs of bruising on her cheek.

"Forgive me, Juliana. I wish I had found you sooner."

"Sin." She said his name softly, her eyes swimming with relief and gratitude. "My cousin—"

"Can no longer hurt you." Alexius removed the rag that held her wrists together.

She winced and rubbed them.

He swallowed, his throat aching with the effort. "How— how badly are you hurt?" Alexius felt helpless. He needed to know what had happened, but he did not want to upset her. "Do we— Should I summon a surgeon?"

Juliana slowly moved to the edge of the mattress. She gingerly touched the corner of her mouth and grimaced. "No. No surgeon. I am unhurt."

"Hardly that!"

She started at his harsh retort. "He frightened me. I have some bruises from the—" Her green eyes suddenly widened as she realized what Alexius was asking of her. "No, he did not touch me that way, though he wanted to. My cousin had— He had plans."

Juliana did not need to elaborate. Alexius longed to pull her into his arms and hold her, but she seemed so fragile and close to collapsing. She had been so brave, had gone through so much. He did not want to shatter her hard-won composure. Instead he threaded his fingers through hers and held her hand tightly.

She stiffened but did not pull away.

Her gaze lifted from their joined hands to his bloodied shoulder.

"Sin, you are bleeding."

Alexius glanced down and frowned. He had been so distracted by Juliana, he had forgotten about the wound. "It is nothing. A slight mishap."

"Sinclair? Juliana?" The marchioness paused. "Oliver?"

Both of them stared at the open door. In the ensuing silence, Lady Duncombe and her daughters had ventured upstairs.

"Oh, my heavens!"

She had stumbled across the unconscious Lord Duncombe.

Alexius held his breath and silently counted the seconds until the lady discovered the damaged door.

Chapter Twenty-four

SIN HAD WANTED to summon the constable.

Juliana had refused.

She had seen her cousin's battered face as they had walked past him in the hallway. Although she was angry and hurt by what the marquess had done to her, Juliana knew that the magistrate's sentence would not be as severe as Sin's punishment.

Besides, the family could not bear the scrutiny of another scandal.

If Lord Duncombe was as intelligent as he had always claimed, he would leave London and distance himself from the vengeful Lord Sinclair.

It might take years for Sin to recover.

Juliana had seen the horror on the gentleman's face when he entered the bedchamber, the fury at what her cousin had done to her.

No, Sin was not the forgiving sort.

"You cannot challenge him."

Sitting across from her in the cramped compartment of the coach with her sister Lucilla sitting beside him, Sin crossed his arms at Juliana's outburst and raised his right eyebrow questioningly.

"Whom do you refer to? Gomfrey or Duncombe?"

"Cease teasing her, Sinclair," her mother said, stirring to Juliana's defense. "She believes you are serious."

Neither the marchioness nor Cordelia had strayed from Juliana's side since they had walked into Lord Duncombe's bedchamber.

"Who says that I am not?" Sin countered dryly.

Juliana tightly clasped the edges of the blanket that had been removed from Duncombe's bed. She had left her evening dress behind.

"And if I say both?"

The white of his teeth gleamed under the warm light of the coach's lanterns. "Then you might not like my answer."

"But—"

"Gomfrey and Duncombe are my business, Juliana," Sin said ominously. "You got your way about the magistrate. Let me have mine."

He spoke so calmly about committing violence that she half-expected her mother to scold him. Maman— to Juliana's surprise—was content to leave the entire matter in Sin's hands.

"You are not a cold-blooded murderer, Sin."

He looked at Juliana in stark disbelief. "You should know better than most that I am capable of anything when provoked."

She bowed her head.

There was nothing she could say to refute his claim. Sin had proved that he could be quite cold and ruthless.

"Sinclair, my boy," her mother said, her voice tinged with unexpected warmth. "How is your shoulder? Should we call for a surgeon?"

Juliana watched as Sin poked at the bloodstain on his coat. When she had asked him about the blood, he had brushed aside the question.

"There is no need to worry. The bullet just grazed me." He peered at his fingers and held them closer to the lantern. "The bleeding has stopped. I will tend to the wound later."

"You were so courageous running after our cousin after the first bullet shattered the urn," Cordelia confessed. "He could have killed you."

Sin looked amused. "He was *trying* to kill me."

Lucilla clapped her hands over her ears. "Oh, I cannot hear another word about this."

"That urn was a Dresden, you know," her mother sighed.

Juliana gaped at the man sitting across from her. "You were shot? Lord Duncombe tried to kill you?"

"Twice," Lucilla added with a ladylike shudder.

Why had no one told her?

Her and Sin's gazes locked. His expression was enigmatic in the shadows. "It takes nerve and skill to aim a pistol at a man. Fortunately, your cousin lacked both. There is no reason to fret, Juliana. All Duncombe did was ruin one of my favorite coats."

It was an attempt at humor. A very poor one, indeed.

Juliana felt her mother's hand on her cheek. "Regardless, you have this family's gratitude. Oliver almost succeeded in marrying my girl. It would have been a dreadful match."

She silently agreed. "He had a spy. Someone he hired to watch us."

The news stunned everyone.

Cordelia was the first to recover. "Did he tell you the name of his spy?"

"No, but it was someone who was aware of Maman's plans to bring us to London. Someone who visited us in the country, and here in London."

No one had a suitable response. Juliana laid her head on her mother's shoulder. She closed her eyes and took comfort in the familiar rumbling and squeaks as the coach brought them closer to home.

"What if the spy was Mr. Stepkins?"

Her eyes snapped opened at Lucilla's question. Juliana could see that the mere suggestion that Lucilla's adoring Mr. Stepkins could be their cousin's spy was distressing to her.

"I met him in the village." She glanced unhappily at her sister. "Cordelia, you were there. He was so attentive, so witty."

"Did he question you about Juliana?" Sin asked, drawing Lucilla's gaze away from her sister's face.

Lucilla made a wordless sound of frustration. "We talked about everything. Naturally he was curious about my family. He was so thrilled when I told him that we would be traveling to London."

Cordelia reached over and touched Lucilla on the hand. "And then, he suddenly stopped calling on you."

"As did Lord Fisken," Lucilla replied icily. "We both agreed that their absence had to do with—"

Lucilla noticed Sin's keen regard and hastily looked away.

Both of Juliana's sisters believed she was responsible for chasing away their suitors.

She coughed into her hand and delicately cleared her throat. "I doubt your Mr. Stepkins was the spy, Lucilla. It could have been anyone."

Without speaking, Sin chastised Juliana with a flinty glance.

She inched closer to her mother's side. The argument sounded weak even to Juliana's ears.

The coachman called out, and the wheels of the coach slowed until they had reached a complete stop. The compartment wobbled as a groom hopped down. The door opened. They had arrived at the town house.

"Will you join us, Sinclair?" her mother asked.

Juliana sensed his gaze still rested on her. They had much to settle between them. However, it would not happen this evening. She refused to give him any encouragement.

Sin must have sensed this, too. As he descended from the coach, he held out his hand to the marchioness. "No, madam, I believe I should continue home."

One by one, Juliana's mother and sisters accepted Sinclair's assistance as they disembarked from the coach. Juliana was the last. As she stepped out, a gust of wind caught her hair, causing the ends to dance on the air.

Before she lost her nerve, she blurted out, "Would you answer a question, my lord?"

"Perhaps."

She straightened her shoulders. "Why did she do it?

Why did your half sister send you to me?" she asked, loathing the slight quiver in her voice.

Sin braced the palm of his hand against the side of the coach. Although she could not see his face distinctly, she could sense his reluctance. "Lord Kyd. My sister loves him. For months, he had become rather secretive. She feared that she was losing him to another woman. When she saw him paying attention to you, she believed that you had stolen him from her."

"Oh." Juliana nodded as if she understood, but she truly did not. She and Lord Kyd had shared an interest in music. He had never shared his private life with her. "You seduced me because of my association with Lord Kyd?"

She felt light-headed and was half-tempted to climb back into the coach so she could sit down.

"I approached you because my sister asked it of me. My sister is all the family that I have left, and she was convinced that you were the reason for the baron's reluctance to press for her hand. She was upset and I was protective." He paused as if measuring his next words. "However, let me be clear. No one rules me, Juliana. Not even my sister. I pursued you because I wanted you. I was not thinking about revenge when I took your innocence."

She did not want to talk about their lovemaking. "You know, Lady Gredell had nothing to fear," Juliana said sadly.

Regret lined his handsome face. "No."

How silly of her. Of course Sin knew. He had breached more than her body. She had let him into her heart. Even if he had not pursued her with calculated malice, he had not considered that by giving in to his selfish desires he had still managed to carry out his sister's petty revenge against the lady she viewed as her chief rival for Lord Kyd's affections.

"Thank you for your belated honesty."

Her thoughts in turmoil, she whirled away from him. Her fingers absently stroked the string of pearls Sin had given her as she stepped away determined to distance herself from the man who had hurt her in a manner far worse than Lord Gomfrey and her cousin.

And then she recalled Lord Duncombe's harsh words.

"I was told that Sinclair gifts all his mistresses with a string of pearls. He has a rather unique manner in which he bestows his expensive gift—"

Juliana turned around and returned to the coach. Sin was waiting for her, watching her expectantly.

"One more thing . . ."

She tugged viciously on the necklace, snapping the string. Loose pearls bounced and rolled off her as she held out the coiled string of pearls to Sin.

"Although I appreciate what you have done for me and my family, I hope you will understand that I never want to see you again." Juliana prayed the darkness hid her tears. "Nor do I wish to keep your beautiful gift. It reminds me that I was no different than any other lady that has caught your eye. So you will have to find another foolish lady with whom to play your wicked games, Lord Sinclair. It is fortunate that London provides you with so many."

He flinched as if she had struck him. When he did not take the necklace from her hand, she moved up to

him, took his hand, and gently pressed the necklace
into his palm.

With the dignified bearing that Lord Duncombe had
once found charming in the thirteen-year-old Juliana,
she turned her back on Sin and walked away.

"So you have been trying to live up to the name your
mother gave you."

Alexius had not been surprised to find Frost waiting
for him. When he had arrived home, Hembry had revealed that he had invited the earl to wait for his friend
in the library. Never one to be idle, Frost had poured a
glass of Alexius's best brandy and had taken it upon
himself to clean his dueling pistols.

"I am too exhausted for cryptic statements, Frost."
Alexius removed his coat and dropped it onto a nearby
chair. His linen shirt was a gory sight. The blood covering the front of his shirt had fused the cloth to his
chest. Thank goodness he had refused Lady Duncombe's
offer to see to his wounded shoulder. Ladies tended to
be a trifle upset and prone to fuss.

He stripped off his shirt, taking care not to reopen
his injury.

Frost glanced up from his work. "Did you not once
tell me that your mother chose the name Alexius because she believed the word to mean 'defender' or 'pro-
tector'?"

"That was what Belle told me when I was a boy." He
grimaced and scraped some of the blood away from
around the raw-looking furrow. "My father, on the
other hand, told me a different tale. This one involved a

Byzantine emperor who usurped the throne from his brother, gouged out his eyes, and locked him away in the dungeon. If he lived today, you would probably nominate him for our little club."

The earl chuckled at the taunting remark. "Charming. Nevertheless, after observing you these past weeks, I am prone to believe your sister's story. You have too much of your mother's blood in you, Sin, and whether you want to admit it or not, your father hated you for it."

The explanation would do as well as any other, Alexius mused. No matter what he had done to prove himself to his father, the elder Sinclair had not been satisfied. In the end, the hate had been mutual.

"Excuse the interruption, my lords."

Hembry entered the library carrying a basin of steaming water and materials to bandage his lord's injuries.

Alexius took the basin from the butler and carried it to the desk. Frost set aside the pistol he was holding and stood up.

"Allow me, Hembry," his friend said, relieving the butler of his burden. "I will take care of your master. He will need a hot meal. I will wager he has not eaten a morsel all day." He pushed a clean towel into the hot water and squeezed out the excess liquid.

"I will see to it at once, Lord Chillingsworth."

To Alexius, Frost said, "Sit."

"Does everyone rush to do your bidding, Frost?" Alexius hissed as the earl unceremoniously pressed the heated towel against the gash in his shoulder. "Christ, have a care. It hurts."

His friend made a clucking noise with his tongue. "You are fortunate that Gomfrey did not shoot your ear off."

Frost assumed Alexius had sought out the man after he had called on the Ivers town house. "When I left Gomfrey, he was in no condition to stand, let alone aim a pistol at my head. No, since we last spoke I have gained a new enemy."

Frost snorted derisively at the news. Water and diluted blood dripped down Alexius's arm, chest, and back as Frost concentrated on his task. "Ah, so you did speak with Lady Juliana. Who shot you, her widowed mother, one of the sisters, or the lady herself?"

"Her cousin. Lord Duncombe."

Alexius recounted the hours after he and Frost had parted ways. By the time Alexius had finished, Frost had managed to do an adequate job bandaging his shoulder.

He leaned over and grabbed the clean linen shirt Hembry had brought him. "So someone had told her about your fondness for quims and pearls," Frost mused with humor dancing in his eyes. "Damn awkward."

Alexius suspected Gomfrey had told her.

With Frost's assistance, Alexius shoved his arm through the sleeve and pulled the shirt over his head. "Juliana tore the string of pearls from her neck and pressed the necklace into my hands." Alexius scratched the side of his jaw, recalling the pain in her eyes and the bruise on her cheek. "I can hardly blame her for being angry about the necklace. It was . . . a cruel jest. One I have played with countless ladies, and yet I did not care one whit about them when I walked away."

"You were an arse."

Alexius's hot gaze locked on his friend's mildly sympathetic expression. "Leave it to you, Frost, to be so elegantly simple when you are insulting me. I know you think me a fool, but I care about Juliana. I hurt her, and my chest aches knowing that she hates me for it. When the marchioness told me that Juliana was going to marry her cousin, I was willing to kill for her. Damn me, I think I have fallen in love with her."

Frost cuffed Alexius on the top of the head.

"What was that for?"

"For taking leave of your senses," his friend replied. "A lady's heart is not worth the grief and loss of freedom. Love ruins a good man." He picked up the dueling pistol from the desk. "You might as well stick the muzzle in your ear and pull the trigger. At least it would be a merciful death."

Alexius laughed and pushed the pistol away from his face. "You must have been hatched from an egg. Is your sister aware of your cynical views about her sex?"

The amusement dimmed in Frost's gaze. "I have done my duty toward Regan. She would be an ungrateful brat to complain."

He said nothing more about the girl. In truth, Regan was probably the only female who had dented Frost's cynical heart. After their parents' deaths, the earl had become her guardian and for years the child had run wild. It was only the insistence of a distant cousin that forced Frost to concede that Regan needed more attention than Frost could provide for her. Ignoring his sister's vehement protests, he had sent the girl away to a girls' boarding school.

Neither sibling seemed happy with the arrangement.

And Regan had yet to forgive her brother for his high-handedness.

Frost crossed his arms. "I assume this business with Lady Juliana is not finished."

"According to her, we are through. It would be kinder to respect her wishes." Alexius thought of the broken string of pearls tucked away in the inner pocket of his coat. He was finished with games.

"Kinder, perhaps," Frost agreed. "However, you have never been sensible about this woman."

"True," he said as a ghost of a smile flickered in his eyes.

Juliana believed that his sister had been the sole reason for his pursuit. Well, that and lust. Alexius had been too angry to contradict her. Nonetheless, ever since he had stared up into the Lettlecotts' hazel tree and seen her startled face, Alexius had desired her. He craved to be near her. Nothing had changed.

"Gomfrey and her damn cousin still need to be dealt with." Alexius would not be satisfied until he had put a bullet in each man.

"In the upcoming days, I look forward to watching your fumbled attempts to win Lady Juliana. And if all else fails, you can use the pistol on yourself."

Chapter Twenty-five

"THERE IS NO need for pretenses," Cordelia said as she entered the bedchamber. "You watched him depart, did you not?"

Juliana could feel the heat of a blush creeping onto her face. "I did no such thing. The man is a liar and an utter beast."

The moment she had heard her sister's footfalls, Juliana had scurried from the window to the chair positioned next to her small writing table.

"Did Maman invite Sinclair into the drawing room?"

"Of course." Cordelia clasped the back of a delicately fashioned oak and brass chair and dragged it several yards until she had positioned it beside Juliana's. "In spite of his obvious faults, the gentleman did rescue you from a disastrous marriage with our cousin. Rest assured, Maman has only partially forgiven him. However, Lord Sinclair will accept any mercy bestowed upon him, since you offer him none." She sat down and fussed with her dress.

A week had passed since Juliana had pushed the broken pearl necklace into Sin's hand and walked away. He had returned to the town house twice, asking for her. This was his third visit to their house.

Although she had refused to come downstairs, on each occasion, Maman and Juliana's sisters had taken pity on him and received him in the drawing room. It was difficult not to feel a prick of betrayal toward her family. Still, it had not prevented her from quizzing her sisters about each visit.

"He seemed well?"

It was the same question that Juliana had asked after each visit.

Cordelia pretended to contemplate her reply. "Lord Sinclair claims his shoulder wound is not troubling him at all. I noticed that his movements as he bowed to us seemed unhindered, so perhaps he is telling the truth."

For once.

Juliana stared at her clasped hands as they rested on the writing table. The man did not deserve her concern, but he had it. Blast him! His death would not ease her heart. Nevertheless, she wished there was something she could do about the hurt and anger that plagued her in quiet moments.

"Lord Sinclair asked for you," her sister confessed without prompting. "Maman told him that you were resting. However, I do not think he believed her."

"I *was* resting, Cordelia." Juliana unclasped her hands and rubbed her temples. "Nor do I care what he thinks." She did not understand why he had returned to their house three times when he had nothing further to gain.

"If it were true, you would not be so sad." Her sister reached over and placed a tiny bundle on the writing table. "Lord Sinclair asked me to give this to you."

Juliana stopped rubbing her temples and stared at the small cloth-wrapped bundle on the table. He had brought flowers on his previous visits. She had assumed he had brought them to soften her mother's disposition. This gift, nevertheless, was different. Juliana picked it up. It was smaller than her fist and secured with a narrow red ribbon. "Was there a message?"

"Yes, but Maman and I thought it rather odd. He said that he had lost his taste for pearls."

"He did?"

Juliana's heart leaped in her chest at the thought that he was giving up his wicked ways for her. It was followed promptly by a scowl, as she reminded herself that she no longer cared how the marquess spent his days—or nights.

"Was that the entire message?"

"He went on to say that it was something whimsical and it made him think of you." Cordelia could not resist leaning forward as Juliana untied the ribbon. "What is it?"

Juliana could not fathom Sin procuring anything whimsical. Nevertheless, she was relieved that he was not returning the string of pearls that she had torn from her neck and tossed at him. She would have taken a hammer to each pearl and pounded them into dust if he had tried.

She unfolded the fabric until Sin's gift gleamed at

her from its green velvet wrapping. It was a gold brooch. Speechless, Juliana gaped at the man's audacity.

Her sister peered closer and then sniffed. "Whimsical, indeed. Why would a spray of gold leaves remind him of you?"

Juliana said nothing. It was a lovely piece, the detail so refined that she immediately recognized the large tooth-edged, heart-shaped leaves. Hazel tree leaves. Nestled within three leaves were a cluster of nuts. Beneath the gold cupules were large nutlike pearls.

Sin wanted her to remember that night in Lord Lettlecott's back gardens. While she had clung precariously to a bough of the hazel tree, Sin and his hostess had chosen the same tree for their tryst. His fortuitous discovery of Juliana's presence had ended his love play with the lady.

Juliana bit her lower lip as she studiously admired the brooch. They had been strangers. Sin had not known her name, and still he had desired her. She had been aware of his masculine appreciation. He had even protected her from Lady Lettlecott's fury and the awkward position of having to explain why she had been spying on them.

As clever as Sin was, he could not have contrived their outrageous first encounter even at his sister's behest.

Still, the gentleman had not been squeamish about mixing his desire for her with his sister's need to vanquish a potential rival. Juliana sighed and set the brooch on the velvet.

"Juliana?"

"Hmm?" Juliana belatedly recalled that she had not

answered Cordelia's question. "Oh, I fear the purpose behind Sinclair's gift is unclear," she lied.

"You are making a fool out of yourself!"

Alexius was not surprised by his sister's incensed pronouncement, only that it had taken her eight days to confront him. For several days he had ignored a dozen of her imperial missives summoning him to her town house. Never one to be thwarted, Belinda had cornered one of his friends to learn Alexius's whereabouts this evening.

If he could figure out which one of the traitorous gents had set about to ruin his evening, Alexius was tempted to return the favor.

"Good evening, Belle. As usual, you look delectable," he said, fingering the twinkling emerald and diamond drops dangling from her ears. "Someone has been generous with you. Lord Kyd?"

Belinda was in no mood for Alexius's flattery. "I have not chased you all over London to discuss my new earrings. What I want to know is, have you taken leave of all your senses? For the past week, my drawing room has been filled with visitors who delight in regaling me with tales about my beloved brother. None of which are becoming to you and the Sinclair name."

"You have never been one to listen to the gossips," he said dismissively.

Belinda grabbed his forearm before he could walk away. "Is it true that you accosted Lord Gomfrey in his library, and then a day later faced him at dawn? Someone told me that your bullet shattered his left elbow."

Alexius clamped his fingers around his sister's wrist and dragged her to the closest alcove. "Have a care, my darling sister. A little louder and I will be forced to leave the country."

"And there are rumors that you are hunting Lord Duncombe, but the gentleman has eluded you."

The recollection of discovering Juliana locked in a bedchamber and tied to one of the bedposts still haunted Alexius. "The gentleman deserves far worse than a festering bullet wound for attempting to violate his young cousin with the purpose of forcing her into marriage."

"Cousin?" Belinda's mouth curled with disdain. "You would not be speaking of Lady Juliana Ivers."

"What if I am?"

"So it is all true," she said, placing her hand over her heart. "When several of your friends told me—"

"Who? Who approached you? I want their names."

Belinda tilted her head as she studied Alexius's intimidating stance. Although she did not fear he would harm her, her unidentified ally would face her brother's wrath if she did not choose her words with care.

"Half the *ton* has been whispering in my ear, Alexius. Do you plan to shoot them all?" She sharply rapped him on the hand with her closed fan. "And for what? A silly miss who parted her legs for the first gentleman who fancied her?"

His sister's hatred toward Juliana was unjust. Nevertheless, Alexius doubted any defense on his part would only increase Belinda's ire. "Hold your viper's tongue, Belle. There are those who might think the same could be said about you."

Hurt burned in his sister's eyes. "Men are so easily beguiled by a comely face. It was apparent to everyone who observed that humiliating display in Gomfrey's theater box that Lady Juliana despises you. What do you hope to gain by this lunacy? The lady's forgiveness by fawning over the lady's insipid mother and sisters? By challenging every man who is sniffing after her?"

Alexius slammed the palm of his hand into the wall above his sister's head. Belinda started at the barely restrained violence. "Lord Kyd's interest in Lady Juliana was business in nature," he said, enunciating each word now that he had Belinda's rapt attention.

The hope that softened her expression was reserved solely for herself. "You cannot be certain—"

"Kyd told me, and he had no reason to lie." Alexius's hand slid from the wall to Belinda's shoulder. "We are selfish people, Belle. Your jealousy and my arrogance ruined a young lady's reputation. Our actions placed her in a position so that she could be preyed upon by the unscrupulous. I cannot wholly make amends for my actions; however, I can try."

"I cannot dissuade you from your fool's endeavor."

"No. Do not stand in my way." Alexius kissed his sister on the forehead and stepped away.

When he turned back toward the ballroom, he noticed Juliana and her sisters. Her discomfort was apparent even from across the room. Alexius leaned against one of the marble columns, his hungry eyes noting every detail.

From behind, his sister asked, "You are not

considering . . . marriage to the chit?" Belinda did not bother concealing her disapproval.

"Do not fret, Belle. Lady Juliana will not have me. Our tainted Sinclair blood ruins us for marriage. You should know this better than I."

Chapter Twenty-six

"HE *IS* HERE."

Juliana felt her heartbeat quicken at Cordelia's whispered words. Her gaze drifted from face to face, searching for the man whom she could never trust. The gentleman her heart could not seem to forget.

"Lord Fisken is near the doors that lead to Lord and Lady Collinge's gardens."

Though Cordelia clasped both Lucilla's and Juliana's hands, it took both sisters to keep her from dashing off in pursuit of her neglectful suitor.

Lucilla squinted at the man. The distance made her long for the spectacles that she usually refused to wear. "Maman said that Lord Fisken would be in attendance this evening. Do you think she sent him a note?"

Cordelia paled at the notion. "Maman would not dare!"

Juliana silently believed Maman would dare anything. This was her daughter's happiness at stake. "He has not moved from the doorway. Perhaps he has not noticed your arrival?" Juliana said to Cordelia, attempting to soothe her frazzled nerves.

"What if he has, and plans to shun her?"

Cordelia swayed. "Oh, I could not bear the humiliation."

Juliana glared at Lucilla. She understood that her sister was still mourning Mr. Stepkins's disappearance, which seemed to confirm that he had been hired by their cousin to spy on the family. Nevertheless, Cordelia needed their support.

"Do not listen to Lucilla. You know that she is blind without her spectacles and is not in a position to judge Lord Fisken's demeanor."

It was the only reason why Juliana had allowed her mother to talk her into attending the Collinges' ball. In the weeks since her arrival, she had lost her innocence, made enemies, been bartered to cover her mother's gambling debt, almost ravished by her hateful cousin, and deemed scandalous by most of the *ton* because of her connection to Sin. Her reputation was in tatters. Any chance to have her musical compositions published had vanished. London was finished with her. A sensible miss would concede defeat and retire to the country.

With dozens of guests weaving between Cordelia and her beloved, Juliana's breath caught in her chest as she watched the nobleman's face shift from boredom to pleasure as he recognized her sister. Cordelia, who never possessed an ounce of patience, brazenly waved at Lord Fisken. The man grinned and nodded toward the open doors, silently inviting her to walk the gardens with him.

Cordelia tore her gaze away from Lord Fisken and looked askance to her sisters. "Should I go or wait for Maman?"

Juliana ached for her sister. She understood the indecision well. "Go to him. There is no harm lingering just beyond the open doors," she said, and then gasped as her sister hugged her. "Either way, you are not alone. We will wait here for your return."

"Thank you."

Cordelia was so happy, she practically floated across the ballroom floor to join Lord Fisken. The man bowed and offered his bent arm to her. Together they disappeared through the doorway.

"Do you think this is wise?"

Juliana gave Lucilla an accessing glance. "Probably not," she said with a shrug of indifference. "We all do foolish things when we are in love."

Lucilla nodded. There was a distinct air of sadness in her gaze as she stared off into the distance. "I shall find Maman, and tell her of Lord Fisken's arrival."

"You might check the card room. Lady Collinge is an avid cardplayer and notorious for her losses. I suspect the temptation to sit at her table was too much for Maman."

Juliana smiled at Lucilla's retreating back; her brisk no-nonsense gait had not changed since she was a girl. It was then that two elderly matrons caught Juliana's eye. Both ladies were staring at her, the one on the right whispering in the other one's ear. The moment they noticed her regard, they turned away.

Without her sisters at her side, Juliana felt defenseless, a pariah cast into a tumultuous sea of the self-righteous. Suddenly she wished that she had Lucilla's poor eyesight so she was blind to the speculation, cruel delight, and pity she glimpsed as ladies and gentlemen walked past her.

"Lady Juliana."

She started at Lord Kyd's voice.

"My lord." She curtsied as he bowed. "I did not expect to see you this evening."

"This is indeed a fortuitous encounter."

He seemed oblivious to the curious glances and whispers. It was not the first time that Juliana silently wondered if Lord Kyd had learned of Lady Gredell's mischief. The gentleman seemed blissfully unaware of the grief his kindness and attention had caused Juliana. If that was true, it seemed cruel to shatter the illusion.

"How so?"

Unable to bear the scrutiny of several nearby guests, Juliana gestured for them to walk the perimeter of the room. She was grateful that he did not offer her his arm, for she would have refused. Lord Kyd simply matched her casual stride.

Without preamble, he said, "I have found you a publisher."

"Surely you jest!" She covered her mouth at her impolite outburst. "Who?"

"Me." His eyes danced in merriment at her speechlessness.

Juliana shook her head in disbelief. "When? How?"

He looked about the ballroom, seemingly reluctant to discuss the details. "Forgive me. This is not the sort of place one discusses business. However, I wanted to assure you that our efforts have not been in vain. I have taken on a partner to share the risks, and your musical compositions will be the first of many works we intend to publish."

Her vision blurred. Although she had trusted Lord Kyd, the countless rejections he had received on her behalf had been discouraging. "This is incredible news! Oh, no!" She brought her fingers to her lips. "I will be leaving London soon."

The baron halted. "This is most unfortunate. Well, perhaps you will reconsider. My partner will wish to meet you and we have much to discuss with regard to our new business venture."

Juliana's throat thickened with emotion. "My lord, you have been a good friend."

Faint lines appeared around Lord Kyd's mouth as his expression sobered. "You are being generous, Lady Juliana. Truthfully, if I had not allowed myself to be distracted by my own ambitions, I might have been a better friend to you and your family."

"I . . ." She trailed off helplessly.

"However, Sinclair settled that business with Lord Gomfrey."

So Lord Kyd knew of the earl. Then he was aware . . .

Juliana straightened as the baron's comment about Sin registered. "What do you mean by settled? How so?"

Lord Kyd belatedly caught on that his companion had been unaware of Lord Sinclair's actions. "Dear me, this is most awkward. I thought your mother had told you that Lord Sinclair had challenged Gomfrey?"

Sin had been willing to take a bullet on her behalf? "No," she said starkly.

"Well, she probably did not want to upset you," Lord Kyd said gruffly. "Sinclair's bullet struck Gomfrey in the arm. The earl will most likely spend the rest of his life thinking of Sinclair every time he raises a wineglass or fork to his mouth.

"Forgive me, Lady Juliana. It was thoughtless of me to speak of the incident." He peered at her, concerned. "You are too pale for my liking. Could I perhaps bring you something to drink?"

She glanced at the open doors to the gardens. Cordelia and Lord Fisken had not returned. "Yes, thank you. That would be nice."

Juliana would have said anything to coax the baron on his way. Why had no one told her that Sin had actually challenged Lord Gomfrey? The blasted man could have been killed!

"Once I feared that you had stolen Lord Kyd from me."

Juliana stiffened as Lady Gredell sauntered up to her.

"Lord Kyd is merely a friend."

"So Alexius tells me," the countess said, stroking the emerald and diamond necklace adorning her throat. "However, I was not wrong about your intentions. Only the gentleman."

One good thing about leaving London was the simple fact that Juliana would never have to encounter the obnoxious woman again. "I must confess,

Lady Gredell, you and your legion of lovers have mattered little to me. Perhaps if you will send me a list of names I will endeavor to avoid anyone connected with you."

"Stay away from my brother, Lady Juliana."

The countess turned on her heel and marched away. If she was truly threatened by Juliana, the lady would seek out Lord Kyd and distract him from returning with Juliana's glass of punch.

She sighed. If Lady Gredell learned of her lover's desire to publish Juliana's musical compositions, their business partnership would end as abruptly as it had been conceived.

"A terrifying creature, is she not?" Lord Chillingsworth observed, his eerie light blue gaze transfixed on the departing Lady Gredell. "In her defense, Belinda has never learned to share her playthings. Sin's interest in you threatens her perfect insular world."

"An intriguing assessment of the lady's character," Juliana mused, her mouth pursed together in distaste for the countess and the gentleman who stood beside her. "And I thought she was simply a shallow, vindictive, selfish woman who enjoyed plucking the wings off anything she considered inferior."

The earl threw back his head and laughed. "So you are not so easily cowed. I deduced as much when I saw you enter the room."

It had taken all her courage to enter the ballroom and place herself on display for the *ton*'s amusement. A part of her still longed to flee, but if Lord Chillingsworth or anyone else thought to intimidate her, they would leave disappointed.

She flipped open her fan and stirred the air around her face. "Since your dislike for me rivals Lady Gredell's, I can only assume you have something to say to me. What is it? A threat, a bribe, or perhaps something not as subtle?"

Lord Chillingsworth's lips peeled back, revealing straight, perfectly formed teeth. Like Sin and their unprincipled friends, the earl was a spectacular example of his strong bloodlines. She might have considered him handsome if not for the mocking contempt that clung to him like an unpleasant stench.

"My dear lady, I fear subtlety is a skill I have yet to master," the earl said; his pale blue eyes glinted with cold amusement. "Sin is here."

At her wide-eyed panicked expression the earl stepped in front of her, effectively blocking her instinctive urge to leave the ballroom.

"Do not fret. I wager, the last thing my friend desires is to cause you further embarrassment. Sin will keep his distance from you and your family."

Unlike his ruthless friends and family.

"Why are you telling me this, Lord Chillingsworth? Did Sin send you or is this some new form of trickery? Like Lady Gredell, I thought you preferred tormenting your quarry? Chivalry does not suit you."

The earl chuckled. "Your opinion of me is appallingly low."

"You stole a kiss minutes after encountering me at the Kempes' ball," she countered. "Nothing you have done since has corrected my initial impression that you are nothing but a scoundrel."

"True," he said with a slight bow. "This might be unpleasant to hear, but I found myself disliking you from the moment I saw you with Sin. I could tell that he had convinced himself that you were to be a simple fuck, a momentary pleasure to satisfy his hunger and his jealous sister's whim. I alone saw through Sin's lies."

Juliana thought of the brooch tucked safely away in her dressing table. She quickly banished the thought. "You were wrong, my lord."

"Was I?" He seemed to consider the notion before he discounted it with a slight shake of his head. "We shall see."

"Pray, let us not mince words. What Sin feels is guilt and a small measure of responsibility most likely impressed upon him by my well-meaning mother. Nothing more."

"Ah. Then you are not troubled by the notion that Sinclair is fighting duels in your honor?"

Lord Chillingsworth was probing for some sign of weakness. She deliberately kept her expression impassive. "I suspect Sin's duel with Lord Gomfrey was not his first meeting at dawn, nor his last. As insufferable as you and your friends are, I would daresay that the lot of you are keeping weekly appointments."

He shook off her insult, letting it roll off him like raindrops dripping from the leaves of a tree after an unexpected spring shower. "You are a stubborn woman."

Before she could step out of reach, he gently took her hand and bowed low. She felt the butterfly caress of his lips across her gloved knuckles. "And beautiful. Traits that tend to ruin a sensible man. There seems nothing to be gained in rescuing a man who does not want to be spared from his fate. I bid you good night, my lady."

Juliana did not attempt to detain the earl.

He was playing games with her, and she was in no mood to humor him. Over the edge of her fan, she was startled to see Sin. Had he observed her exchange with his friend? Apparently so. With swift, powerful strides Sin crossed the ballroom until he had caught up to Lord Chillingsworth.

Their exchange was brief. Sin's abrupt violent gestures revealed that he had not sent his friend to speak on his behalf. Lord Hugh and Lord Sainthill joined their friends, and briefly the argument escalated. She could almost hear Sin's voice above the strains of the orchestra. Suddenly Sin glanced at Juliana, and their gazes locked. She felt the impact all the way down to her toes.

She was the first to look away.

When she risked another peek, both men had left the ballroom.

Juliana told herself that the cold, hollow feeling in her stomach was relief that Sin had not tried to approach her.

From across the room, Cordelia appeared at the threshold with Lord Fisken. Her face glowed with undisguised affection for the man at her side. To the right, her mother and Lucilla were making their way to the happy couple. If there was a wedding to be planned, her mother would be intolerable to live with until she had found husbands for her other two daughters.

Juliana remained where she was, invisible and unimportant, content to watch her family's jubilation from a distance.

Chapter Twenty-seven

A WEEK AFTER the Collinges' ball, Lord Fisken formally solicited Lady Duncombe for her elder daughter's hand in marriage. The marchioness welcomed her future son-in-law warmly, believing the family's financial woes were coming to an end.

Cordelia was happy. While she and Maman planned for the autumn wedding, Lucilla had set her cap for a Sir Charles Stansbury. She had been introduced to him by Lady Collinge. Almost twelve years older, the reserved gentleman seemed rather enchanted with Lucilla's bubbly nature. Maman pronounced them a perfect match. However, Juliana was not so certain.

Her sister's enthusiasm could oftentimes be wearing on the nerves.

Especially when Lucilla seemed determined to have her way and the rest of the family was inclined to indulge her.

"Oh, you must come," Lucilla wheedled. "We will have such fun at Vauxhall."

Juliana had wanted to walk the gardens with Sin. She imagined it would have been a rowdy, crowded fair. No doubt she would have loved it. The music and the fireworks would have delighted her, and knowing Sin, he would have charmed her by stealing a kiss when no one had been looking.

"I am certain you will. Nevertheless, I prefer to remain at home this evening."

"Maman," Lucilla wailed, her high pitch causing the four ladies in the drawing room to wince. "Tell her that she *must* come with us."

Juliana sat at the writing table with several blank sheets of paper scattered across its surface. While her mother and Cordelia worked together embroidering a tablecloth, Juliana had sought solace in her music.

Her efforts were dismal at best.

Cordelia lifted her gaze from her work. "You are troubled by Lord Duncombe's letter."

Two days after the Collinges' ball, a messenger had arrived with a letter from their cousin. He expressed regret for his mistreatment of Juliana, and his desire for the family's forgiveness. Maman had tossed the letter into the fire and turned the messenger away.

"In part," Juliana admitted.

Lucilla flounced to the window and peered down at the street. "Our cousin cares naught for us. What he does fear is Sinclair's aim."

"I have to agree with our sister, Juliana," Cordelia said as she dug into the basket of thread beside her. "Lord Duncombe wrote that letter to appease the marquess.

Otherwise, it will be years before he will be able to visit London without fearing retribution from Lord Sinclair."

Juliana conjured the absurd image of Sin gripping a pistol as he chased her cousin down the streets of London. She bit her lower lip, torn between laughter and tears.

"Girls, you are frightening your sister." The marchioness jabbed her needle into the linen and reached underneath to pull it through. "Juliana, Sinclair has proved quite capable of handling himself on the dueling field. Gomfrey learned a painful lesson: that the marquess is not one to be trifled with. If Oliver possesses one ounce of wit, he has already left London for Ivers Hall."

"Lord Fisken will be joining us later at Vauxhall," Cordelia announced. "He has expressed a desire to become better acquainted with the family."

Not to be outdone, Lucilla added, "Miss Povey will be performing as a soloist. Sir Charles heard her sing at a benefit, and claims her voice is divine."

"Oh, and we should wear masks." Cordelia raised her eyebrows in an exaggerated manner, eliciting a giggle from Lucilla. "Our arrival will be heralded by the *ton* as exotic and mysterious."

Juliana lowered her head to conceal her grin. Her sisters were hopeless.

"You will join us, Daughter," her mother said, taking the decision out of Juliana's hands. "I will worry less if the family is together."

"Duncombe has left London."

Alexius raised his arms, allowing his valet to fuss

over the fit of his coat sleeve as he quietly digested the news that Duncombe had eluded him. "Are you certain?"

Vane crossed his muscular arms, straining the seams of his elegant coat. "I hired a Bow Street runner to ensure our inquiries were discreet. I believe you are acquainted with my contact."

He frowned. "Who?" His valet pushed Alexius's arms down to his sides and tugged on the coat's cuffs.

"A Mr. Stepkins."

Alexius's eyes flared in recognition. "Lady Lucilla's Mr. Stepkins?" Well, it certainly solved the mystery of the man's sudden disappearance.

Vane cocked his head and cracked his stiff neck. "Months earlier, Lord Duncombe employed him to watch over the family. It appears the marquess did not trust the widow to follow his orders."

Alexius's visits with the marchioness had revealed the lady was as stubborn as her youngest daughter. "Did Stepkins know Duncombe's whereabouts?"

Vane shook his head. "No. Stepkins considered their business concluded when Duncombe separated Lady Juliana from her family. He was concerned that if the family complained, he would be charged with kidnapping."

"Enough," Alexius softly entreated, moving away from his persistent valet and his boar-hair brush.

"At my urging, Stepkins checked the Duncombe town house. The house was empty. When he took Lady Juliana, I doubt the gentleman planned to linger."

So Duncombe was the coward Lady Duncombe accused him of being. Alexius walked over to the wardrobe and opened the double doors. Instead of the frustration simmering in his gut, he should be feeling elation. In spite of her cousin's wrongdoing, Lady Duncombe had not been enthusiastic about Alexius putting a bullet into the man. She had warned Alexius that Juliana would not approve of his need for revenge.

The lady had made it clear that there was very little about him that she approved of. Encounters with his sister and Frost had not improved Juliana's opinion.

Alexius opened the top drawer within the wardrobe and retrieved several black velvet masks. He accepted his hat from the valet and handed one of the masks to his friend.

"Where are we going?" Vane asked.

"Let us stop at the club and collect the others," Alexius said as he walked through the doorway, knowing curiosity would prompt Vane to follow. "I feel like prowling Vauxhall this evening."

Wearing a dark blue evening dress, Juliana slipped her mask over the upper portion of her face. The blue velvet mask had been adorned with gold sequins, seed pearls, and downy ostrich plumes. In a nervous gesture, her fingers caressed Sin's brooch as she strolled along Vauxhall's pathways with her mother and sisters. Juliana was not certain what had prompted her to pin the delicate trinket to her bodice this evening. Her mother and sisters had complimented Juliana on her decision but, for once, did not mention the marquess.

"Do you see him?" Cordelia demanded, unhappy

with her mask because the eyeholes had been cut too small. "He promised to join us."

Lord Fisken would be difficult to find among the thousands of people in attendance. The revelers were a mix of masked merrymakers, members of the lower class and the fashionable. The latter did not seem to care that they were mingling with their inferiors. Amusements and strong spirits were enjoyed by one and all.

"In this throng, the sensible approach for Lord Fisken would be to search for us near the orchestra."

When Cordelia did not agree, Juliana glanced back at her. The poor thing was still struggling with her exotic mask. "Here, permit me."

Juliana repositioned her sister's mask. "Better?"

"Yes, thank you."

"Hurry, my girls," their mother implored, quickening her pace. "Do you not hear the music? We are late!"

"Maman, there is no cause for haste," Juliana said, her voice rich with laughter as the marchioness revealed a goodly portion of ankle to anyone curious enough to watch the harried quartet. "Music is for one's ears, not eyes."

"I will tolerate none of your cheek, Juliana." Her mother gave her an exasperated look. "Poor Lord Fisken will think that we have abandoned him."

Dear heaven, Juliana silently mused, spare her the misery of fretting mothers and anxious sisters in love. They entered the Grove; the twinkling lights of the pavilion and music beckoned. Beneath the colonnades, people sampled their supper boxes and washed their meal down with punch or wine.

"Thank goodness," Lucilla muttered, relieved that she and her family had arrived at their destination slightly ruffled but relatively in one piece.

Juliana closed her eyes and savored the music. It flowed through her and was as heady as wine to her senses. Music was something that she understood. It humbled and awed her and brought comfort to those who despaired.

She opened her eyes as the final notes of the piece waned. There was a brief pause while the musicians shuffled papers and readied their instruments. Amid the laughter and the low din of hundreds of conversations, there was anticipation in the air.

"It appears we have not missed Miss Povey's performance, after all," Juliana said, not really addressing anyone in particular.

Her mother placed her hand on Juliana's shoulder in a comforting gesture. This prompted Juliana to turn her head to the side and kiss the older woman's fingers.

The orchestra began to play.

Juliana's head snapped upright at the first familiar notes. This was her sonata! With her hand over her mouth, her brilliant green gaze shifted from Lucilla, her mother, and Cordelia.

This was Juliana's composition that she teasingly had named "Passion." She had composed it solely for the pianoforte. However, someone had altered her arrangement so the fluid notes of a violin and flute blended harmoniously with the pianoforte.

The beauty of the piece overwhelmed her.

When the trio had finished, everyone applauded with

such enthusiasm, Juliana could no longer fight back her tears.

"Maman," she sobbed, removing her mask. "How is this possible?"

Lucilla and Cordelia removed their masks. There were joyful tears in their eyes, too.

The marchioness untied her mask. "Your beautiful music was meant to be shared, my girl. Oh, how proud your father would be!"

Juliana gave her mother a fierce hug. "How did you manage it? Who did you bribe?"

Lady Duncombe pulled back from their embrace laughing. "No one. I wish I could take the credit. Nevertheless, I was only responsible for getting you here in time for the performance."

"And you saw how well that went," Cordelia teased.

Juliana's forehead creased in puzzlement. "Then who? Lord Kyd?"

The marchioness waved her hand in a careless gesture. "Granted, he had his hand in this business. Still, there is another . . ." She let her words trail off as she nodded shrewdly at someone who was standing just beyond Juliana's shoulder.

No, it could not be . . .

Juliana whirled around, her heart in her throat at the slightest chance she might be wrong.

Dressed magnificently in black, Sin tugged the black velvet mask from his face. His hazel green eyes flared in fierce pleasure as he noticed that she had worn his brooch this evening. Extending his bent arm, he said huskily, "Care to walk with me beneath the stars, my bewitching *lybbestre*?"

Chapter Twenty-eight

A SPEECHLESS JULIANA was a small wonder to behold. However, Alexius did not expect the lady to remain docile for long. With Lady Duncombe's blessing, he had tucked Juliana's arm into the crook of his arm and led her out of the Grove.

"I do not understand," she said finally, her voice cracking with emotion. "Why did you do it?"

Privacy was elusive along the main walkways, so Alexius tugged her off the path lit by variegated lamps and into the shadows a small, narrow copse of elm trees provided.

Alexius wiped the tears on her cheeks away with his thumb.

"There, there, love, I did not mean to make you cry," he crooned, and kissed her tenderly on the lips. "You have shed enough of them on my behalf."

Juliana shuddered. "If you did this out of pity—"

"Not pity," he said, cutting off her accusation. "I did this— I know about your business venture with Lord Kyd."

"How could you?"

Alexius smiled at her outrage. It was a sign that his *lybbestre* had recovered from her shock and was ready to engage him as his equal. He wanted to win her fairly.

"I am Kyd's silent partner in his publishing venture."

"What?"

The lamps from the walkway provided enough light for Alexius to glimpse Juliana's disbelief. She gave him an unladylike shove. Laughing, Alexius stumbled back against the trunk of an elm tree.

"How could you?"

He gently folded his hand over hers and held it over his heart. "How could I not? I know little about composing, but your music was meant to be heard beyond your mother's drawing room. Forgive me for not truly understanding until now what it meant to you."

"This is unlike you," she said, shaking her head. "This is another one of your games—"

Alexius seized her by the shoulders and spun her about so that her back was pressed against the trunk of the tree. "You are correct. I do want something from you. I would give away my fortune and title to claim it. I want your forgiveness."

"Sin—"

"Not Sin," he said bitterly. "Sin was taught selfishness from the cradle. It is all he ever knew until he glanced up and saw you in the Lettlecotts' hazel tree. He would tell you pretty lies, and manipulate you until you gave him what he craved."

He bowed his head, lightly touching his forehead to hers. "However, Alexius loves you. He longs to hold you in his arms each night. He will fight your battles, and grant all your unspoken dreams."

Alexius traced the arch of each eyebrow with feather-like kisses.

"Granted, Sin is as much a part of me as Alexius," he said, slightly amused by his flaws as much as he was about his tarnished virtues. "Nevertheless, neither side can be whole without you. If you will have me, I wish to marry you."

"Oh!"

It was not the response Alexius had conjured in his mind.

She hiccupped and reached for her reticule, realizing belatedly that she had dropped it when she saw him in the Grove. Most likely her family had retrieved it.

Alexius retrieved a handkerchief from the inner pocket of his coat and handed it to her. "You cannot forgive me," he said dully.

She grimaced, looking as tormented as he felt. "My lord, it is not so simple."

"It never is, my dear cousin," Lord Duncombe said, pressing the muzzle of his loaded pistol to the back of Sin's head.

Juliana watched in horror as Sin slowly straightened. He would have stepped away, in a noble attempt to protect her from the discharge of her cousin's pistol, but she grabbed Sin's hands.

Mute fury burned in Sin's hazel green eyes. However, Juliana shook her head and would not release him.

Lord Duncombe chuckled at their silent deadlock of wills. "Juliana has a stubborn streak that can oftentimes be troublesome, can it not, Sinclair?"

Without taking his gaze from Sin's head, her cousin said, "Be a good girl, and move away from Sinclair. That is such a lovely dress. If I grow impatient, I would not want to muss it with your lover's blood and gore."

"Heed him," Sin said tersely, his eyes willing her to comply.

Reluctantly Juliana let go of Sin's hands and took several steps to the right.

"Not too far, Cousin," Lord Duncombe scolded. "You will be unhappy with the outcome should you think to run for help."

In the distance, fireworks exploded overhead. The spectators cheered with each salvo, drowning out the orchestra. The walkway was empty; the shadows reaching across the pebbled path reminded her of spectral fingers. Even if Juliana could have cried out to a passerby, her cousin would discharge his pistol and Sin would be dead.

Juliana licked the dryness from her lips. "Cousin, I beg you to end this madness. Lower the pistol, and I—I will leave with you."

"No!"

She ignored Sin's guttural outburst.

"You asked for the family's forgiveness." She cast a nervous look at Sin. "You have it. Please."

Lord Duncombe sneered. "I doubt your lover will be so generous. Sinclair and his friends have been scouring London for me, though I have managed to elude them for more than a week."

Sin crossed his arms. Juliana silently marveled at his composure. Though he was noticeably enraged, one would never guess that he was concerned that he had the barrel of a pistol aimed at his head. "Who helped you? Stepkins?"

"Lucilla's Mr. Stepkins?" Juliana asked, grateful that her sister had swiftly recovered from her loss.

"Stepkins is a Bow Street runner," Sin told Juliana. "Or was. Magistrates tend to frown upon kidnapping and murder."

"Enough!"

Juliana visibly flinched at her cousin's thundering order.

"How I eluded you and your friends is not important," he said, digging the barrel of the pistol into the back of Sin's head. "Juliana, come to me. Regrettably, Sinclair is about to face his demise at the hands of a footpad."

"No!"

For the first time, Lord Duncombe stared at her, his face twisted with hurt and disbelief. "Do you love him so much that you are willing to die in his stead?"

Juliana somberly nodded. "Yes."

Her cousin's eyes flared at her insolence. A growl rumbled in his throat as he redirected his aim at Juliana's horrified face.

Sin did not hesitate.

He slammed his arm skyward, altering Duncombe's aim. Juliana covered her ears and screamed as the pistol discharged harmlessly into the air.

Or so it had seemed.

Her cousin's face went white and he staggered back a step. Sin plucked the pistol from the marquess's hand before he thought to use it as a club. Lord Duncombe collapsed in Sin's arms.

Juliana started as she realized that they were not alone. Three men seemed to rise up from the shadows. They were Sin's friends: Lord Vanewright, Lord Sainthill, and Lord Chillingsworth. Clutched in Chillingsworth's lowered hand was a pistol.

"Did I kill him?"

Sin crouched down and lowered the injured marquess to the ground.

"Time will tell."

"I will find a constable," Lord Vanewright volunteered. He set off down the walkway at a brisk pace.

Lord Chillingsworth did not seem to care one way or the other if her cousin perished. He pointed the pistol in Sin's general direction. "Christ, Sinclair, I thought you were planning to talk the bastard to death."

Sin glared up at his friend. "I was keeping him distracted so one of you could knock him out before Juliana taunted him into shooting her."

Sin's angry gaze narrowed on her. His expression softened. "So you love me."

Juliana almost choked on her tongue. The man was an arrogant beast to tease her after everything they had been through. Overcome with a nauseating wave of dizziness, she brought her hand to her head and swayed.

"Catch her!"

There was nothing Juliana could do to prevent the cloying blackness from swallowing her.

Chapter Twenty-nine

IT HAD BEEN a difficult night for everyone.

With her hand on the balustrade, Juliana slowly climbed the stairs as feelings of uncertainty threatened her newly won composure. It had been humiliating to awaken to the acrid scent of hartshorn as her frantic mother wafted her favorite silver oblong-shaped vinaigrette under Juliana's nose.

A large crowd had gathered around them. The curious came to see the dying man. Though to be fair, there were some who just wanted to help. There had been familiar faces, and sober ones of authority. In the confusion, her mother and sisters had bundled Juliana into a coach with the assistance of Sin's friends.

No one seemed to know Sin's whereabouts.

Hours later, when a constable had knocked on the front door of her family's town house, Juliana had to accept the fact that Sin was deliberately distancing himself from her and her family. As she thought about those frightening minutes when her cousin aimed the pistol at Sin's head, she realized that Sin and his friends had set a trap for Lord Duncombe. The outcome had not gone according to plan.

Juliana padded silently down the hall until she reached the bedchamber. She raised her fist to knock and then lowered her arm until her fingers closed around the latch. The battle she was about to initiate would not be won by fairness.

She opened the door and stepped into the dark interior.

"You should be in bed."

It was hardly the welcome she expected or deserved; however, Juliana was willing to make allowances. She stepped back into the hallway and retrieved one of the lit lamps.

"Good evening, Sinclair," she said brightly. "Thank you for inquiring after my health."

She set the lamp on the table beside Sin's bed.

The marquess cursed under his breath and rolled away from her. Juliana pursed her lips as she watched as he stood and wrapped a sheet around his waist. She had not considered that he slept naked in his bed.

"Juliana." He sat on the edge of the mattress and held out his hand. She joined him on the other side of the bed and placed her hand within his, trying not to wince at his bone-crushing grip. "Are you hurt?"

She gave him a lopsided smile. "Only my dignity. I have never swooned in my life, and I found the experience rather mortifying."

Juliana had hoped to make him smile. Strangely, her small attempt at humor only seemed to make things worse.

The gloom of the bedchamber cast Sin's face in shadows. There had been a time when she would have backed away from his forbidding expression.

"Your cousin is dead."

"I know," she said softly, and sat down on the mattress beside Sin. "A constable came to the house."

Sin's exhale was a weary sigh. "There will be an official inquiry. However, I doubt the magistrate will hold Frost responsible. After all, the man did save both our lives."

Juliana silently agreed. She was not certain that she would ever like Lord Chillingsworth, but she was grateful for his timely assistance. "Did you think that I would blame you?"

Sin played with one of her blond curls. She had not bothered pinning up her hair, because she knew he liked it best when it was down.

"The plan was to lure Duncombe out of hiding. I had expected Duncombe would follow us. The loaded pistol pressed to my head was unforeseen."

Juliana curled her fingers over her lips and giggled.

Sin pushed her onto her back and braced his arm against the mattress to prevent her from sitting up. "The swoon must have addled your brain if you find any of this unpleasant business humorous."

She looked up at him with tears and haunting images of the incident swimming in her green eyes. "I found nothing amusing about my cousin's desire to shoot you. Or me."

Her heart had stuttered painfully in her chest when Lord Duncombe had aimed the pistol at her head.

"Hush; banish what might have happened from your thoughts," Sin said, affectionately brushing the errant strands of hair from her face. "You are not responsible for your cousin's actions."

"Neither are *you*."

His eyes narrowed and he cocked his head to one side as he realized she had neatly maneuvered him toward the point that she wanted to impress upon him. "You think you are so clever."

"I have learned from a master. I have been studying your technique for weeks," she said cheekily.

Some of the shadows faded from his eyes. Sin untied her cloak, and what she was wearing underneath had him swearing. "Christ, what possessed you to wander the streets of London in your nightgown?"

"Oh, do not be so prudish," Juliana admonished, shrugging off her cloak. "The cloak covered me from head to ankle. Hembry did not even notice my attire when he opened the door and let me in."

Her nonchalance pricked Sin's temper. He pulled her up so that she was sitting on the back of her heels. "If word of your mischief gets back to your mother, she will lock you in your bedchamber for a month."

Juliana bit her lip to hide her smile. Her beloved rogue was sounding awfully like an irate husband. She tipped her chin in a haughty fashion. "Not if you marry me, Alexius."

Sin froze at her declaration.

Brazenly she pulled off her nightgown and tossed it onto the floor.

Next, Juliana opened her hand and wordlessly revealed the tiny white plume Sin had discarded that awful night at the theater.

His eyes flared in recognition.

Juliana squealed with delight as Sin released the sheet at his waist and lunged for her, covering her with his hot, naked body. The plume danced on the stirred air and then floated to the floor.

The feather forgotten, Juliana made a low approving sound in her throat as Sin's arousal brushed her thigh. She bent her knee and shifted her leg, a silent invitation.

"I might be persuaded," he murmured, crushing her lips with a devastating kiss.

After several breathless minutes, she gasped, "I love you, Sin." Juliana dug her fingernails into his back as his thick manhood filled her. She wanted him to understand that she craved his wicked nature just as much as she hungered for the tenderness he reserved only for her.

Sin's hazel green eyes gleamed possessively as his fingers caressed her cheek. "And I love you, my beautiful *lybbestre*."

Read on for an excerpt from the next book by

ALEXANDRA HAWKINS

Till Dawn
with the Devil

Coming soon from St. Martin's Paperbacks

GABRIEL WAS ONLY half serious about ravishing an innocent miss. He really craved a lady greedy enough to grant his every wicked whim without question. Gabriel openly prowled the ballroom, searching for a familiar face or a new one that tempted him.

His expression must have hinted at his dangerous mood.

Gentlemen and ladies separated, giving him a clear path. Several mothers seized their daughters by the arms and dragged them away for fear his mere presence might tarnish their daughters' reputations. Others shyly glanced away as he passed. Gabriel heard the gasps and whispers in his wake. Scandals never truly died. They were akin to dust on old flooring that, when stirred, choked the air whenever anyone dared to tread over them.

And then he saw her.

With Theodore Enright.

Well, well . . . this is most unexpected, Gabriel thought. Lady Harper's little ball was riddled with surprises.

Standing near a wall of potted plants, a blond-haired angel dressed in a charming white satin frock with light blue Claremont braces, and matching bows and ribbons at the bottom of her skirt, appeared to be hanging on every prosaic word Enright was uttering. Gabriel shook his head in disgust. Snatching the beautiful blonde away from the preening dilettante would be a pleasure. In truth, he was doing the chit a favor, though he doubted she would thank him for it.

"Enright."

Gabriel watched with a bland interest as the dark-haired gentleman turned a sickly pale green.

"Y–you!" he sputtered.

Concern furrowed the blonde's brow as she peered intently at her companion. "Mr. Enright, are you ill?"

Gabriel looked hard at woman. Her concern for the sniveling bastard irritated him. "There is nothing wrong with him that a little fresh air will not cure. Is that not correct, Enright?"

"Yes." Enright retrieved a handkerchief from the pocket of his waistcoat and blotted his upper lip. "With your permission, Lady Sophia, I will escort you to your friends."

Gabriel's dark blue eyes narrowed on Enright's pinched face. "Do not trouble yourself. I have come to claim a dance from Lady Sophia." He extended a gloved hand, but the lady rudely ignored it.

"Dance?" The lady wrinkled her nose. "I must regretfully decline, my lord . . . ?"

"Reign," Gabriel politely supplied. "And I really must insist."

Lady Sophia squeaked as Gabriel shackled her wrist, and pulled her into his arms. Not expecting his high-handed maneuver, the lady stumbled and her walking stick went skidding across the polished marble floor. Without the stick as support, she was forced to embrace him to keep from falling on her lovely backside.

The blonde straightened, but his iron grip on her wrist prevented her from stepping away. "Oh, I do beg your pardon, my lord."

"See here, Reign," Enright said, working toward righteous indignation. "Lady Sophia is *not*—"

"Your concern, Enright," Gabriel said, displaying plenty of sharp teeth. "Leave at once, or I just may decide to spare Lady Sophia and play with you. The choice is yours."

"Mr. Enright?" Lady Sophia queried hesitantly.

"Forgive me, Lady Sophia," Enright said, backing away. As Gabriel had assumed, the coward was more than happy to leave the lady to meet her fate alone. "The devil take you, Rainecourt!"

"He already has, Enright," Gabriel drawled. "And he is looking forward to meeting you."

Rainecourt.

Sophia tugged, attempting to free herself from Reign's unyielding hold. She was convinced this man was intimately acquainted with the devil. And curse Mr. Enright for abandoning her to a *Rainecourt*.

This is the son.

She had forgotten that the Earl of Rainecourt had had a son. How old had Reign been when his father had cold-bloodedly murdered her parents, and then had taken his own life? Twelve? Thirteen?

Reign started to pull her toward the other dancers. "I have promised you a dance."

"That is hardly necessary," Sophia protested, barely keeping up with him. "If you could help me find my walking stick, I will leave you to pick a fight with someone who has actually offended you."

Reign abruptly halted. He caught Sophia before she went sprawling forward onto the floor. "You are the clumsiest creature I have ever encountered."

His insult was just too much to bear.

"Ooph! My eyesight is ruined, you horrid man!" Sophia seethed, resisting the urge to hit him with her reticule. "You are walking too fast and everything is scrambled. And—and I want my walking stick!"

Reign waved his hand over her eyes.

Exasperated, she said, "I said, 'ruined', not 'blind', you twit!" Utterly provoked, Sophia slapped his arm with her reticule.

Where was Fanny or Griffin? Why was Rainecourt just staring at her? Good grief, had she just made a complete fool out of herself in front of Lady Harper's guests? She could not stop her mutinous lower lip from quivering.

"Do not move," Reign ordered as he backed away.

Sophia dutifully stood there trembling and imagining the worst. Blinking furiously to battle the tears that threatened to fall only added to her humiliation. Through the watery blur, she overheard Reign as he exchanged a few pleasantries with a helpful gentleman who had retrieved her walking stick from the floor.

Reign held up the white and gold stick. "I have it."

Not feeling gracious, Sophia snatched it from his hand. The smooth firmness of the painted wood clasped within her palm calmed her. It helped to banish the vulnerability she was feeling, and gave her the strength to find her way back to her friends without the assistance of the Earl of Rainecourt.

"Good evening, Lord Rainecourt," Sophia said, grinding the tip of the walking stick into the floor as she stepped away from the infuriating gentleman.

The earl caught her elbow. "And what of our dance?"

Sophia was getting weary wrestling Reign for her freedom. "I do not dance."

"Nonsense. Your vision is impaired, not your feet, Lady Sophia," Reign said, leading her away from the edge of the ballroom toward the other dancers.

A waltz was playing. Staring at the flashes of movement and color made her head spin. No, she could not do this. Not with so many people looking at her. Sophia locked her ankles together, refusing to move.

"No."

Reign did not seem to comprehend the meaning of the word. With a soft sigh of impatience, he captured both of her hands. He guided the hand holding the walking stick to his shoulder so her stick dangled down his back. To keep her from pulling out of his brazen embrace, he placed his free hand on her waist.

"What are you doing?"

"The waltz," he said, immune to her outrage. "This is not the time to fuss. People are watching us."

She ceased struggling at his announcement.

"How many?"

Reign grinned, melting away the grim lines around his mouth. "Enough. Everyone is curious. They will think I chased Enright off because I wanted to claim your first dance."

Sophia did her best not to notice how handsome the man was when he wasn't glowering at everyone. "That was not the reason why you ran Mr. Enright off."

As they stirred the air with their movements, Sophia noted that Reign's scent differed from Mr. Enright's. It was heavier, a heady mix of musk, wood, and smoke. She tried not to inhale too deeply.

"No, I ran Enright off because I despise the sniveling bastard." They slowly circled about with the other couples. "Of course, only you and I know the truth."

"You honor me," Sophia said, her voice laced with sarcasm.

Reign tossed his head back and laughed. "More than you know, my lady. Lord and Lady Harper's guests are watching you with interest. Who is Lady Sophia, the mysterious lady who lured the Earl of Rainecourt out onto the ballroom floor to dance the waltz? I wager half the *ton* will be knocking on your door tomorrow afternoon."

Gracious, her brothers would be furious with her if what the earl said was correct. More importantly, they would be upset when they learned that Lord Rainecourt was the reason. "I do not want to be mysterious or fascinating to the *ton*, my lord!"

"Liar," the earl countered, his amusement taking the sting out of the insult. "All ladies crave attention."

"Perhaps I am a different sort of lady, Lord Rainecourt," she said, mildly peeved with the earl's opinion.

"Reign," he pleaded, infusing enough charm into the request that Sophia could not think of a reason to refuse him. "Mayhap you are correct, dear lady. After all, you have managed to do the impossible."

"Now you are teasing me."

"A little," he conceded. "However, I cannot resist. Your cheeks turn a delightful pink hue and your blue-green eyes sparkle like a chest of priceless gems. It flatters a gent to think all that beauty shines for him alone."

Sophia glanced down and would have stumbled if Reign had not pulled her closer.

"Now you truly flatter me," Reign said, smoothly setting her apart without missing a single step. "The secret is to keep your gaze on my face. I am tolerably good-looking, would you not agree?"

Sophia bit back a smile. She did find him more than tolerable in looks. Not that she would dare admit it. "You want compliments? I thought you told me that it was only the ladies who craved attention?"

"Only a fool would not desire a beautiful lady's notice," he said lightly.

Was Reign actually flirting with her? The deadly intent that had driven the man to separate her from Mr. Enright had vanished, and now she was uncertain of how to proceed. After all, once the earl learned of their connection, their friendly alliance would come to a sudden end.

"Ah, now you are frowning. What are you thinking about?"

Sophia gave Reign what she hoped was a scolding look. "It is rude of you to inquire."

The annoying shadows and blurs that obscured her vision ebbed and flowed as they circled the ballroom with the other dancing couples. Focusing on Reign's face helped to quell her frustration. It was no hardship to study such masculine beauty. Dark brown hair that was as rich and thick as molasses. Strong cheek bones, and a fine blade of a nose, but it was his eyes that drew her gaze, ensnared her. Framed by dark, thick brows and long lashes, his dark blue eyes were an unfathomable sea of restraint, confidence, and intelligence. During their brief encounter, Sophia had glimpsed in those beautiful dark blue eyes cold, mute fury, calculation, humor, and—even though it rankled to silently admit it since it was directed at her—pity. What she now saw in his gaze wasn't pity. It was frank appreciation for the lady in his arms. Sophia's stomach fluttered like restless butterflies in a cage at the thought that Reign's interest was more than gallant flattery to bedazzle his dancing partner.

Reign ruined her speculative thoughts with his next words. "Squinting like that should give you a megrim."

Sophia's lips parted in surprise at his rude observation. Perhaps she had been wrong about the appreciation. "Forgive me. It is the reason why I never dance. My eyes . . ." She let her explanation trail off into silence.

His hand flexed, and then tightened over hers. "So you were telling the truth. I thought you might have exaggerated your claims in an attempt to refuse my invitation."

Invitation? The man had literally dragged her across

the ballroom floor to join the other dancers. "Why would I decline such a polite invitation, Lord Raine-court?" she asked a tad too sweetly.

The earl had the grace to wince. "If you wish to berate me for my boorish behavior, let us adjourn to a less public setting," he muttered, taking charge of the situation in his usual highhanded manner. He took Sophia by the elbow and escorted her away from the dancers.

"My lord—Reign, I cannot just leave the ballroom with you!" Sophia protested.

"No one will object, Lady Sophia," Reign said, guiding her toward the open doors that led to the garden terrace. "My reputation does provide certain benefits, and I am selfish enough to savor them."